"*Singer Distance* is a surprising, captivating, surpassingly intelligent novel, and I mean it as a great compliment when I say that I'm not quite sure where it came from. The narrator who leads us through its pages insists that he is one of the world's carpenters rather than one of its architects, but the reality that surrounds him is extraordinary, and so too, therefore, is his story. On the macroscale, it's a story about the interpersonal pathways that connect one planet to another and the interplanetary gaps that separate one heart from another; on the microscale, about what it feels like to occupy a single life, and how difficult it is to tell, when you're in the middle of it, whether that life is being wasted or fulfilled."

—**KEVIN BROCKMEIER**, author of *The Ghost Variations*

"*Singer Distance* pulled me in from the very first page. I fell in love with the characters—who are full of mettle, vitality, and human chaos—and the audacity of the book's alternate history, wherein contact has been made with a civilization on Mars, but that contact leaves humanity with more questions than answers about the nature of the universe. This book is a love song to our desire for understanding, the scientific drive for progress, and the thread of faith that runs through both. An outstanding debut novel."

—**ADRIENNE CELT**, author of *End of the World House*

"An inventive and heartfelt novel about the search to understand both the universe and ourselves. The best sort of mystery, one with big ideas at its center. "

—**KATE HOPE DAY**, author of *In the Quick*

SINGER DISTANCE

Published by Tin House, Portland, Oregon

Distributed by W. W. Norton & Company

Library of Congress Cataloging-in-Publication Data

Names: Chatagnier, Ethan, author.
Title: Singer distance / Ethan Chatagnier.
Description: Portland, Oregon : Tin House, [2022]
Identifiers: LCCN 2022022421 | ISBN 9781953534439 (hardcover) | ISBN 9781953534514 (ebook)
Subjects: LCGFT: Thrillers (Fiction) | Novels.
Classification: LCC PS3603.H379773 S56 2022 | DDC 813/.6--dc23/ eng/20220523
LC record available at https://lccn.loc.gov/2022022421

First US Edition 2022
Printed in the USA
Interior design by Jakob Vala

www.tinhouse.com

Excerpt from *Dear Friend, from My Life I Write to You in Your Life* by Yiyun Li, copyright © 2017 by Yiyun Li. Used by permission of Random House, an imprint and division of Penguin Random House LLC. All rights reserved.

SINGER DISTANCE

ETHAN CHATAGNIER

 TIN HOUSE / Portland, Oregon

For Ishmael and Colette
Keep looking up with me

"What a long way it is from one life to another, yet why write if not for that distance."

—YIYUN LI, *Dear Friend, from My Life I Write to You in Your Life*

"The mathematics of the Martians is a curious language, a thing that asks us to affirm contradictory truths. It asks us to see closeness in distance and distance in closeness. It tells us we must stop seeing the two as different. Perhaps, like a patient with his crutch, we are not ready to give up our way of understanding distances. We lust after what we might gain from such an understanding, but meanwhile fear what we might be asked to forsake. I for one feel ready to throw it all away, my old understanding of the world, in order to gain a new one. I would very much like to."

—FLORENCE REDGRAVE, radio interview, 1936

PART I
LOVE BETWEEN EQUALS

As soon as I saw the light off the side of the highway, I felt myself falling in love with it. It was too far from the road to be a town and too high up to be a farmhouse. The light was the wrong hue anyway. We'd passed many roadside lights in this week of night driving, and without realizing it I had become fluent in the language of them. This one was a word I couldn't translate. No town huddled next to it. No road branched off toward it. Its unknowability, its unreachability, compelled me. I felt the urge to veer toward it.

Crystal slapped my shoulder and told me to wake up.

I gripped the wheel tighter and told her I wasn't sleeping.

"You were drifting," she said without judgment.

"Not much to hit out here."

"Lucky for you."

"The only thing you could hit out here is a pothole, and those are in the road."

"You're assuming the space is empty because you can't see what's in it. You should know your way around that old fallacy."

"I'm comfortable with the inference," I said. "I saw what this state looks like in the daytime."

Crystal said she could drive, since I was falling asleep. No, I said. Stopping would wake the others. I told her again that I hadn't been sleeping, but felt less certain this time. I felt fresh now, set in a state of magic alertness, a headspace as clear as the sky after rain. I peered into the darkness north of the highway, looking for the light. I checked for it in my mirrors. It was gone. It might have been a dream, or it might have been in my blind spot. We were in an old newspaper van with tiny mirrors. The whole thing was a blind spot.

We were on Route 66 somewhere west of Oklahoma City, sometime past midnight in the waning days of 1960. Our self-appointed mission was unknown to anyone but the five of us in the van. Ronnie, Otis, and Priya were dozing in the back, but to me, in those hours, there was only Crystal. I looked at her there, barely lit in the cab of the van but still glowing. She'd started college at seventeen and grad school at twenty-one. Twenty-four now, she was the youngest of us by four years. She didn't look it. Her eyes were young and her smile was young, but light creases were appearing on her face. Her hair hadn't blanched but it had dulled, some of its color draining away even in the two years that I'd known her. She'd be gray by thirty. My mother was like that. She looked older than she was but wore her age well, as if the signs of it were fine accessories she'd graduated into. Smile lines were the best makeup, my mom said, and no amount of cosmetics would cover up a lifetime of frowns. Like fine wood or leather, she and Crystal were both improved by the slight sense of wornness.

4

I did know not to say that to a woman, even if I thought it was a beautiful compliment.

Johnny Preston was on the radio but hardly existed. Our friends sleeping in the back of the van hardly existed. I lived for these nights with no one but me and Crystal, the darkness of the expanse erasing everything but us. A road can be the connection between places or the distance between them, and as deeply as I longed to reach our destination, I also longed to drive this one forever. I'd volunteered to drive the night shifts. I was a natural night owl, I'd said. They all knew otherwise, but no one else wanted to volunteer. Those moments were perfect, just the two of us awake in the pocket universe of the van.

Otis snored, we'd discovered, but at highway speeds you could barely hear it. The lightest breezes sounded like waterfalls when they broadsided the van. He was turned toward the wall of the van, his oversized frame taking up more than a third of the mattress. His feet stuck out from the bottom of his blanket, resting against the cold metal of the van's back door. Ronnie slept in the middle, crowded closer to Otis than he would have liked in order to allow Priya, sleeping on the other side of him, a buffer of respectful space. No matter how we arranged it, you could smell other bodies while you slept. This was the close-quarters traveling that came with long-shot missions and desperate hopes.

I thought about what I could say to start Crystal talking. I often said things just to hear her respond to them. Not only to hear her voice, but also to see her way of thinking. It was a game I played with myself, to say something I thought interesting, something I thought I was interesting for knowing, so I

5

could see how far beyond me she was. We'd been together for a year and a half, but I still felt the same need to prove myself that I'd had when we started dating. I'd fallen in love with her in our first semester, listening to her translate our professor's complex ideas into simple analogies so the rest of us could get it. The brilliance radiated off her, but she was so unaware of it, or so used to it, that she inhabited it as casually as an old sweater. The great, unexplained miracle of my life was that she'd said yes to a date. I'd come to understand that I'd always feel like this around her, this blend of torture and rapture.

I mentioned the rumble strips that had recently started showing up on Boston's freeway on-ramps and off-ramps. In a few decades, I said, they'd be everywhere. They seemed like some utopian metro extravagance now, some city planner's splurge, but the economics were there: fork out for them once, and for every prevented accident, you didn't have to pay police to come monitor it, you didn't have to call in a tow truck and cleanup crew, you didn't have to pay for litigation.

"You're imagining a safer future for yourself," she said.

"And everyone in the van with me."

Did I know, she asked, about the musical road in Denmark? It used bumps, like road braille, to play a melody. You could do the same thing with those grooves. Change the size and spacing of the grooves to control the pitch, then arrange those pitches in a pattern to create the timing. They'd hardly look like anything more complex than a railroad track, but could contain a whole song. All you had to do was drive over it. Imagine every highway in America, she said, with its own song coded into the grooves of its shoulder.

"You'd be encouraging people to drive on the edge of the road," I said.

"Well, you could build them in the lanes."

"Awful hard on the tires."

"Stop ruining the fun."

But this was the fun. She liked to be pulled down to Earth a little. Then she hopped right back up into the clouds. She'd been more alive since we left Boston, more intense. The moments of quiet poetry that would slip out of her on late nights or cold walks, often with me as the only witness, were now bursting out of her all the time. The rare shooting star had become a meteor shower.

She went on about how incredible codes were. They looked the same, inscrutable, to most bystanders, but any short strip could be a song, a message, or a unique identifier. At that time, barcodes were only in development. I don't know if she'd read about them or had conceptualized them wholesale in her own mind. The latter wouldn't have surprised me. She could have been a millionaire at twenty-four if she'd turned her mind to practical things. Not that I wanted her to.

Otis's snore took over the vanspace. A sawing exhale, an interminable pause, a gasping inhale. Our vehicle, a snub-nosed newspaper delivery van from the late forties, wasn't as wide or tall as the vans in the coming decades would be. We'd all had to push to wedge a single full-size mattress into the back, which was a small cavern with a low ceiling. The whole thing rattled from the ten years it had spent delivering the *Boston Globe*, treading paved streets and cobbled ones. It was both remarkable and disturbing that Otis's sleep sounds could compete.

"Code that," I said.

Crystal leaned toward the windshield and looked up, as if she could see Mars from the car.

"I just love the humility of codes. The difference between looking at a sheet of music and hearing that music performed. Wouldn't it be a tragedy"—she said, changing her train of thought—"if we finally figured out the Curious Language, only to be killed in a highway crash?"

"That's an awfully generous *we*. And my driving is fine. There's nothing to hit out here."

"How long until someone else would solve it?"

"Centuries, maybe."

"Don't flatter me."

"Decades, at least. It's been decades since the Richter Site."

Off to the left, some creature's eyes, low to ground, reflected the headlights for a moment.

"Let's hope we're not in a Shakespeare play," I said.

"Do you think all lives can be classified as either comedy or tragedy?"

"Everything goes to tragedy. That's the direction of the universe."

"That's such a boy thing to say."

"But there's room for comedy on the way."

"What's your favorite?"

"*King Lear*. You?"

"*Midsummer Night's Dream*."

The night that couldn't seem to get any darker seemed to get darker before it happened: the black sucked inward, it deepened, and then a flash cracked the horizon in half. The sky bleached on either side of the bolt, then lavender turned blue again, and the black soaked it back up. The cab was silent, as if the flash had ionized all the sound in the car. No one woke, but Otis's snoring had let up at some point without me noticing. Crystal stopped speaking and stared straight ahead. I thought for a moment that she'd been stunned somehow, hypnotized, by the flash. That her mind had been knocked out of her body. Then I looked at her lips and saw she was counting Mississippis.

"Don't bother," I said. "It was too far away."

She put her hand on my leg.

"It proves me right, though."

"About what?"

"You can't see the clouds, but they're out there."

I wanted to tell her she was wrong. A bolt-from-the-blue could strike twenty-five miles from a cloud, from an ostensibly clear sky. I caught myself before I said it, before she could smirk and point out the heavy lifting my *ostensibly* was doing, before she could quote my words back at me: "twenty-five miles *from a cloud.*"

But I did want to hear her talk more, so I told her about the rumors that the government had tried using nuclear blasts to communicate with Mars in the early 1950s, out in the New Mexico desert we'd be crossing the coming day. They'd used low-kiloton explosions in a sequence adapted from Morse code, hoping the blasts would be so bright the attempt would be impossible to ignore.

She snorted.

"That's like writing a love letter with your dick," she said. "No wonder they didn't get a reply."

9

*

"There are Martians?" Crystal had asked her father many years ago, after the Soviet attempt of 1948. He'd come home to change from the suit he wore to his day job to the coveralls he wore to his night job. As usual, she'd cooked a dinner for him to eat between the two, which he sat down to devour the moment he came in the door.

Picture Crystal at her worn-out kitchen table, age eleven, hearing about Mars for the first time. Picture what the world looked like to her in the cramped, one-bedroom apartment she and her father shared until he was able to secure a professorship and move them into a house. The only window was the one over the transom. The world looked like walls. It looked contained. Alone in the apartment, penciling in her homework, she had heard about the Martian civilization for the first time, a nasal voice trumpeting out of the radio: *The Soviets are trying to do what scientists have not attempted in a generation. Will they succeed, or will Mars stay cold as ever?* She didn't know what to make of it. The Russians, carving some kind of strange message into the Siberian woods? Trying to signal another planet? American kids learned the history of our attempts to communicate with the Martians in third grade. It was rote to us, but to Crystal it must have been the first time the world looked open. When she was in second grade her family had been focused on outrunning the Germans, fleeing Poland for Belgium and then Belgium for the United States. She'd missed hearing about Mars in school, and it was one of many things lost to the chaos of rebuilding. No one had time for history, let alone astronomy, in those years, and the Martians had been quiet for so long nobody talked about them.

At their table, her father chewed his mashed potatoes longer than mashed potatoes take to chew. Back home, he had been a professor of statistics, but in the United States, until he could find a professorship, he was a bank teller and a night custodian at the high school. He stuck his fork into a big cabbage leaf and turned it upright. His voice changed to his professor voice: cautious, Socratic, and laden, it always seemed, with traps. Crystal imitated it whenever she told this story.

"Some people think they're all gone. Something went wrong. Their agriculture collapsed. Their atmosphere was poisoned. They stopped responding so completely. They went so quiet."

He paused, raising his brow to let her know he was assessing her, seeing if she'd take the bait. She was a stoic kid, she said. She revealed nothing. I never knew if I bought that. She was the opposite of stoic now—sometimes dreamy to the point of unresponsiveness, but never walled off.

"Those people don't want to accept that we didn't measure up to the challenge."

He explained that Giovanni Schiaparelli, the astronomer who first noticed the formations on Mars in the late 1800s, had taken them as waterways, seeing shadows he thought were lakes and seas. Percival Lowell later interpreted them as irrigation canals, drawing water from the poles to the central plain. Over time, other astronomers started to take in the built environment, however crudely they could sketch it after stepping away from their telescopes. All this stuff the rest of us learned in third grade, Crystal heard first from her father sitting at the dinner table, untying his tie while he ate.

By the late nineteenth century, most scientists had accepted the possibility of Martian life and had come to think we needed a sign, something big enough to catch their attention and unique enough to demonstrate our intelligence. There was talk of a giant circle, the most perfect shape in nature, a shape evoking peace and harmony. But it was decided that a circle risked being mistaken for an impact crater. Instead, the Dutch astronomer Flavius Horn oversaw the carving of three parallel lines into the Tunisian desert in 1894. The giant tally marks, each a hundred miles from end to end, were filled with petroleum and set on fire at the moment of Mars's direct opposition. Months passed, Mars receded out of viewing distance without a response, and the project was taken for a failure.

"They didn't see it?" Crystal had stopped eating by this point, and was staring evenly at her father.

He put his fork down, held a finger up. His signal to be patient.

The next favorable opposition of Mars was two years later, in 1896. When the planet came around to us again, he told Crystal, the astronomers of the world took to their telescopes, each hoping to sketch out the new definitive map. What they saw made them break down in tears: cut into the red plain of Mars, in sharp, intentional relief, were four perfectly parallel lines.

*

When we'd left Massachusetts at the beginning of the week, Cambridge had been sunk under snow. Little wood-sided bungalows poked their heads up from under the blanket, their windows gleaming day and night. The wet, black asphalt of streets crisscrossing in neat geometric shapes here, then spiraling elsewhere in some unknowable logic, fossils of some older pattern: the rows cows used to graze, the path some influential colonist liked to take downtown. Even MIT's campus, with its mix of Doric and utilitarian buildings, even the connective tunnels underneath with industrial piping winding overhead, seemed of a piece with the still, frozen surface. You climbed up a stairwell into the bracing air and the mind didn't pause.

The road we were traveling now seemed a different planet than that. Morning sun put a glow onto the wide distance, a red-orange that made me think of an oven preheating. Stretches of the highway had earlier been flanked by mottlings of sagebrush, but this morning it was bare. There hadn't been enough winter rain yet to bring the grass up. The dusty landscape was free of anything but hills as low and graceful as sea swells on a calm day, punctuated only by occasional roadside curiosities. In Illinois we'd seen Abraham Lincoln statues and giant soda cups. A gas station in the shape of an observatory dome. On this desolate stretch, the sights were even weirder. We'd passed scrapped cars painted to look like they were faces kissing, a large wooden carving of a marmoset, and strange, abstract sculptures I couldn't parse at all. We passed a pair of water barrels, each suspended on seven legs, that reminded me of the tripods from *The War of the Worlds*.

Otis was the last to wake. I pulled to the shoulder when he did. Crystal wasn't so fresh now. She'd stayed up through the night with me, but she'd been in a quasi-sleep road trance for the last few hours, not saying anything, staring ahead into the darkness, then grayness, then brightness of the landscape. When I pulled the van over, she turned her head toward me, blinked her bleary eyes, and smiled like she'd just woken up.

She and Priya tore away a few sheets of toilet paper each and took off to the side of the road to pee. Since there was no longer any brush to hide behind, we boys went to stand on the other side of the van. We were in the road, but there was no one coming. You could see a car twenty miles off. It was the morning of Christmas Eve. Everyone crossing this highway for normal reasons had done so days ago. We had the strange terrain to ourselves, and after Elk City, it was only going to get more deserted. Crystal jogged back to the van to grab the roll of toilet paper.

"Emergency," Crystal said, "for Priya."

"Before coffee?" Ronnie said.

"Don't tell her I said that."

Crystal disappeared to the other side of the van again. When they were done, we took our turn. Then we got back on the road. In the rare hour we were all awake, we crowded around the center console of the van like it was a campfire and passed around a bag of trail mix. Ronnie was behind the wheel now, with Priya shotgun. Crystal and I were in the back because we hadn't slept, as was Otis because his sleep wasn't restorative. You had to subtract all the time he wasn't breathing, which was more like death than sleep. People like to say they'll sleep when they're dead, but if there's one thing I learned from Otis it's that death isn't restful.

Otis was a big, awkward guy. You might be intimidated by him until you saw him try to open a door. He had huge, fluffy sideburns that were going white early, and a pair of wire-rimmed glasses from 1952. He took up a quadrant of the vanspace, the same amount Crystal and I occupied squatting next to each other, her arm against mine. While we cruised along the highway, he read an Isaac Asimov book and Ronnie sang along to the radio. Priya bobbed her head to it, slightly, when she thought no one was looking. The sun was behind us, but we squinted at the brightness of the naked landscape in front of us. We all cheered when we saw the sign for the Texas border. The great thing about Oklahoma, Priya said, was that each state after it got a little better. Ronnie asked if Crystal and I were going to sleep. I'd been doting on Crystal. He'd been doting on me. We'd always had each other's backs, but on the trip he seemed to think I needed extra.

"Let's get breakfast first," I said.

"Hope you like dirt."

"There's a diner and a gas station in about thirty miles."

"They might be closed for the holiday," Priya said. She had appointed herself the skeptic of the trip. She and Crystal had been roommates since the beginning of grad school, and she hadn't seemed to notice me until I started dating Crystal. The change had not made her hostile, but did make her orient herself against me as a kind of check against my influence.

"They're not," I said. "I called to ask before we left Boston."

They weren't closed. They were almost empty though. There was one old guy at the bar with a coffee and a yolky plate. There was a waitress filing her nails who didn't look up when the bell on the door jingled. We were five MIT grad students, PhD

15

candidates in pure mathematics. In Cambridge, we were brilliant because our brilliant professors had anointed us as such. In Cambridge, we were the next generation. Out here we were five wooly kids in a van that smelled like newspaper, dressed like we were going on a field trip to a dairy. Grubby jeans, worn sweaters, faded T-shirts. We had nothing but an idea that might be crazy, and it was a delicious feeling, being unsure if our own greatness was a secret or a myth.

I took a few steps toward a large, empty booth, and Ronnie followed. He was my closest friend in the program. He was down-to-earth like me, practical. Most people in the program came from money. He came from Chicago, and in fact from Chicago State University. He wasn't on the Ivy track like so many of us. He didn't catch the math bug in earnest until his undergraduate years, when a professor noticed he had a talent for it. Of the five of us, he was also the most prolific eater. Once our food came, he tucked away his biscuits and gravy and his pancakes before I'd even finished my eggs. I'd known he could eat, but what I didn't know before the trip was how well Priya could put it down. Maybe it was the travel hunger, but she was the only one of us to finish all three of the heaping plates that constituted a standard breakfast order. With her British accent, her small frame, and her neat fashion, it was hard to imagine her plowing through a meal like that until you saw it, after which it was impossible to forget.

As the rest of us sipped at coffees, Crystal started in on what we had been talking about the night before, about roads and codes and music. "Think of a violin in its case, unplayed," she said. "The violin and the bow are the same matter when they're dormant as when they're played. When you combine the two, when you do so in a patterned way, you create a whole new thing, a thing that isn't matter. But it's not just energy either, it's energy that contains the pattern that was played. Waveforms in the *shape* of the pattern. It's information in the form of energy, but also information that disappears instantaneously, that leaves no record or shadow or residue. The code and the music are opposite sides of the same coin: the symbols that can't be music on their own, the music that can't outlast the present without being coded. The Curious Language is like that—"

"Haufmann-Eisen spatial mechanics," Otis interrupted.

"We've been through this," Crystal said.

They had been through it—many times. Haufmann-Eisen spatial mechanics was the technical name for the Curious Language. It was the name the academic journals used. It was what universities called their departments, at least those that still had a department. Most schools had let them atrophy in the last decade. Otis hated "the Curious Language" because it was what you'd see in a popular magazine, a nickname derived from the musings of the earlier mathematician Florence Redgrave. Otis thought it was too bohemian, a froufrou term used by people who cared more about poetry than math.

Crystal never called it anything else. First of all, she'd argued, Haufmann and Eisen didn't solve anything. Just saying that something that doesn't make sense does make sense wasn't the same as making sense of it. More importantly, we didn't know what its creators called it. They certainly didn't name it after two middling Earth mathematicians—*Two of the most famous*, Otis had interjected—so if we couldn't know what they'd called it, why not call it something that captured what it was? Math was called the universal language, but the Martian math wasn't universal. It wasn't universal because of us. We didn't get it.

Otis forked at his pancakes. Crystal's confidence flustered him.

Mathematicians had known all along that the last branch of mathematics the Martians carved into their planet's surface—this one far more advanced, reflecting the progress we'd made in our communications with them since those first four perfectly parallel lines—had to do with distance. The equation seemed to indicate there was no difference between a near infinite distance and an infinitesimal one. That distance did not exist as a constant, or not only as a constant. The great supposed breakthrough of Haufmann and Eisen was an argument that this meant distance did not exist at all. Distance was a construct, an illusion. That was thinking around the problem, Crystal said. That was important men deciding that if they couldn't explain something, it must be unexplainable.

For months now, Crystal had been telling us the Martian math did not conflict with our understanding of distance, as so many people thought. It rotated distance to reveal a new dimension of it we hadn't been able to see yet. It was more like the played violin versus the unplayed violin. A distance being traveled is different from a distance being measured.

"So is a distance being traveled infinitely small or infinitely large?" Ronnie asked.

"It depends which angle you're looking at it from."

Ronnie laughed.

Cute that she was still trying to explain the Curious Language to us. The better she came to understand it, the more convinced she was that the rest of us could grasp it too. She didn't get that she was drifting toward it while the rest of us stayed stationary.

"No," she said, not wanting Ronnie to resign himself. "Now think of a record. The code isn't two-dimensional like a sheet of music. The shape of the matter is the code. Rick, think of the musical road we were talking about. When no one's driving over it—" But she'd already lost them. She'd gone through so many examples trying to get us to understand. Priya was usually the one to ask the questions that probed closest to the bone, the questions that injected Crystal with a sudden enthusiasm to keep explaining. But Priya was quiet now, looking down at her hands on the table. Sometimes the enthusiasm was enough to make Crystal seem crazed. She had a fork in one hand and a syrupy knife in the other, and she was waving them around like an orchestra conductor. Ronnie excused himself to the bathroom to avoid the lecture. Otis still wanted to debate semantics.

She'd even lost me, in the sense that I'd take her word, at this point, on any of it. I believed she understood it even if I couldn't. What I understood was that the measurable distance to Mars was calculable but the distance of the journey there, to us, was infinite. I also understood Crystal's position. Being the only speaker of a language across an impossible distance was lonely enough to make anyone feel crazy.

By the time we'd finished eating, I'd had six cups of diner coffee and had to pee. The bathroom was a closet around the back that you had to exit the restaurant to get to. I waited outside the door longer than it could possibly be taking Ronnie to do whatever he was doing in there.

Crystal appeared around the corner of the building and before I could say anything, she was pushing me back against the wall, leaning her body into mine and kissing me aggressively. This hunger was another of her traits that had become magnified on the pilgrimage, another interior light that could no longer be contained. I wasn't going to complain, though of course there were few opportunities to take advantage of it. I returned her kiss. She sucked on my lip. Her hand moved to the front of my jeans and I wriggled away from her. There may have been a door between us and Ronnie, but he was less than ten feet away.

"You're exhausted," I said.

"I'm impatient."

"Not like this."

Before she could assail me further, we heard Ronnie unlatch the door. Crystal took half a step back, leaving her hands on my hips.

"Hey," she said to Ronnie.

"Hey," he said, glancing away.

"My turn," I said, escaping into the little bathroom and latching the door behind me. I could hear her talking to Ronnie outside. I put my ear against the wood to listen to what I already knew was not an apology.

"The groove in a record looks like a uniform line, but really—" she was saying. She was carried away, her voice no less thrilled than when she'd accosted me a moment ago.

*

After the initial Martian response—those four parallel lines—in 1896, interplanetary signaling had progressed in a fever. It was like everyone on the planet had a new best friend. By the time of the favorable opposition of 1899, dozens of messages had been carved into the skin of the Earth. Great Britain, France, the Austro-Hungarian Empire, the Ottoman Empire, Russia, the Arabian kingdoms of Hejaz and Nejd, China, Japan, Mexico, and many other nations and kingdoms had written something on their territory that they would light on fire when the opposition came. The inscriptions included words of greeting, a pentagon, a short poem, numerals, and national symbols—but Mars had already added its own communiqué to the Acidalia Planitia. There were now three lines of text, each one governed by a rail across the bottom of it, with symbols etched in glowing blue curls. They sprung off the rail in figures that looked no more or less foreign than a human language one was unfamiliar with. But their special location and that phosphorescent glow gave them the impact of magic runes.

The first line of text contained twelve different symbols. The second had five symbols. The first and third symbols were the same, and matched the second symbol from the first line. The second and fourth symbols were new ones, not included in the first line. The fifth symbol was the fourth symbol from the first line.

The third line contained four symbols. The first and third symbols were the same, and matched the third symbol from the first line. The second and fourth symbols matched the second and fourth symbols from the second line. There was no fifth symbol, but the rail continued, leaving a blank space running to the same length as the line above.

The debate over how to approach this message seems so silly now, in retrospect, only because the correct solution was confirmed and spotlit by history. Consider a scrap of text from any foreign language and the countless things it might mean. No one even knew at the time whether each symbol was a letter, a word, a numeral, or some other unit of meaning. There was heated debate over whether extraterrestrial life would first communicate with us through language or mathematics, with humanists and scientists falling into predictable camps.

But the patterns were in the message.

Within a few months a robust plurality had settled on this interpretation:

$1\ 2\ 3\ 4\ 5\ 6\ 7\ 8\ 9\ 10\ 11\ 12$
$2 + 2 = 4$
$3 + 3 = \underline{\quad}$

Our first true message from the Martians: *Pop quiz, kindergartners.*

That response was so significant it briefly united the world—or at least the world's scientists. The British insisted that the scientific community present a unified solution, not some fractious patchwork of camps and theories. They suggested that the most sensible choice of who should deliver it was Great Britain. The rest of the world, for whatever reason, went along with it. Nations across the globe donated their soldiers to the effort of digging the answer into the desert of British Sudan.

In the Martian symbols, we wrote: $3 + 3 = 6$.

And, for good measure: $4 + 4 = 8$.

While the soldiers dug, the academics, plus a few obsessed noblemen, scrutinized Mars through their finest telescopes, looking for a new message. There was none in the days leading up to the next opposition, but after the petroleum filling the canals of our Martian numerology was lit at the central moment of the opposition period, astronomers started making reports of a blue dot. Then the blue dot stretched. They wrote of standing for hours while the lines slowly traced their way into the surface, looking away only to sketch the designs carefully onto their easels.

Years now passed in pairs. That was how often Mars, with its longer orbit, was usually in opposition. We passed kindergarten arithmetic. We passed third-grade geometry. In the year 1903 we passed middle school algebra. Later in the aughts, we were showing we knew differential calculus and equations essential to Newtonian mechanics. In the teens, we were quizzed on elements of the zeta function and polynomial rings, fields in which we had only recently made the breakthroughs that allowed us to respond effectively. We passed those tests too.

It was a lively time, by all accounts. We had found our equals in the universe, right next door.

Our equals. We always wanted to think so.

*

Walking out of the diner, Ronnie held back, grabbing the sleeve of my jacket while the others went ahead to the van. He looked worried, like he was a doctor about to give me bad news.

"She okay?" he asked.

"She's good. She's stressed, excited. Who wouldn't be?"

"Who wouldn't be. That's the point. That kind of stress can crack people."

"She's got a lot riding on this."

"Exactly."

I looked at him. He looked back at me.

"She's not acting like herself."

"She's more herself than ever," I said. That was true, but it was also another way of not being yourself. Of not being able to restrain yourself in the ways people usually do. I saw in Ronnie's face that I hadn't allayed his doubts at all. I saw they were serious worries, less a fleeting consideration in response to seeing Crystal accosting me by the bathroom than the product of studied observation.

"I'll keep an eye on her. She just has to get through the next few days and then the weight lifts."

The others were waiting by the side of the locked van. Crystal leaned against it and the wind scattered her hair across her face. She was full of energy. The rest of them looked tired, and so did I, but she had something igniting her inside. She looked enraptured, but I wondered if someone else would say she looked crazy. I wondered if I could interpret her correctly. What kind of wild was she? What kind of judge could I be?

I tossed the keys to Ronnie.

"You drive. I'm tired."

He passed the keys to Priya and took shotgun. Otis climbed in the back with us again, ready for the first of his four naps. He pulled his grandmotherly knit blanket over himself and turned toward the passenger wall of the van. Crystal and I crawled under my thick Mexican blanket, heavy as a dentist's lead apron, and she lay close to me, leaving a little aisle in the middle between us and Otis. It didn't take much to get to sleep after a full night of driving. The van lurched into reverse and coasted onto the freeway and we were out. Not even the seizing engine of Otis's lungs could keep us awake.

The van stopped hours later, and Ronnie and Priya woke us for a peanut butter and jelly lunch break on the side of the road. Ronnie said we were out of the Texas panhandle and into New Mexico. The girls peed in the desert, then we peed in the desert. We climbed back into the van without ever fully waking up. Ronnie took over driving, Priya became the passenger, and Crystal, Otis, and I resumed our sleep shifts. The wheels touched the asphalt and we were out again.

Crystal remembered her dreams. I was used to her waking up and acquainting me with the wilds of her subconscious. She'd give me a whole picaresque string that seemed like it must have taken more than eight hours to dream, and she'd be able to tell me what stood in for what else, who had the appearance of her piano teacher but was, emotionally, her mother. She could decode them so well, but still spoke with a kind of wonder, as if her own mind was a mystery to her.

I've never remembered mine. Aside from some odd nightmares in which I startle awake picturing the thresher that had snagged my arm in the dream, whatever plays in my mind through the night gets sucked into the pillow. But I know that I do have dreams. I wake up with the feeling of them, the residue.

25

I can tell when I wake up how the dream has positioned me against the day.

The van was quiet when I woke again, or what had become our default of quiet. No one was talking. The radio was off. Priya preferred silence, and Ronnie humored her when he was the only one awake. They stared straight ahead. Otis was flat on his back in the middle of his side, lying in the position and manner of a corpse in a casket, with the exception of his open mouth. After several days on the road, we'd fallen into sleep routines, and this wasn't our usual wake-up time. The sun wasn't pouring through the westerly windshield. The hour was too early in the afternoon. And whatever my dream had been, it was incomplete. It had the feeling of being interrupted, of being thrust into a space that was not a dream but was as confusing as one.

I was, I realized, awake because of Crystal, who had huddled into my big spoon. She pushed her backside against me. She curled her hips forward then pressed them back against me again. She worked into a rhythm, grinding back against where I'd already grown uncomfortably hard in my jeans. Her arm winged down on the arm I had wrapped around her, pinning mine there and pressing my hand to her sternum. From behind, I saw her head resting against the pillow at an angle that imitated sleep, but I knew she was not asleep. Her movements spoke the language of consciousness. They were an attempt.

Her arm let go of mine and wandered back behind her. She unbuttoned my pants and tugged down the zipper. She slipped her hand inside my underwear and wrapped it around me. It was warm under the thick blanket but her fingers were extremely cold. They started to warm as she traced them along me. Then she grabbed it like a handle and twisted it up and out of my pants, where she started stroking it more thoroughly, intentionally. I kept waiting, hoping for and against the moment she stopped. I thought I knew what she was trying to do. She was trying to tease me into a tryst later, trying to drive me crazy enough to take her behind a rest stop bathroom, and I didn't doubt it was going to work because I already felt crazy.

She let go of me. I felt relief and agony. She fiddled with something around her hips. Then she took hold of me again, scooted herself back, and I was inside her warmth. I inhaled sharply. I didn't move but she moved for me. Slowly at first, in long, undulating movements. In other circumstances I might have made a joke about an unplayed violin versus a played one. My fingers gripped her collarbone. We could hear the pavement rushing by two feet beneath us.

"Not like this," I whispered, though I didn't mean it.

"Just like this," she whispered back.

A pothole jostled the van and it felt incredible. It had been a week for us. Four days on the road, plus the two before we left, when I was too consumed by the packing and planning to pause for thirty minutes, and she, besides, was looking over her diagrams, plagued again by the feeling that she had missed something. This was a sort of homecoming. I gripped her tighter and joined her movements with my own. She moved my hand between her legs so I could touch her.

I realized too late that I was bumping her knees into the side of Otis's body. He started to stir, his head turning toward us. He lifted one groggy eyelid, then the other. Finally, both at once. He started to realize what he was seeing. We were covered by the blanket, but it was clear on our faces.

"Gross," he said. He lumbered up to squeeze as much of his big body as he could between the two front seats.

Caught, I wanted to stop. I did stop my movements, but she redoubled hers, and nothing in the world could make me stop her. She pushed my hand away to stimulate herself with her own until she couldn't take it anymore. I saw her biting her lip to keep silent but felt it in the way her rhythm went erratic, turning into heaves and shudders that pushed me over the edge as well.

The others all looked straight ahead, quite conspicuously, at blank New Mexico. They weren't saying anything. The radio wasn't saying anything. Shame flooded me. The tawdriness of it. Crystal reached for the roll of toilet paper. She wadded a bunch together to make a pad in her underwear and sat upright against the back door of the van. She leaned her head against the cold metal and closed her eyes, no trace of shame in her face. Within minutes she was asleep.

I was still under the blanket, tugging my clothes up, damp against them. I knew I wasn't going back to sleep. Ronnie turned the radio on loud enough to compete with the highway noise. The airwaves gave us Connie Francis and Paul Anka. I watched the three up front. Their heads swiveled right in unison when we passed gas stations or roadside diners, some of them strung with Christmas lights. I couldn't see the lights from my spot on the mattress, but I'd seen enough of them along the way to know.

We'd also seen rooftops painted with Martian numerals. There had been a lot of those houses in Pennsylvania, where Lucas Holladay was from. I guessed there would be lots in

Flagstaff too, so close to the Richter Site. We didn't know much about the limits of Martian telescope technology, but these rooftops were almost certainly too small for them to read. The roofs were also too small to write anything complex, so they directed simple arithmetic skyward. It was like walking into the most advanced math seminar in the world and shouting out, *Three times three equals nine!* But there was something I loved about the sentiment, something I felt kin to. It was country manners: the need, if someone else was in the waiting room, to strike up a conversation.

Occasionally, I saw Priya's head swivel on its own to the left. To me. She couldn't help glancing back, not at Crystal but at me, with something like worry, something like pity, in her eyes, and I knew that the thing on the brink of happening this whole trip had happened in a way that was permanent. We were not a group of five anymore. They were a group of three now, and we were a group of two.

*

The first time the Martians asked a question we couldn't readily answer was in 1922. It drew upon the general theory of relativity, but included elements that Einstein had not considered. The Martians seemed to know that the power of our observatories was scaling up. They wrote their messages smaller now, allowing for more intricate equations. Their latest would have filled up half a sheet of lined paper if written in normal print. This was when many scientists began to get bitter. If they had a more advanced system of mathematics than we did, why didn't they provide us with it instead of taunting us? But Einstein was said to be tickled by this. Crystal said it was because he didn't want the answer given to him.

At the oppositions of 1926, 1928, and 1931, we had no solution for them. Astronomers scrutinized Mars for updates. Perhaps they would offer a clue? They did not. We had not given them a solution, so they did not overwrite their question. The text on Mars stayed the same, only a little less bright. Whatever technology they used to illuminate their phosphorescent blue writing, it faded a little each time we saw it, disappearing ink in slow motion.

By 1932, Einstein thought he had worked it out in conversation with Arnold Richter. Richter arranged for the construction on the display site in the Arizona desert to begin in secret, waiting for Einstein's arrival in the United States. Einstein had kept his theories on the subject entirely private. Hitler, ascendant in Germany, would never have let him set foot in a port if he knew Einstein held the secret to communication with aliens. Einstein took his professorship at Princeton in the fall, Richter oversaw the construction of Einstein's proof, and during the 1933 opposition they set it aflame, surprising the world.

When the message was lit, Mars was silent for a day. Many had wandered away from their telescopes by the time the response started up, a dozen glowing points of blue that lengthened and curled in a synchronized array, as if one complex mind were drawing the signs simultaneously using a dozen pens in a dozen hands. First, they were lightning bugs waltzing across the surface of Mars, and then their curls linked and intersected and the rails along the bottom line of the numerals gave the framework for their equations. We didn't know why they'd taken hours to respond. Some supposed they no longer had faith in us. Imagine asking a student for the solution to seven squared and waiting ten years for them to answer.

Only with the brightness of the new blue did we really see how faded the old writing had become. You could barely see it, and only if you took pains to look past the new writing. But who cared to look back at all that? It was a moment of victory. We'd passed that test.

Of course, there was another.

*

Before night descended, the sky gave us a gift. The horizon glowed like molten iron. It was orange at the margin and patched with bolts of red. Above it, rags of clouds glowed purple from underneath, as if they were soaking up the depth of the higher sky and had to vent it. I was driving now, and Crystal was shotgun. The night shift began again.

But the other three were all up, crowding in behind the seats for a view out the windshield. We'd been crossing the desert for two days so we all knew how special these sunsets were. We'd carry the miracle of them back to New England, so when the cold silver lid was buckled over us the next two years while we compiled our dissertations, we'd have a fire to dream of. We were still split, I knew, a component broken down into constituent parts, a number broken into its factors, but for half an hour the Arizona sky—that was it up ahead, the state of our destination—had the nuclear force to hold us together.

31

Even if it did not have the power to embolden much conversation.

Then it was dark. The others' eyes in the rearview, lit by a passing truck, lost a wakeful openness. Their doors had closed, and no one wanted to say anything.

Ronnie and Otis very conspicuously flipped the mattress.

They arranged themselves as they usually did. Otis caught the side of the van and Ronnie settled in the middle. Priya took the left side, a spare blanket laid between her and Ronnie as a buffer. I reminded everyone this was the last night sleeping in the van. Tomorrow, we'd crash at Crystal's father Karl's house in Albuquerque. We'd enjoy home-cooked food, hot showers, and our own places to sleep. Ronnie grudgingly admitted he needed a shower. Priya joked that she needed him to have a shower too, and that Otis was on the list as well. It got quiet and I could hear them thinking that Crystal and I needed a shower most of all.

"Can your dad cook?" I asked Crystal.

"Do we have to stop at his place?" she asked.

"I told him we were coming. You don't want to?"

"We've been in such a rush to get to Arizona. Why slow down now?"

"I figured everyone would be worn out from the road by then. We all need a chance to refuel." That was not my primary reason. I'd thought Crystal would want to see him, though that wasn't my main reason either. "It's almost Christmas. You want to pass through your dad's town without seeing him?"

Priya announced, definitively, that if some people in this van didn't get bathed as soon as possible she'd be jumping out the back door. The matter was settled.

More quietly, I asked Crystal about her reservations. She loved to quote Karl, imitating his jokes and monologues in a thick but refined Polish accent. She'd made him sound funny, loving, and supportive in all her stories about him. He *was*, she said, but had I ever had an overly energetic teacher? They were the best ones, I said. But he's like that all the time, she said. He was always running a lecture hall. He might as well have a podium attached to his chest. And he would be even worse with all of us there. He loved a crowd.

If he was in a good mood while I was there, I thought, so much the better for me.

The darkness over the highway had deepened, and the three in the back were sleeping once again. The pocket universe was back. Only stray glimmers of highway light made Crystal and I anything more than voices. The radio was static. Crystal turned it low, but not silent. It blended with the rustle of the road. We talked about what we'd do after all this panned out. We'd have any jobs we wanted, I said. Harvard, Oxford. "You can make them take me as a spousal hire." She neither flinched nor smiled at my implicit proposal, though I'd been hoping for a clue.

"We'll have to go into hiding," she said. "The kind of attention we're going to get." It was nice to talk like this, unbound by the doubts the others harbored. "Einstein was already Einstein when he got involved. We're kids. We're nobody. People are going to love us. People are going to hate us."

A question occurred to me that I should have asked earlier. "You have anything we should patent before this is out in the world? I know none of us is in applied math, but this has got to have some implications for, like, air travel."

33

She stroked my temple.

"My practical boy. Airfare will be the same."

"Shipping? Communications?"

"Try power generation."

"Shit, Crystal. We should be all over that."

"You don't want to be in that. You want to be a professor so you can flatter yourself about not seeming like a professor."

"Hey now."

She was right.

"I'm a good teacher," I said.

"You are," she said. "Much better than I am. You're like a Trojan spousal hire."

She smiled. So she did notice.

"Who was your best math teacher?" I asked. "Who hooked you?"

"My dad."

"Me too. But I mean schoolteacher."

"My high school physics teacher was pretty good. Lots of fun experiments. Even if it was stuff I already knew."

"My dad always made math seem useful. It was my seventh-grade teacher, Mrs. Cruz, who made it seem beautiful. She liked to talk about how shapes have different dimensions of information coded into them, how you have to change the angle from which you look at them to catch it all. You would have liked her."

"Maybe if I'd had her I'd be a better teacher."

"She told us the two sides of an equation are in love with each other. To stay in love, they have to maintain their balance. What one loses, the other must lose. What one accepts, the other must accept. I felt like she defined love and algebra for me at the same time."

"No," Crystal said. "Love can't exist between equals. Love is feeling like they're real and you're fake. Like they're a variable and you're a constant. Like they're so far ahead you could never catch up to them your whole life." She said it so dreamily, as if she were offering up something hopeful instead of cynical, as if she hadn't just sucked all the air out of me. This woman we all knew was the best of us was saying that one partner runs ahead of the other without looking back.

I let a dark Arizona mile pass.

She saw my face contorting, trying to marshal a counter-argument when she'd just described exactly how I felt about her.

"QED," she said.

"If that's true, only one partner can ever really be in love."

"Exactly."

I felt like crying. Now she seemed more spooked by what she'd said, staring out the window away from me. After a minute she said: "You have to feel like they're infinite and you're nothing. I know because that's the way I love you."

*

Karl Singer, Crystal's father, was an almost-famous professor of statistics at the University of New Mexico. It was the first professorship he secured after his bank teller years, and he'd never left it, though he could have leapfrogged higher. He liked living in a place, he said, that no one would ever want to invade. After a year of hearing Crystal tell stories about him, he seemed like he was doing an impression of her impression of him. I'd always assumed she played up his accent for comic effect, but in fact it was stronger than she was able to successfully imitate. He let us in, calling us the Great Unwashed, and sat us down at a table crowded with fine china and glasses of cabernet franc. He lifted a lid off a leg of lamb, releasing a cloud of rosemary-infused steam. Crystal was right. We were Karl's captive audience and he delighted in having us, launching into stories about Crystal's youth before we'd even sat down. How, when her mother left, Crystal had just taken over running the household without being asked. How in high school she'd begged and begged for a record player. How she sprinted ahead of her classmates in math. How she'd disappear on long walks and he'd just have to trust that she'd wander back home. And because it was Crystal, talk about her youth led to talk about Mars.

"Why do they only send math?" Karl asked. "What ever happened to the liberal arts? I'm a statistician but I still read poetry."

He went all the way back to the beginning, to Schiaparelli and Lowell, and I remembered Crystal once describing him as a guy who had to tell every story from the beginning because he didn't have faith that anyone else could tell it to his standards. I kept an eye on her as he added his color commentary to the history we all knew. Crystal's posture was a barometer of her mood. Relaxed, she was languid as a cat. She slouched. She curled into the recesses of chairs. When her mind was excited, she'd lean in toward whomever she was speaking to. Her hands would move in front of her body. But I'd never seen her like this. As Karl dove into the Soviet attempt of 1948, as world history intersected with her personal history, she stiffened into royal propriety, uncurling slowly like something drying out in the sun. He talked about Crystal's shock, her wonder, when the curtain was torn away for the first time. She was never the same after that, he said.

"Oh, come on," she said. "I was the same kid. It's normal to get interested in the sudden news that there's another civilization in the solar system."

"She was always looking elsewhere. Always chasing something."

"Can we move on?"

I saw the strategy behind her phrasing. Karl loved moving on.

Enough about the failures, he said. Albert Einstein got a question from the Martians in 1922. General relativity. He'd already been working on it and it still took him a decade to figure out what they meant. He answered them in 1933. Our greatest mind, and even he had to stretch to reach that one. Immediately they tasked us with a longer, more complex problem. Crystal took issue with Karl's phrasing. "More complex is actually more simple," she said. "You have to get *around* your mind's ability to complicate things. When you can do that, all math is intuitive."

"Most of us can't do that," Karl said, "so let's call complexity relative. The Theory of General Stupidity. Where were we?"

"Einstein," Ronnie said.

Einstein gave up, Karl said. He didn't throw his hands up in frustration. He just stepped down like the heavyweight champ he was. He thought about it for two years—everyone waited on him—and said he wasn't so young anymore and his mind wasn't so flexible. You get too used to the way things appear. He wouldn't be the one to do it, he said. Karl grinned, before delivering what Einstein supposedly also said: "Heisenberg won't be the one either."

The Heisenberg quip was apocryphal. Besides not being Einstein's style, Einstein had made the statement about himself in a taped interview, and hadn't mentioned Heisenberg at all. But Karl was having so much fun I didn't want to spoil it, and I had an interest in staying on his good side.

"Einstein wasn't troubled by it," Karl continued. "A Buddha, that one."

Everyone else was. People started getting mad at the Martians—*mad!* As all poor students are when a teacher pushes them. Why can't you give me a clue? Why can't you pop the answer in my mouth like a little candy? A student this semester— Karl was retired but taught the same course load he always had—had asked him why he couldn't round up an 87 to a 90. He'd plucked an apple from his bag and asked the boy if he could turn the apple into two apples. Even good students and great scientists were mad. "Crystal was mad," he said. "She wasn't even there at the time, but she was mad when she heard about it."

"No," she said, her eyes flaring, "I was really, really sad."

"You were grumpy. Trust me."

She opened her mouth to object, but Karl beat her to it. Twenty years of silence, he said, shifting his voice into a minor key. Twenty-seven now. They were supposed to be our neighbors. You can't blame people for feeling that way. People kept trying, at first. The Royal Swedish Academy of Sciences, 1935. Fire on snow. Those breathtaking photos. The Germans in 1937. Their scientists knew they didn't have it but the Nazis whipped them into it. Their failure enraged the Führer. We carved out the Grand Falls in 1941. It was a long shot, but we weren't in the war yet. People still felt like we had to keep trying, even if there was a growing impression that attempts signaled hubris more than ambition.

The blue was fading. Every two years, a little harder to see. But then it would refresh every four oppositions or so, bright blue again, until it once again faded. No one knew why they were doing that, bringing the color back. I've been teaching long enough to know, Karl said. He sat up and cleared his throat like he was taking the podium. He rapped his knuckles swift and hard against the dining table, startling us.

"Earth? *Earth?* Are you still working on this?"

"Don't make light of it, Dad. It was hard for a lot of people." Her voice took on a defeated tone, her frustration giving way to sadness.

"I remember. Poor girl," he said, turning to the rest of us. "She was there for Lucas Holladay. Lucas Holladay broke her heart."

"We all were," Priya said.

"He broke mine," I said.

"Mine too," said Ronnie.

"I ain't sayin' nothin'," Otis said.

No one cared in 1941, Karl said. Everyone was sending their sons off to war. Everyone was fleeing a homeland with their valuables sewn into their clothes. This one—Karl pointed his thumb at Crystal—was a toddler. The three of us were living in a cold basement in Ghent on a potato a day. I didn't give a damn about Mars. No one cared about a telescope. No one had the time to look upward, especially at a planet that was like a woman who had stopped answering your letters.

I couldn't tell whether Karl was really mad. He was practically spitting the words out, when a minute earlier he'd been ridiculing anyone less beatific than Einstein.

"You're trivializing," Crystal said quietly.

"Trivializing! Talking about the war?"

"It's in your tone."

"My *tone*?"

"You could be less of a showman."

She got up from the table, folding her napkin neatly and placing it on her chair. The forced poise with which she walked out of the room was like a distress signal. I knew right away I needed to follow her. I did, hearing him resume, as I walked into the hall:

"We were lonely. They'd made the whole planet lonely. If we could . . ."

Crystal's childhood room was utilitarian. There was not much in it. A small, high window let in the barest scrap of light. The covered bulb in the ceiling didn't add much. I don't know what I'd expected—posters of Elvis? calculations chalked to the windowpanes?—but there was nothing on the walls, and hardly any furniture. There was one little bookshelf as high as my hip with books filling but not overflowing its two shelves. On top of it was a framed picture of her mother, who'd gone back to Europe in early 1952 with all the finality of a divorce, but without the effort and expense the paperwork would require. Crystal sat on a twin bed, made up neatly with a lavender quilt.

"It's a story to him."

"He tells it pretty well."

"Lucas Holladay did break my heart."

"A whole generation. The Lost Generation of mathematicians."

"If this doesn't work I'm going to break my own heart all over again."

"Don't let them get to you."

"Who?"

"The others."

"They don't think it'll work?"

"I don't mean that. I mean, think about the math. Do you get it? Don't think about the people, think about the theory. Do you have it?"

She smiled. She straightened. Her posture inflated.

"Think of the story you'll give him," I said.

She leaned against me. I wrapped my arm around her and we sat like that a while. We could hear when Karl rose to dramatic points in his monologue. We heard when our friends laughed aloud. Eventually we heard plates being scraped.

"You okay here?" I asked. "I need to talk with him before he goes to bed."

"Please don't scold him on my behalf."

"I'm not going to."

"It won't work."

"I don't think anything could change him. He's a fixed entity."

"He is. Don't butt your head against it."

"Likewise."

Karl and my three friends were out on the back porch. Karl pointed out constellations the others all knew, identifying the bright white dot of Venus. He joked that there were Venusians

41

too, but they were dumb as rocks. Couldn't even count. Every word our parents utter is personal, but Karl's storytelling wasn't so bad. Crystal was too close to it to see it for what it was: he was reenacting the best part of his life, which had been raising her.

I waited in the kitchen, hoping he'd come in alone. He had a glass of wine that was almost empty. He asked them where we were heading, again? We were on a pilgrimage to the Richter Site, Ronnie said, playing it coy, as we'd discussed. Crystal had made us all promise to keep our real motive secret. It would be unbearable if he doubted her, she'd said, and more unbearable if he believed. Karl said they'd made the Richter Site a national monument. The numeral trenches filled up with water when there was a desert rainstorm. People came from all over to swim in them. They didn't know the beds were still soaked with creosote and petroleum. Or they did know, and the temptation to swim in Martian equations was too strong to resist.

Finally, he came back in. The other three stayed out back. I'm sure they were happy to have a break from him. For his part, he seemed happy to have a moment alone with me as well. I asked if I could pour him another glass of wine. Only if I joined him, he said. I emptied the bottle of red into our glasses and we sat down at the table.

"There's something I've been wanting to ask you," he said. "How's my girl doing up there in the tundra?"

"The professors love her. She's the star."

"Not how her work's doing. How she's doing. She eating enough? Getting along okay?"

"She's been good. We're really happy together."

42

"Mmhmm."

"She's eating plenty."

"She's different, Rick. This is the first I've seen her since undergraduate. More serious. Less flexible. She was never a sensitive one. She laughed more."

"We've been driving long days. I don't think you have anything to worry about."

"Everybody gets serious in graduate school, I guess. I thought I was the Genghis Khan of statistics. Still, a father worries."

"That's only natural."

He drank from his glass and I matched him. He swirled what was left in the globe in front of him. I didn't try to match that, knowing I'd end up splattering the table. He looked me over some.

"I bet your parents don't worry about you," he said. "You're not that type."

"They don't."

It's farmhouse law that if a husband dies first, his widow will live another thirty or forty years, seemingly invincible. The flip side of that law is that if the wife dies first, the husband must follow within a year. Three years earlier, my mother had died four and a half months after being diagnosed with pancreatic cancer. She'd barely been having stomach pains a month before her diagnosis. Eleven months later, my father obeyed the law and had a heart attack. He wasn't too proud to call 911, but he was gone by the time the ambulance got out there, his mouth still white with chewed aspirin. I didn't tell any of that to Karl. Taking his compliment as my opening, I asked:

"After this trip, I want to ask Crystal to marry me. I want to ask you for your blessing."

He swirled his wine on the table again. He looked me over. "Sure, I guess."

"I was hoping for a more enthusiastic response."

Now he gave me a different look, between men, a look that didn't size me up but spoke to me out of eight years of de facto divorce and a house that was not empty tonight only because my friends and I were in it. It said: *There's only so much you can do in this world. There's only so much you can expect.*

"It doesn't really matter. Who's going to measure up to her?"

"Fair enough. I don't plan to."

"I was a very good scholar. You're probably an even better one, to be where you are. But she's a real thinker."

"But I do plan to take care of her."

"Okay," he said. "You have it. A more enthusiastic response. A partnership is about who takes out the garbage. The two might take turns dumping out the can. One might dump it out every time. It doesn't work if you both wait for the other to do it. If you can manage that problem, you can figure out the rest."

Instinctually, I looked at his trash bin, which was slightly mounded. A dented Coca-Cola can was on the floor next to it. He saw where my eyes went.

"Ha!" he shouted, slapping me on the shoulder. "I like you."

Then he cast his gaze down the hall where her door was still closed, and he looked divorced again. He said: "I think you're going to be the one taking out the can."

*

On Christmas morning, 1960, I was in a phone booth in Flag-staff, Arizona, yelling at a man I'd never met. The phone booth was at a gas station across the street from the warehouse where we'd parked. This town was the last stop before the end, and the beginning of the plan in so many ways. We all felt how close we were. The nerves were getting to Crystal even more. I could see her throwing up her oatmeal on the other side of the parking lot. Priya was there holding her hair out of the mess, rubbing her back maternally.

I should have been the one there, but the man I had hired to deliver the trucks and materials had forgotten to leave the keys in the lockbox. The moving truck and the water truck were both there, and we found the lockbox strapped to the moving truck's ball hitch. The code he'd given me opened it. There were just no key rings inside, so we had two trucks we couldn't drive. We couldn't even open the door of the moving truck to check the inventory.

"The trucks *are* there," the guy said.

"What fucking good to me is a truck I can't start?"

"It's Christmas morning, man. I've got my kids here."

"Christmas morning was always the plan. We agreed on Christmas morning. You added an extra fee because of it."

"I'll forfeit the fee. First thing tomorrow I'll—"

"Listen, Mars is at opposition in five days."

"*What?*"

"Nothing. We're just—we're on a very tight schedule."

"Let me see what I can do."

"Let *me* see what *I* can do about your next installment check."

45

"It's going to take me an hour and a half."

"That's unacceptable."

"I live an hour and a half away. What do you want me to do about it?"

"Fine. Drive fast."

I felt about ready to throw up my own oatmeal. I'd never planned anything the way I'd planned this trip. I'd calculated miles and driving time. I'd ordered Yellow Pages from a dozen states and called diners and gas stations along the route to see when they'd be open. I'd planned extra food for today, knowing all the restaurants would be closed. A ten-gallon drum of extra fuel, since the gas stations would be closed too. I'd had the van packed before finals, idling outside Priya's last exam. Personally, I would have skipped finals to buy us an extra day, but we would have lost Otis and Priya in the balance.

I had not planned on this shithead forgetting to give me the keys.

A steam vent in me opened and I slammed my fist into the side of the van, putting a dent into its broad green flank. Ronnie told me to keep it together. He angled his head toward Crystal, indicating whom exactly I wasn't helping. I told him I was good. I said we were all wound up tight.

"I'm not," he said.

"Me either," said Otis.

I updated them about the drop-off situation.

"What are we going to do for an hour in Flagstaff on Christmas morning?"

"Want to go caroling?" Otis said.

No one felt like singing, but we didn't have much else to do besides walk around. This was a popular stop on the Route

66 corridor. We were up in the high desert now, in ponderosa pine country. The trees poking their fingers up above the town showed us the most green we'd seen since Illinois. Above the skyline was an actual mountain. Had no one told it what state it was in? The roads were emblazoned with Route 66 shields. The signs on all the businesses had the same. A-frame lodges proclaimed vacancy. A burger joint had its menu items hand-painted on its siding planks: the Sixty-sixer; the Mother Burger. The touches of kitsch were balanced by the natural beauty, and in the end it was charming.

Off the main strip, little wood houses painted a variety of colors lined the streets. The sky was big above their low roofs. Christmas lights strung along their eaves seemed to connect the whole block, except for a couple of houses where a bulb failure had caused the entire string to fail, lost teeth in the row. With-out snow on the ground, the Christmas lights read like costume jewelry. It seemed like it was March and everyone had forgotten to take them down. But all the little windows were iced yellow by the light from inside. We couldn't see the families around their trees, the pajamas and presents, but they were in there. Or certainly not out where we were. There was not a child on a bike or a dad mowing a lawn or a family walking a dog. There was not a sound. There was not a soul outside except us.

Otis kept singing "O Come, O Come, Emmanuel" in his most operatic bass, but he only knew the words of the title, so he just stretched out the closing "-el" more and more. It hap-pened, of course, that Crystal and I fell behind the other three. Celestial groups moving at different speeds. They were a house or two ahead of us.

47

"If you want to avoid the attention of cracking the code," I said, "we could just stop here. We could have our own little 950 square feet and live anonymously in it. We could both teach math at the local high school."

"You know about my teaching skills."

"I could teach math. You could do whatever you want."

"I can barely pay tuition."

"I could sell my parents' house, buy one of these. I've already sunk almost the price of one into this mission."

"All the more reason to finish it."

"Sunk-cost fallacy."

My dad would've killed me for using my inheritance on this trip if he hadn't died to give it to me. This was absolutely the last thing he would have wanted me to spend his savings on. Even considering the truck rental and the agricultural equipment. But I could see my mom winking at me from over his shoulder, signaling me to go for it.

She'd say, *Do anything for love.*

I'd say, *This project is bigger than love.*

She'd say, *It can be bigger and smaller at the same time. Love mixes into our actions. Our actions mix into love. They're not separate entities.*

I'd say, *Thanks, Mom. I love you. I miss you.*

"I'm just fantasizing," I said. The part I didn't say: if she weren't trying to shoot for the moon, she wouldn't be putting me at risk of failing her. "It's a nice thing to think of. You and me. A fireplace. Kids someday. You'd have a secret knowledge in the world. You'd be the only one in the world who understands the math."

"That's a terrible secret."

"It's romantic."

"I want it out of my head, Rick. I can't sleep right, can't eat. I'm all over the map. My head's not on straight. All of them see it. Let's just get it done."

"We will. We are. Five days."

She was quiet, hunched, but at least seemed mollified. She began walking faster, working to catch up with the others. We kept strolling the neighborhood. *Emaaa-nuel. Emaaa - aaaa - nu - eeeeeel.*

"Otis, shut the fuck up," Ronnie said.

I stopped in the middle of a dead intersection.

"Look."

I pointed up along the avenue. Peeking above the tree line west of town was one of the white domes of the Lowell Observatory. Its influence was one of the reasons the Richter Site had been put out here. Percival Lowell built it after taking inspiration from Schiaparelli's maps and the writings of Camille Flammarion. He had recorded some of the clearest sketches of the Martian numerals there in the early years. This was one of the key places keeping watch on the red planet, and would've merited a pilgrimage in its own right if we'd had a day to spare. Pluto had been discovered with one of these telescopes. I wondered if I might be able to sell the rest of them on a visit on the way back. Probably not, I decided.

The powerful telescope in the dome was pointed way past Mars. To think that it was focused on Uranus and Neptune now, looking right past our nearer neighbor, seemed ludicrous. I wanted to break into the building and reorient it toward

Acidalia Planitia: watch this spot. We all stopped for a minute to look at this dome that looked into space.

"We should get back to the warehouse," Crystal said.

*

Lucas Holladay was an associate professor of theoretical physics at Duquesne University in western Pennsylvania. He wore brown suits. His dissertation, published in 1946, had not been influential. He hadn't published anything since. He hadn't advanced toward tenure. His department chair considered him unserious, but students flocked to him. Teaching in a tan blazer over a lime-green turtleneck or other outfits of the sort, he was both a little comic and a little dapper. He was each in a way that disarmed the other. A lank switch of chestnut hair swept across his forehead, keeping him youthful even in his forties, and his voice made him sound like a man who could clean a carburetor and drink a cognac at the same time. When he asked his students to imagine they were in a blacked-out train car—an adaptation of one of Einstein's thought experiments on general relativity—they closed their eyes and imagined. A five-hundred-seat lecture hall would go silent.

It wasn't just his voice. He had a way of speaking about science that none of them had heard before. Their high school teachers, their other professors, listed dates of discovery and molecular formulas as if reading instructions out of an almanac. The first day of each semester he'd wait until everyone was seated, even allowing a few extra minutes for the stragglers, before speaking. He wouldn't begin with the course title or a warning about the difficulty of the class, but with a question:

"Have you ever stopped to ponder an egg? The egg you eat for breakfast?"

He would hold up an ordinary egg he'd brought.

No?

It's an incredible physical object. Hard on the outside. Liquid on the inside. Two different liquids: a ball of liquid inside a sea of liquid inside an oval wall. On a biological level it's simple: one big cell. One of the only cells you can see without a microscope. Or eat, without a very small fork.

The egg needs to be strong enough to get out of the hen, but delicate enough to be broken open by the beak of a chick that wasn't even there when the whole thing started. Now, we think of an eggshell as an eggshell, but I want you to consider the *shape* of the eggshell. Is the force required to crack it the same at the tip as it is at the belly? Imagine, if you will, a perfectly spherical egg . . .

He was always asking his students to consider an object, to close their eyes, to imagine. His voice and his way of speaking magnified each other, working together like the lenses of a telescope. His point about the egg was that we look past science every day. It's mixed into everything. Because it's so easy to generate the force required to break an egg, we don't feel the need to understand it. And yet, no one cracks an egg at the tip, because we have some innate feeling for the physics of the egg.

He'd toss the egg to a student in the first row. No one ever dropped it.

They had not known—maybe no one had known—that science could be so human.

I remembered him from my high school years, his voice flowing from the radio into our living room, the question for which he became famous: "Do you ever feel alone in the universe?" By the 1950s he had former students who'd gone into broadcast radio, students who remembered closing their eyes to listen to radio plays as children and now remembered closing their eyes in Lucas Holladay's lecture hall to think about trains and eggs and spinning disks.

He became a frequent guest on *The Colbie Monk Radio Hour*. My dad would never have let me listen to it, but he also would never stop my mother from doing anything that brought her joy. She loved to sit at the kitchen table with a cup of coffee and the newspaper crossword, the radio running. I'd lie on my belly on the living room rug, reading a detective book and watching the happiness she took in that simplicity, as if no luxury could be added to the moment without subtracting from it. Her pupils would drift to the top corners of her eyes and her pencil would droop in her hand, and I wouldn't know if she was getting lost in Lucas Holladay's voice or searching for the answer to a clue.

By the late 1940s, my dad and I had lost something in our relationship. I was a teenager, no longer his apprentice, no longer held in high regard, no longer entitled to a reservoir of patience and grace. He'd lost a certain softness with me, and I came to realize that I had been one of his only sources of softness in the world until I aged out of it. I lost it too, feeling I was supposed to be an island now, to need nothing. I didn't lean on my mother in those years, though she invited me to. But I don't know what would have happened to me if I hadn't had those afternoons when we relaxed in adjacent rooms, a clear line of sight between us, and I could be assured by the silent warmth of her presence.

We listened together to Lucas Holladay's distant voice pulling the poetry out of a Slinky, teaching us when a bowling ball was different from a feather and when it was the same. He asked us to imagine our garden hose. He explained toast. Late in the interviews he would say the words *fluid dynamics* or *thermal transfer*, but not until we knew the science. Not until we understood it as if we always had, as if knowing were an inborn state.

Do you ever feel alone in the universe?

Eventually he would get to that question. He managed to sound even more excited about it than about toast. "Let me tell you something you haven't heard me talk about, but that I think about every day. Do you ever feel alone in the universe? Because I do sometimes, but it's crazy. Crazy to feel alone in the universe when we have a neighbor. Let's talk about the odds of life. There's a very narrow band of planets that will support life in all of space. It's a Goldilocks universe. That one is too hot. That one is too cold. No food here. No water there.

"Of all the planets in the solar system, and all the planets that may be orbiting all the stars we can see in the night sky, there is exactly one, other than our own, that has given us the slightest inclination that it harbors life. The odds alone of another planet doing so are, pardon the term, astronomical. The odds of the *planet next door* hosting intelligent life are—that's not luck. That's a miracle. It means something."

"Not all life on Earth is so intelligent, Dr. Holladay," Colbie Monk said. "Just yesterday I saw a man trying to lift his car onto the jack."

Lucas Holladay to the rescue. He defended the intelligence of people. We had our foibles, certainly, but he had the privilege of teaching young people, which allowed him to witness wonders of curiosity, intelligence, and insight every day. The problem was too many teachers treating students as stupid for not already knowing what they were there to learn. Teach people like you'd teach a precocious child and they'll rise to your expectations. Treat them like defective adults and they'll turn their backs on you.

Teaching was the perfect example for what we should do with the Martian math, he said. When his students didn't get a concept, he didn't want to see them go silent and give up. He wanted to see them try again and again. He wanted them not to accept not understanding. The only way forward was to keep giving your next best wrong answer.

"We're not their students, are we?" Colbie asked. "Many people don't want to be looked down on."

"Looked *down* upon? To be a student is a wonderful thing!"

"Now, Dr. Holladay—"

"How does anybody learn except by being asked a question they can't yet answer?"

"I don't mean to say—"

"We know what it's about. We know what it says. We just don't know how to make sense of it yet."

"*Do* we know what it's about? I don't," Colbie said. His voice was tinged with annoyance, either at being interrupted or at being confused.

"It's about distance, Colbie. We don't understand it right. You're sitting across the table from me here in the studio. Two people, next to each other. The Martian math tells us that we're no closer than if we were hundreds of miles apart. Now, I can see you. I could reach out and clap you on the back if I leaned forward. So I don't know what it means to say that the space between us is both great and small. I like you a lot and I think we're always at handshake distance. But there are two ways of understanding it and they seem to contradict each other and they don't. We just need to wrap our minds around why not."

They cut his segment short. Colbie was curt in closing out the interview. He did not like being railroaded. But the audience response was overwhelming. The phones were already lighting up, and with extra time to fill, there was nothing to do but answer them. People called in from all corners of the country. Housewives, fathers, high schoolers. They didn't understand, they said. But they wanted to.

The next time Holladay was on the show, he said he wanted to talk about a person's relationship to science. He talked less about the Martian math than about Einstein. Einstein riding his bicycle around Bern, losing himself on the map as he lost himself in thought. Not hunched over a dim candle scratching with a pen, not in a university cloister, but feeling the cool Swiss air rush against his face, his feet tracing perfect conjunctional orbits. He asked himself what it would be like to ride a beam of light. What it would be like to race a beam of light and look over at it. He made one of the great discoveries of physics by asking, *What would light look like from the side?* He looked at things from different angles. He rotated them in his mind. He rotated himself around a bolt of lightning and let the light race toward him in all directions.

That was what we had to do, Holladay said. We couldn't beat the problem into submission. We had to play with it instead.

He returned to his favorite example. Imagine an egg, he said. Hold it vertical, little end up. Draw a line around it—a belt. What do you have? A circle, right? A ring. At the widest part of the egg you have a bigger circle. At the smaller parts of the egg, the circle gets smaller. But things get much more exciting when you tilt the angle at which you circumscribe the egg. Tilt the angle and you have a strange, oval loop, but not a perfect oval. These were approximations, he said, of what mathematicians call conic sections, slices of cones—a very interesting field of mathematics, and one related to the orbits of planets. But an egg was even more interesting. Slice it one way and you have a circle. Slice it another and you have an irregular oval. Change your angle and the orbit distorts and flexes, something different from a circle and something different from an egg. And when viewed as a whole, it's something singular in nature: no way to describe it but as an egg-shaped prism.

"An egg contains one baby chicken and infinite math," he said. "What we need to do is look at this egg from more angles."

"But what does it mean? What does this tell us about the Martian math?" Colbie asked. "That's what our listeners have been calling in to ask."

Holladay laughed.

"Well, I haven't solved it, Colbie. Though I do admit I've been thinking about it a lot. The enthusiasm of your listeners is contagious! To all of you listening, your fire is my fire. I don't know. I don't know! But that's what's so exciting about it. It could be anything. It could have implications that outrun the wildest magical thinking. Einstein's theories unlocked the terrible power of the atomic bomb. Maybe solving the equation will give us the ability to cross great distances. Maybe they're being poetic, saying, *We're not so far away as we seem.*"

"Poetic? The beings that have only ever sent us math problems?"

"Math is as curious a language as poetry, my friend. It contains as many mysteries."

When the radio hour ended, I looked up through the open doorframe into the kitchen, where I saw my mother holding a brown egg aloft between her finger and her thumb. She held it where the afternoon sun poured through the window, giving the egg an orange glow. I watched her rotate it this way and that, shifting the tilt of its axis and peering at it closely. When she saw me observing her, she smiled sheepishly and hunched her shoulders inward, like a child caught in the midst of some embarrassing but minor offense. I shook my head.

She set the egg gently on the counter and smiled at me in a way that only she ever did, a smile of infinite understanding that I wanted to hate but couldn't help but love. Her smile that knew who I was on the outside of the egg and who I was on the inside of it. I felt myself flush and put my nose back into my book.

A few minutes later she went back to her room, leaving the kitchen empty. I moved to the space she'd just deserted and picked up the egg. I held it up to the light.

*

We waited another twenty minutes for my liaison to arrive. He showed up on a bicycle. His hair was unbrushed, his stubble unshaved. I'd thought he would look professional, but he looked like one of us, five days into our drive.

"You biked here?" I asked.

He waited to catch his breath.

"Just from Bellemont."

"Why didn't you tell me you didn't have a car? We could have been there and back in thirty minutes."

"You weren't in a very receptive mood."

"Because you were delaying us. That would have saved us time."

"More flies with vinegar, man."

"You mean honey?" Priya asked.

"Yeah, honey. You want to give me a ride back then? My bike will fit in there." He nodded at the van.

"Excuse me?"

"You said it's only thirty minutes."

"That would have been saved time. Now it's lost time."

"Bah, humbug," he said.

He tossed a heavy key ring my way, and by the time I caught it he was hoisting himself onto his pedals.

"Where do you think you're going? I need you to stay for inventory."

"Christmas morning, man. Kids."

He was up and coasting away. I shouted after him: "If anything's missing, I'm calling you back out here."

His voice was already small in the distance: "Nothing's missing. Mail me the check!"

Sorry, I told the group. There weren't a lot of options as far as professional fixers in northern Arizona.

Crystal was sitting on the bumper of the van, eating handfuls of granola from the bag, replacing the oatmeal she'd thrown up earlier.

I unlocked the back of the moving truck and swung the doors open, terrified the inside would be nothing more than a scatter of used napkins. What I saw instead was as neat as the aisles of a professional stock house. It looked as if it had been assembled by someone as organized as, well, myself. The supplies were arranged in a U shape, with an aisle large enough to walk in down the middle. The right-hand side was lined with big red fifty-five-gallon drums of a special additive I'd ordered from DuPont. They were stacked double and belted to the wall by a rope tied to cleats at the front and back. On the left-hand side was a wire shelving unit for smaller supplies, the front of it crisscrossed with bungee cords to hold the items in place.

I had checklists written out on clipboards. I passed one to Ronnie and climbed into the truck. Ronnie started counting the drums. I knocked each one on the middle and top to ensure they were full. He tallied the count on his page. He also had the fuel on there, twenty five-gallon drums of diesel and forty ten-gallon barrels of gasoline. I took the caps off a few and smelled them.

"All good," I said.

Ronnie didn't respond, so I said it again.

I looked over my shoulder. He was distracted by something at the door of the truck.

I saw Crystal there, the top half of her showing above the bottom of the trailer opening. She was weeping quietly but so intensely I couldn't see her eyes. Her bottom lip pushed upward.

Her brow pushed downward. Her face crumpled. I jumped out of the truck and took her in my arms. "Jesus, babe," I said. She heaved against me, sucking in her breath. I hadn't seen this woman cry before, except a few stray tears one night when she talked about her mother leaving. I'd seen her eyes light up like dark windows when she was burning to share a thought. I'd seen her go far away when she was thinking of something she'd rather not. I'd seen her tongue trip over itself when she was trying to explain something that mattered to her.

This was the first time I'd seen something erupt from her.

I looked at the others around us. Ronnie was still in the truck with his clipboard. Priya had her arms crossed and was chewing her lip. Otis had a finger in his ear. They stared at the two of us like we were an accident on the side of the road. No one moved to help, to join. Looked like I would be handling this one without backup.

"It's all here," I told her. "Everything's going to plan."

She couldn't talk yet.

"It's going to work."

She said something unintelligible.

"What?"

"Happy tears," she managed. She turned her ear to my chest. Her respirations calmed. "Love tears."

"Take a clipboard," I said. "It's better to have something to do." She listened and tallied the count as we checked the shelves on the other side of the aisle, which mostly contained supplies for living five days in the desert: potable water, beef jerky, oatmeal, trail mix, bread, toilet paper, toothpaste, three tents, five sleeping bags, an extra spare tire for the van, folding chairs, sun

hats, two pipes and some fabric we would use to build an awning off the side of the van—even in the winter, you couldn't sit
in that sun all day—flares, backpacks, salt, signaling mirrors. A
camera and more rolls of film than we could ever use. It was all
there, labeled in marker on strips of masking tape.

"It's perfect," I said.

Crystal said she was sorry. "Look at all this," she said, gestur-
ing at the assortment of supplies. "How did you do it? You made
everything appear three thousand miles from where we started."

"Twenty-five hundred."

"Without you we wouldn't have anything but a sketch on paper."

"That's still all we have. But not for long."

A shudder rocked her. I was asking her to believe. Meanwhile, I was imagining her as a carpentry stud bearing too
much of a load from above. I was picturing a board snapping in
half at the midpoint. I was trying to figure out how to take on
some of that weight.

"You're a genius," I said. "You figured it all out. I'm just running support."

"You have a genius for organization."

I laughed.

"That's like having a talent for grocery shopping. It's a nice
way to say I'm a responsible dope."

"No, I mean—"

"Don't worry. It's how I like to see myself."

"Hey, Rick?" It was Otis, hanging his thumb at the cab of
the moving truck. "Can I drive the big truck?"

Yeah, I said, giving Crystal a little space. She'd recovered
herself. I told Otis to knock himself out. *Oh yeah!* he said. Just

slow on the turns, I told him. It's not a Pontiac. He and Ronnie moved their personal bags to the trucks while I scanned the inventory one last time and closed up the moving truck. Crystal headed back to the van and I separated out the key rings.

"Everyone know the way to the site?"

"Uh, yeah? The same road we've been on for four days," Otis said.

"Stop at the giant black letters in the ground," said Ronnie.

Crystal came out of the van with her two binders of notes under her arm. She was headed in the direction of the water truck. I trotted over to intercept her. I asked what was up. She said she was going to ride this last stretch with Ronnie. She wanted to look over her notes. To refresh. To double-check. Ride with me, I said. I'm a good sounding board. She laughed. No one would have guessed she was breaking down fifteen minutes ago.

"We talk too much."

"I can be taciturn."

"I talk to you too much."

I didn't want her to go with Ronnie. I wanted her next to me. I didn't want to be parted for a minute or a mile, and, especially now, I wanted to be where I could keep a watch on her.

She kissed me on the cheek.

"I can't help it," she said. "You drive me to distraction."

Off she went to the far side of the water truck. I rambled to the van and hopped in the driver's seat. The passenger door opened and Priya got in. I remembered the way she'd looked at me when I started dating Crystal, like I was some hole in the ground out of which a rodent might appear. The gaze wasn't hostile, but was prepared to be. It was watchful, patient, wary. That was the look she was giving me when she climbed into the van.

*

Think of an egg. Think of a Slinky. Consider the mirror on a moving car. Imagine a kite on a string. The notches on a tape measure. The distance around a cupcake versus the distance across it. The minute hand and the hour hand of a clock. Have you considered a simple water glass? Have you considered a thread as it weaves up and down through cloth, traveling one distance to make another?

For a year, Lucas Holladay tried to explain the Martian math. To understand by explaining—he was clearly stumbling in the dark. He knew he was, and he wasn't shy about it. He laughed as he talked himself out of each analogy on live radio, as he explained how it didn't, after all, resolve the contradiction at hand. He was ostensibly on the show to discuss other facets of science, but callers each time wanted to know, or if not to know to at least hear him trying, because when he was trying it all felt closer. Closer in a way older folks remembered from their childhoods. Closer in a way this generation had never known.

This was the period during which Crystal came to listen to him. She was turning the dial alone at her house—her mother had left years earlier; her father was usually on campus—when she heard the honeyed voice essaying about quantum entanglement, the choreography of particles. He said it had the wrong name. Quantum entanglement made it sound deeply understood, cataloged, when it should really be called what Einstein called it: "spooky action at a distance." It wasn't pithy, but it was just right. Crystal was already intrigued. When the calls coming in directed the conversation to the Curious Language, which she'd been obsessed with for four years, she was hooked.

During the early days of our courtship, we talked about Lucas Holladay a lot. We talked, mostly, as if things had turned out rosy. What inspired her about Holladay, she said, was that he was never bored or jaded with the world. He never turned off his seeking-eyes. He was always chasing understanding.

I told her she sounded like him.

"I'll take the compliment."

We were across the Charles River from campus, lying in the grass of the esplanade on a cool autumn day. The river crept by, crew teams crawling along its surface like caterpillars. Above it we could see the campus, where we typically cloistered ourselves. Even now, we'd escaped it only to get a better view of its domes and columns. The esplanade's trees were saturated with a vibrancy of color I had never seen on the West Coast, their pigments pure as an ideal. I told her how sad it made me that my mother had passed before she'd had the chance to come see this. I told her about how my mother had loved Holladay's radio appearances, how I'd pretended not to. She was always reaching out to me, I said. She let me be distant, but always left a light on for me to come back.

We'd been dating for four months then. We were starting to open the deeper vaults.

"Can I tell you a secret?" Crystal asked. "A secret I think your mom would have liked?"

She told me then that she was working on the Martian math. Actively working on it. Trying to figure it out every day. She was working harder on it than her dissertation. This really was a secret because in that era, working on the Curious Language was like working on warp speed or time travel. It was the domain of kooks, cranks, and deluded prophets. The field was already on the downswing when the Holladay fiasco cast it down seemingly beyond redemption. All the academic departments and institutes on Haufmann-Eisen spatial mechanics that proliferated in the 1920s had shuttered, and now even students of the most closely related branches of study, differential geometry and general topology, were sometimes looked at askance. Crystal was doing work in both of them. If she weren't the star of the program, doing more important work in two fields than any of the rest of us were doing in one, she never would have been allowed to.

"Isn't it frustrating, trying to solve it?" I asked.

"It would be more frustrating to understand it."

"You can't mean that."

"The chase is the best part. Is it better to be traveling on a road or at the end of it?"

"Depends what's at the end of it."

Once she'd confessed her secret project, she began talking to me about the Martian proof all the time, trying out different analogies, talking herself out of them. She used echolocation. Her own ideas bounced back to her off me, reflecting a skepticism I didn't care to exercise. She imagined the critiques I would have made were I not so clouded by love. It didn't matter to me whether she ever solved it, so long as I could listen to her trying.

What I was trying to unpack was much closer to Earth. My father was living alone now in a little farmhouse north of Lodi without the softening balance of my mother. He'd been a gentle man when I was little. Somewhere along the line he started to feel assailed by unseen enemies. Some hostile vibration in the atmosphere resonated in him, but skipped Mom and me. I told Crystal late one evening about the summer some college students made crop circles in our cornfield. I'd stood next to him on top of the tractor shed, surveying the damage. A part of me wanted to believe it really was an alien landing. No part of him did. It's crazy, I said to Crystal, how you can stand three feet from someone but feel miles apart if they're turned away from you—

"Wait, what did you just say?"

"They made a figure in the field. You know, crop circles, made to look like an alien—"

She didn't stop me, but I trailed off on my own because she looked so far away. I didn't dare interrupt her. Eventually she shook her head. She said she should go. It was late. She was thinking crazy.

"Stay," I said.

"I stayed last night."

"Stay every night."

"I'll stay tomorrow."

She knocked on my door at 9:30 the next morning. She looked like shit. Her hair was a tangle of hay. Her eyes were so puffy I thought someone had hit her. She handed me a sheet of paper with neat rows of Martian numerals in light blue ink. She asked me to look over it.

"I can't read this."

"Sure you can. Anyone who's taken an interest in the language knows the numerals."

"I learned how to read music for middle school band. Now it's more like translating."

"So: translate."

"I can't with you staring at me like that." She looked hurt.

"I mean, it's going to take me some time. A day, probably."

"It's one page."

"I'm a slow learner. And I do have to sleep."

She gave me the day. I skipped class to spend it laboriously translating the Martian numerals to human numerals. After a first pass I had to go to the library to find a resource to consult for some of the more complicated figures. Sigmas, zetas. I also discovered I'd mixed up the symbol for seven with the symbol for nine and had to redo much of my work. When the translation was complete, I stared at it for nine hours. She did stay, as she promised she would, and she stayed out of my way. A silent presence, observing without lurking. She set cups of coffee in front of me, plates of food, and retreated back into the wallpaper. I wondered if she was showing me how she wanted to be loved. Did I talk too much?

"Is my translation right?" I finally asked, when I felt I couldn't make any more progress on my own.

She checked it over. "You really did translate the whole thing," she said. She could look at a page of Martian numerals and read them as fluidly as Arabic numerals. She'd done the work directly in Martian script. She hadn't needed to translate as a half measure. But she confirmed my transcription.

"I don't understand this line," I said.

"That's *the* line."

"I know. I don't get it."

She launched into the first of her many attempts to explain it to me. Not the calculation but the concepts it represented, the way it resolved them. She asked me to imagine the shape of a key. She asked me to imagine my toothbrush. She asked me to imagine a rolled sheet of paper.

"Have you ever felt—" she asked.

"Like I'm alone in the universe?"

We both laughed. I'd caught her in the moment.

"Not when I'm with you," I said.

Then I gave her the kind of kiss you remember, a kiss that contained more, for me, than the sheets of paper in front of us that had decoded one of the great mysteries of the universe.

*

The stretch of Route 66 on the other side of Flagstaff was slated to be bypassed in the next few years. Where it swept northwest, bent toward the gravity of the Grand Canyon, it passed through Peach Springs and Hackberry, by Grand Canyon Caverns and of course the Richter Site. The more direct route would pass from Seligman straight to Kingman, and so that was where Interstate 40 would go, putting a tourniquet on ninety miles of gas stations and motels and quaint Old West tourist towns. Crystal might have said these places were living off light from a burned-out star. Light takes eight minutes to travel from the sun to Earth, so if you look at it one way there's a grace period between when the star stops burning and when the light runs out. But if you look at the first moment without light as the first possible information heralding the end of the star, there's no time in between the star's collapse and the light running out. The eight minutes carry the moment of collapse on their backs.

But Crystal wasn't in the van with me. She was thirty feet behind me in the cab of the water truck with Ronnie. In my side mirror I could see a swish of hair that looked vaguely like hers. I mentioned my Route 66 thoughts to Priya, just to see how she'd respond. While Priya was never prone to the same bouts of poesy as Crystal, she was the most socially adept person in the program—not the hardest crown to wear in a community of professional mathematicians, but still: she was easy to talk to. Except she had spent most of our trip looking like she had a stomachache. A certain amount of that could be written off as the travails of travel, the indignities of the road, too much time in the close-quarters company of smelly men, but something had clearly been bothering her.

"I know you've put a lot of planning into this. I hope you have a plan for if it doesn't work," she said.

"Why come all this way if you don't think it'll work?"

"I do think it'll work. Don't get me wrong. I wouldn't be out here if I didn't think it was going to happen. But an outside observer would bet on our failure. No offense, but you're a little lovestruck. You're taking a lot on faith. We didn't bring this to our professors because we know it might fail."

"We didn't tell our professors because we know it might succeed. No one else is going to get the credit for what she figured out."

"What she *might* have figured out. The whole world is peppered with little scraps of math people have carved into their backyards, thinking the same thing we think. Mars has been silent to all of them. So what are you going to do if Mars doesn't say anything back to Crystal?"

I stared at the road. The sky was rippled with a sheet of threatening clouds. I didn't tell Priya my thought that rain was a thing I hadn't planned for. If it rained on the wrong day, it would wash away everything we wrote before it was exposed to the sky.

"If it doesn't work," I said, "then I'll hold her. I'll make her soup. I'll talk to her professors. I'll keep the fire going in her bungalow and food in the fridge. If it doesn't work, I'll do what I need to do. But I can't be there without being here first. This stop has to come first."

I'm not sure I liked Priya interrupting the faith, the little world it created when Crystal and I believed in it together. Crystal believed she had it right, but broadcasting it was my idea. I was the one who told her that if she had it, she couldn't just keep it in her notebook. She had to see for sure. She was the one who said she didn't have the resources to sketch it and no institution was going to put that kind of money on the theory of a twenty-four-year-old grad student.

I was the one who told her anything was possible.

*

My mother woke me in the middle of the night, her eyes shining with a secret. She pulled me out of the room. Across the hall, I could see my dad's bare feet in the moonlight, splayed at the foot of their bed. From the living room I could see the flickering black-and-white light of the television. We sat together on the little oval rug in front of the set. The volume was so low our slightest movements erased it. The darkness outside the windows was complete. I knew where the barns and silos of our neighbors should have been, but could see no trace of them.

The set was tuned to a late-night show I hadn't known existed. I didn't know there was any programming at that hour. I'd assumed the networks went to static after 10:00 PM. But here was the host, a funny, confident man in dapper glasses holding court over the night owls. His guest that night was Lucas Holladay. Holladay was saying he wanted to speak to a big audience because he had big news. Was this about that Martian mathematics? the host asked.

"It is," Holladay said. "And the news is I've got it. I figured it out."

The audience gasped. I might have too. Holladay turned to the camera.

"Grab a sponge," he said.

My mother hopped up and ran to the kitchen. She returned a moment later with the sponge in her hand. Holladay asked us to consider the distance between one corner of the sponge and the opposite corner. Think of the thread a droplet of water would have to travel to get from one corner to the other. Now compress the sponge. Is the distance between the corners the same? It's shorter, is it not? If you're really squeezing, the distance is almost nothing now. But the same distance, the same thread that a water droplet would have to travel, is coiled inside that smaller

71

distance. Two distinct, unequal distances exist at once. They are both correct.

My mother looked at the sponge as if it were a holy object. I did too. I finally felt I understood the contradiction that had been baffling me.

Holladay switched to talking about optics. We weren't sure why. His friend at the university was a very famous professor of optics, he said. One of the best. The professor told him that the previous displays had been written on a scale that was pure overkill. They were much larger than they needed to be because of inefficient design. Writing with fire in the middle of a red desert? Grab an orange crayon and see how well it shows up on a sheet of red paper.

"You don't think the Martians saw the Richter Site?" the host asked.

"I'm not trying to suggest that. Brilliant minds went over it. They knew it could be seen from space. My friend's point was that the letters need not be so gargantuan if you use a contrasting color. You could go a tenth of the size."

"I don't know about you, but that sounds to me like it would mean a tenth of the cost."

"Not even a tenth of the cost! You're dealing with area—square numbers. The decrease in expense is exponential. Costs could be a hundredth of what they once were. Now take a blue crayon and mark that same sheet of paper. Watch it leap off the page. From the very beginning, they haven't spoken to us with fire. They've spoken to us in blue. Let's speak blue back to them."

"So what burns blue?"

Holladay laughed.

"We're a nation of pyromaniacs. Who needs to burn anything? Let's talk to the Martians for the cost of blue cloth. I've
already begun raising funds for the project. With a few hundred
thousand dollars—"

Now why, the host asked, was his university or the government not sponsoring his project, if the costs were so much lower?
Holladay laughed. Well, he said, that was his fault. The bean
counters had inspected him and found him wanting. You see,
he wasn't an endowed professor at Oxford or Harvard. He didn't
publish in the journals those folks published in. He preferred
talking to the people over other mathematicians. He didn't have
a résumé worth the kind of investment they needed. I'm not the
type of man they can imagine solving the problem, he said—not
a grizzled old academic, not some hoary elder astronomer, just a
man who's let the problem live in his brain every day.

The host flashed an address on the screen for those who
wanted to donate to Holladay's project. It didn't take long. People
sent envelopes with two or three dollars. Kids sent silver dollars
they'd been given for their birthdays. Holladay delivered his spiel
to Colbie Monk, to Lester Ferris and Tom Castaneda and Steve
Allen. He did a tour of regional radio markets. People liked him
even more now that he was asking for money. So many asked if
they could volunteer their labor that he started keeping a list. In
the three months after the *Tonight* appearance, Holladay raised
more than $430,000. That, he said, would buy a lot of blue cloth.

On a warm day in June 1954, Holladay, his volunteers, and
an army of news reporters converged on the site he'd chosen,
a hayfield in eastern Ohio. A farmer there had donated the

use of his two thousand acres of property and even disced out the designs Holladay had sent to him. Into those carved-out designs, Holladay and his team unrolled long skeins of azure fabric, staking them into place. The line of each numeral was hundreds of yards across, so even with hundreds of volunteers it was a big job. The weather was nice. The volunteers who weren't commuting rolled out their sleeping bags inside the symbols and slept under the stars.

Filling the symbols in took three days. The front pages of the newspapers showed the progress of the project. It looked as if the gargantuan numerals were slowly being filled by a giant fountain pen. People sat by their radios, by their televisions. My mother left the radio on while she did the dishes. I came into the kitchen to fix a snack, and sat there doodling Martian equations long after I'd finished. The updates were not particularly exciting—*they've finished the next symbol; they've completed the second line of the proof*—but we listened as if it were the World Series and we'd put down money.

And now all eyes turn to the sky. But all eyes didn't turn to the sky. They finished on a Wednesday, a day ahead of the opposition. With no fire to light, there was no climactic moment to wait for and no significant difference in visibility between that day and the next. The display on Wednesday would offer ninety-nine percent of the clarity Thursday would. There was something magical, though, about the absolute moment of opposition, something primal. The atmosphere was ritual—festival. Volunteers had brought fiddles, banjos, flutes, saxophones, bongos. They made crazy, half-discordant music in the letter spaces. They couldn't light campfires in a hayfield, so they pointed the headlights of their cars into the common area where the impromptu band had formed, and they danced into the night. That's where the famous photo was taken, the one that later became the famous poster, of volunteers dancing joyfully on the azure field.

You could see Mars with the naked eye—not that it was red, not whether it was inscribed with blue, but a light in the sky too bright to be a star. If you could sit and observe for months you could watch it trace its retrograde loop, swinging back eastward as Earth's orbit overtook the red planet's, like a backstitch. Even the enthusiasts who'd lugged out a sixteen-inch telescope in the bed of a GMC pickup, a beast the size of an artillery cannon, would only see a bouncy ball of marbled red, perhaps an unreadable smudge of blue if the response came.

The eyes in the observatories of the world? Those were pointed skyward. Disdain Holladay as the academics did, belittle him as a slick-tongued outsider, many of them believed. Those who didn't watched just as eagerly to debunk him. On the ground, the people who'd built the display had their hearts in the sky but their eyes on each other. Nine months later, there was a small but definite fertility spike that got the nickname "HollaBabies."

He was the thing no one was keeping their eyes on, the man who'd put it all together. Not the night before the opposition. Not the day of, when no response came. Not the second day. Such delays had happened before. It was not until the third day with no response that the question was whispered by so many people that it became the voice of the crowd: Where was Holladay? Runners crossed every letter of the display. They searched the nearby woods. News vans drove to his house in Ross Township to find it empty of people and half empty of things. Clothes were gone from his closet, his dresser. The toothbrush and toiletries were gone from his bathroom. There was no note on the door or the table. Dishes were dirty in the sink. The trash can was full and it stunk. Lucas Holladay, along with whatever was left of the $430,000 he'd raised, had disappeared.

*

The Richter Site was gouged into the desert south of the highway. From the road, we couldn't see the depths of the trenches, just ripples, divots, stretching off into the bright horizon. The site's form was obscured by our angle of observation, which was like standing on the edge of a giant sheet of paper and trying to read what was written on it. Looking at the engravings from this unreadable angle called to mind Crystal's idea of a song embedded into the rumble strips of roads, a song you couldn't hear unless you ran your tires over it. Despite our tight schedule, there was no getting around stopping to look at it, carved here in the middle of nowhere like the least attractive wonder of the world. It was where Einstein's last solution went. It was the last place we called out to Mars and they called back.

The government had designated it a National Historical Landmark, but didn't seem to be doing much to maintain it. The dirt road that split off the highway to the edge of the site was rutted with the treads of occasional traffic. There was only a small wooden sign with the name of the site branded in, no map or aerial photograph or explanatory panel. There was a crumbling shack that I supposed was once a public bathroom. There was also a well with a pump. I checked that it still worked. Water poured happily out of the spigot. That was good. That was important. The public seemed to have done more to maintain the environment. As we neared the edge of the closest numeral, we saw a pool ladder set up to descend into it, though it was hardly necessary. The numerals averaged only two-and-a-half feet deep at the edges. Strings of buoys stretched across the dry bottom, dormant swimming or kayaking lanes.

The scale was the impressive thing. We were looking at an eighty-kilometer man-made lake in the shape of a transliteration of a sigma from a language that originated from thirty-five million miles away. This was only one of almost two hundred characters in the array. If they were canals, which they almost were, they'd be the longest and most intricate system of canals ever built, a larger project than the Roman aqueducts or the Dutch dike system. For a band of travelers who grew up the only kids in their towns who understood that a person could love mathematics, there was a beautiful affirmation in seeing our love carved so indelibly into the skin of the planet.

But there was something ugly about it too. Burned out the way they were, the trenches looked clawed into the ground. They were marbled black tarry holes. It wasn't a hot day, but we could smell the creosote baking. As inhospitable to life as the desert we'd driven through was, these seemed against life. Anti. We'd burned the dirt. Where the oil soaked down through the tar cap, nothing would grow in our lifetimes. Looking at it, I couldn't help but agree with what Lucas Holladay had said. This was no way to talk to anybody. We should be speaking blue to them.

We would be.

We crossed the highway to get to the north side of the road. Our eighty-kilometer side of it, our blank canvas. Our operating theory was that if there were watchers on Mars, if there were still citizens of that place who believed we were worth a second look, the place they were most likely to have their gaze trained was the last place humans had passed their test. We drove a mile north of the road, not wanting travelers—or, mostly, cops—to stop and ask what we were doing. No one from the highway was going to bother us much when we were just dots in the distance. If you were on this road, you were going a long way. No one would want to take a detour.

We had thirty-two characters to write. Crystal's whole proof was two pages, but she said there was one line we could write that would demonstrate our understanding beyond a doubt. It was the one she had said was *the* line, the one I didn't understand. The one that understood distance in a way that, as far as we knew, only one person on Earth could.

Funnily enough, our first step was to measure the distances we'd be writing on. We could proceed well enough on the part of it we grasped. We were Newtonian mechanics in the age of relativity. I had bought four tellurometers, state-of-the-art surveying equipment, the fanciest ingredient in the recipe. Mapping out the spaces right when you're working in two dimensions but exist in only one of them, in terms of relative size, is both more important and more difficult than most people realize. Ronnie wondered at one point whether we could wing it. I asked him to imagine driving his car into a cornfield and writing a legible sentence with it.

Working in two teams, we first measured the bottom rail that would connect the numerals of her proof, planting flags at each corner. We divided that into thirty-two segments to account for all the characters we needed to draw. Then we measured, very carefully—I checked and rechecked our right angles maniacally, exasperating everyone—fifty kilometers, a little over thirty miles, west of the rail. Our sentence ran north–south, the only way to fit it between two ridges of mountains. We planted a small flag every kilometer of the way, and a large flag on a ten-foot post at the corners of each of the thirty-two rectangles we created.

That took us into the midafternoon. After we broke for lunch, Ronnie and Otis took over the tellurometers and worked to plant flags at the corners of each square kilometer within the rectangles, turning the field into a grid. A grid that corresponded to the graph paper in Crystal's notebooks. While they took off in the van to measure it out, Crystal, Priya, and I readied the agricultural equipment we'd be using as our pen. This was a territory more familiar to me. We had a center-pivot irrigation system— thank you, Frank Zybach—rigged up for lateral movement. It was basically a long array of sprinklers on a rail with a wheel system on both ends. That was the modification. Center-pivots have wheels only on the circumference end, like the pencil end of a drafting compass. I checked the welds on the modified side. They looked solid. Assembly was required, though. The whole array was a kilometer wide, divided into one hundred ten-meter segments to fit in the trailer. We had to fit and fasten them all together and then wind the irrigation lines around it.

Everything I saw so far was making me happy except the cloud cover.

The clouds hadn't split open, but they hadn't scattered either.

We'd tow the rig with the water truck at one end and the moving truck at the other. The big hassle would be driving the water truck back and forth to the well pump every kilometer or so, but there was no chance of keeping enough hose to cover the distance from the well to the top of the letters. When Otis and Ronnie returned from gridding the first rectangle, they helped me dump the first fifty-five-gallon drum of our additive into the water tank. I used an aerator to circulate the water. The water in the tank turned the color of lapis lazuli.

Priya and Crystal took the van to start gridding out the next rectangle, while Otis and Ronnie got ready to drive the two trucks. I manned the machinery and coordinated the trucks, walking backwards in front of them, waving them faster or slower to keep their pace parallel. We started with the rail of the equation, the bottom line. We needed a stroke width of seven kilometers to be sure our writing was legible from Mars, which meant we had to snake our irrigation rig back and forth seven times to create one line, but at least for this first one it was straight forward and straight back. We had to fill the tank ten times to make the seven passes, but that was a better rate than I'd estimated. More happy news.

The sun was a few hours from setting when we started the rail and an hour from the horizon when we finished, but the desert light wouldn't empty out much until the horizon snuffed it out in a flash. We ate dinner around a campfire before that happened, our bodies aching from the labor. We'd forgotten it was Christmas. Forgotten it was anything but the day our work began. Truth be told, I'd been worrying about the way the solution was soaking into the dirt, a low-blue tint that looked dirty. It looked more like a stain on a shirt than a pen on paper. But as we were setting up our tents in the last of the day, the light draining swiftly when the sun touched the horizon, we saw the glow effect take over: the solution springing to life with the comforting warmth of a night-light. By the time we'd set up camp, nightfall was complete, and the blue glow a blaze stretching miles off into the distance like a runway to heaven.

The five of us gathered to stare. Like the Richter Site, it felt monumental. It felt beyond the human, and particularly beyond anything five math students could put together in a day. I can't deny that I felt a certain smug satisfaction about pulling it together. That didn't stop me from thinking what the others were thinking: *They have to notice this. There's no way they can fail to notice this.*

Ronnie said he wasn't sure he'd be able to sleep, given how bright the glow was. I reminded him he'd been sleeping two feet away from Otis's irregular snoring for five days. He could sleep through anything. He and Otis had a tent. Crystal and I had a tent. Priya had her own. She was probably happy for the independent sleeping space, but I felt bad for her. Not bad enough to share, though. Not bad enough to ask Crystal if she wanted to bunk with her roommate.

I was still greedy for her. I wanted to lie next to her and, if I'm being honest, to hear some compliments on how my plans were coming together. It would have to wait until the morning, though. When I got into the tent, she was already asleep, dozing under the Mexican blanket. I curled up behind her, and soon I was too.

*

Thunder woke us. Morning light illuminated the tent walls. Crystal stepped outside the tent to scan for more lightning. It was a favorite phenomenon of hers: its unpredictability, its power and echo. I was more worried about where the storm system was. I poked my head out of the tent flap. We still had cloud cover, but it looked to be the lighter tail end of it. The thunderheads had passed southeast. There was a chance they were snowing on Flagstaff right then. Another bolt. Crystal and I both caught it. She started her count, and this time I let her. Seven miles. I could live with that.

Priya was working her way out of her tent. Ronnie was up, wrapped in a blanket but starting a fire and gathering breakfast. Otis, of course, slept away, the only one of us immune to thunderclaps. It was Boxing Day, Priya said. Then she had to explain what that was. We ate. Ronnie jostled Otis awake for some lukewarm oatmeal. Then we got to work. We had to draw eight characters a day or the equation would be incomplete at the moment of opposition.

I've always enjoyed work. Despite all the bellyaching when I was a kid, I loved when my dad wrangled me into his projects. I mourned them when he stopped inviting me. He was of the generation that never said *I love you*, but the love was in those projects. The projects were our relationship. And the problems, the things that disrupted the projects, those were what gave them the purpose. The troubleshooting was what gave them meaning. Painting a house wasn't that interesting. Nothing went wrong.

I had to say, though, our smooth sailing so far was one of the best feelings I'd ever experienced. I'd never enjoyed work as much as this. I didn't know if the others had grown up the way I had. Crystal was the most self-propelled student I'd ever seen, but in terms of labor, I'd never seen her pick up a wrench. But the four of them seemed as tuned to it as I was—to the art of figuring out what needed to be done and doing it. Otis was happy as hell in the cab of the moving truck. The clouds cleared midmorning and the sun warmed us up, even if the temperature was mild. Ronnie, Otis, and I tied our T-shirts around our heads. Priya drove the water truck to the pump and came back with her hair soaked.

We were as dirty as beggars, but we were grinning. We lunched when we got hungry, got back to work, and stopped for dinner when we were hungry again. We finished ten characters the first day after the rail, nine the next. Traffic on the highway picked up. We could see cars slow down as they passed our stretch, their drivers presumably looking out our way and wondering who the hell was watering the desert. In a week they'll know, Crystal said. We didn't fiddle or dance. No one wanted the spectacle of Holladay's event anymore. That taste had turned sour. But the intimacy here could kill you—an individual achievement composed, somehow, of five. Once again, genius or madness was a secret we held close. Crystal wasn't fraying now. She was joyous. The others weren't worried about her anymore. Priya kept glancing at her, but even if she hadn't suspended her concerns, she'd put a pause on them for now.

On the third evening, Ronnie took the van out to Peach Springs and came back with two chickens from the market. We roasted them over the campfire and ate them with our hands, pulling the quarters apart. With her nerves resolved, and the rumble of van travel absent, Crystal was ravenous. She seemed to be making up for all the food she'd thrown up or avoided eating along the way. Otis claimed the necks and gnawed on them a long time. We washed our hands from the water tank and climbed to the top of the moving truck to get a better view of the work we'd done. The angle was still shallow; we couldn't read it, per se, but we could see that it snaked and turned like some kind of capillary system, that it branched into the distance like a vein of glowing ore in a mine. Crystal brought her notebook up there, comparing her designs to what we'd drawn.

Crystal and I made love in the tent. We both smelled like chicken skin. The next day we had four characters to write, half a day's work. It was the day before the opposition. We emerged in the morning to a new storm system blowing in. It wasn't over us yet, and it was a pale silver, but it was headed our way. Despite the risk it posed, I was half happy to see it. We'd worked the last two and a half days in full sun. We were all peeling somewhere or another.

By noon, when we finished, the clouds were overhead. They didn't look that threatening, and even if they were, my fear of the rain had been replaced by a faith in the five of us. We could do it again if we had to. We'd find the money. We'd get the equipment. We already had the plans. From the top of the moving truck, we looked out over one thousand square kilometers of painted desert. It was less impressive in the bright wash of day, but the numerals still glowed with a faint warmth under the cloud cover.

I told them anyone who wanted to could nap. The women, before they napped, drove the van back across the highway to bathe at the Richter Site pump. Ronnie and I took the trucks and the irrigation rig to go back over the numerals we did the first day after the rail, to make sure their glow wouldn't fade. Crystal, Priya, and Otis were all asleep in separate tents when Ronnie and I returned at 5:15, the sky just beginning to go pink.

I woke the three of them and pulled us all to the top of the moving truck. Otis grumbled and Priya asked what the rush was. I didn't tell them, but they saw me grin when we heard a buzz approaching from the east. This was my tour de force, scheduled for 5:40 PM, when the last lick of daylight would be just enough to make out the hulking moving truck and five figures standing on top of it. We waved as the little Cessna did its first flyby. I saw it bank a little to get a camera angle on us. It circled around to a higher altitude, halfway between the ground and the clouds, to catch a picture of our writing. Then it pulled around again, much higher and farther out, apparently needing more distance to capture the full scope of what we'd done.

"Jesus, Rick," Crystal said. "How much did you pay for that?"

"It's worth it," I told her. "It's for posterity."

I was telling all of them, really. I wanted Ronnie, Priya, and Otis to feel the weight of what we'd done here. I felt like the three of them only half got it, mostly because I myself had been able to hold the magnitude in my head only in rare moments. If Crystal's math was right, we'd just changed the course of human history.

In the morning, opposition day, we took more pictures before the sun got high enough to wash out the glow. These weren't from a hired plane. They were with the Nikon SP I'd brought. I gathered my friends together in front of our work. They put their arms around one another's shoulders. Ronnie and Otis were on the outside. Ronnie tried to look dignified but the joy kept breaking through. Otis had a big goofy smile. Priya was radiant. Even against that backdrop, Crystal was the focal point, looking as often as not halfway past the camera. Her smile seemed like something out of old Hollywood. With her willowy silhouette and the flutter of her long hair in the breeze, she looked like a painting of a druid.

This was the picture we'd send to the newspapers, our proof of concept. Show your work. Crystal was seven weeks pregnant in that photo. Too early to show. Too early to know, if your attention was trained elsewhere. I wouldn't know about our daughter for another thirteen years.

PART II
IMPOSSIBLE DISTANCES

I remember running home.

My father loved to hit me with riddles and brainteasers. Easy ones when I was a child. In elementary school, I figured out that the surgeon is the mother, the golden treasure is an egg yolk, and time devours all things. A clock has two hands and a face but not much else. You light the match first. Later I learned to measure a liter by pouring backwards with jugs. That was the only time we measured in liters at the farm. Everything else was gallons or acre-feet.

I had a wooden Tower of Hanoi toy: three vertical pegs with discs of increasing diameter. You had to move the stack of discs from one peg to the other without ever putting a larger disc over a smaller one. When I mastered a stack, my dad would add a new disc to it. After doing so a few times, he had to re-build the set so the larger base discs could fit next to each other. He took the original dowels and nailed them onto a two-by-four, extending each by a few inches so the top discs wouldn't overflow the pegs. By the time he revised the set, I already had an instinctive grasp of how it worked. I stumbled sometimes and had to backtrack, but I knew the direction I was heading. Soon after, I worked out the algorithm for moving the discs with enough clarity that I could articulate it. I stopped short of sketching out an equation, but when I explained it to my dad he was impressed. He hugged me and said he didn't need to build my tower any higher. Adding more discs would take more time for me to solve, but it wouldn't require any new thought from me. I gushed with pride.

Our house was a quarter mile back from the road, but I always felt like I was home the moment I rounded the mailboxes and my feet hit the gravel of the long driveway. That driveway was where I built my endurance. My dad's refrain: "Run and get the mail." My first inclusion in adult business, still undertaken with a child's energy. The small give of the piled rocks, the satisfying sound of each step. It announced your pace. I was in seventh grade the day I ran home so eagerly that my pace was double-time.

My history teacher had related one of Zeno's paradoxes that day in a passing digression, then patiently repeated it when I asked him to explain it again at the end of the class period. I'd been turning it over in my mind so intently I didn't catch a word from the second half of the lesson. I hadn't been able to resolve the conflict. What excited me so much was the prospect of offering my father, for the first time in my life, a riddle that he couldn't solve either.

I had to catch my breath when I found him washing a pair of boots out behind the tractor shed. Is your mother okay? he asked. He could tell I'd been running much harder than usual.

He slapped some cold water from the utility sink onto my cheeks, and I explained the paradox to him.

That which is in locomotion must arrive at the halfway stage before it arrives at the goal.

If a runner wants to cross a field, he must first make it to the halfway point before he can get to the other side. But he has to get a quarter of the way before he can get halfway. He has to get to the one-eighth mark before he can get to the quarter distance. You can keep subdividing the journey ad infinitum. So, motion is an illusion. Any journey is composed of infinite stages, so no journey can be completed.

He stopped to think about this. He took a moment of pause to gather his thoughts.

"I knew you wouldn't be able to get it!" I said, with some amount of glee.

He held up a finger and kept gathering his thoughts, mowing the problem down with his scythe. Finally, he said:

"That's not a paradox at all. It's easy to explain."

He explained that the dichotomy wasn't just in splitting the distances into smaller units. There was also the hidden dichotomy separating the distance from the motion. Notice the puzzler mentioned the distance but not the motion across the distance for most of the explanation. Zeno, or whatever his name was, was like a magician holding the real card behind his back. He didn't want you to think about how you cross the distance, because if you think about the distance and the motion at the same time, it's easy to parse.

As the divisions get infinitely smaller, the steps get infinitely larger in proportion.

He paraphrased it in the drawl he used when he pretended to be folksy:

"Cutting a steak into smaller pieces don't give you more steak, son."

He clapped me on the shoulder. I turned to walk back to the house, dejected. Then he called out after me. Remembering my taunt, I think, he called out without warmth.

"Is that why you ran here so fast? Thought it was impossible to get all the way home?"

*

Mass is relative to movement. Time is relative to speed. Everything is relative to memory. This part of the story starts with a letter I sent to Palo Alto even though events began weeks earlier:

Dear Crystal,

I just dropped you off at Logan and sat down to write this as soon as I got home. You're probably not even in the air yet, but already you feel so far from me. When something is out of reach it doesn't matter whether it's by inches or leagues. You're sealed in a capsule on a journey that won't end until you're in California, and so you're already there. And this letter being written before you take off will not arrive until a week after you land. Any response you send will not arrive for another week after that. Probably longer, given how long it will take you to run out for stamps when it sits lower on your to-do list

than unveiling the secrets of the universe. Scratch that.
I'm putting the rest of my stamp booklet in the envelope.
A self-serving act of generosity.

You promised to cook for yourself. I'm including a
few simple recipes from my mother's clippings for you
to start with. Beef stroganoff with egg noodles. One-pan
chicken and potatoes. The pot roast will last you most of
a week. None of them will steal too much of your time,
and anyway Einstein ~~and Lucas Hol~~ *exalted the merits*
of distraction. The majority of my own breakthroughs,
I think, have come while washing the dishes. Writing
all this has me imagining you stirring a saucepan and
decoding the miracles of mathematics at the same time.
Your job to make it a reality.

With infinite love,
Rick

*

When I moved back into the farmhouse where I'd grown up,
two years after the road trip to Arizona, the first thing I did was
order new gravel for the long driveway. The old gravel, pressed
flat into the dirt beneath it, was more mosaic than road now.
The delivery took three weeks, and I had plenty to do in the
meantime—plenty more pressing than the road, in fact. I re-
hung sagging doors. I patched the roof. I cut rotted subflooring
out of the bathroom, where a toilet seal had failed. There was
an endless catalog of other projects to work on. I'd been renting

the house for four years without checking in on it. I'd had other things to worry about. So, apparently, had the tenants. That was okay. I'd come to take comfort in things that were straightforwardly mended.

But ordering the gravel took emotional precedence. Driving up to the house and seeing a road the color of mud was like driving into a memory and finding it in disrepair. I wanted the road to be what it had been when I was growing up: a long welcome mat. I loved gravel. Old gravel is the dusty gray of backcountry granite. New gravel, like the day the trucks came and dumped two piles along the drive, shines blue like river rocks. It changes color in the rain, then shines in the sun, and you can smell the rain a few days later when you walk on it.

On an afternoon in 1968, a blue Chevy van crunched down the driveway. That was the other thing I liked about gravel. It announced visitors. The sound of tires would make me look up to see who was coming and decide if they were friend or foe. I didn't recognize the van, but was envious of how spacious it was compared to the secondhand newspaper delivery van we'd had to use for our trip. I walked to my end of the driveway to greet the vehicle. Four guys and one lady emerged. For the most part they were a little shaggy. They looked two days past a hot shower. The one who stepped forward to speak for them was clean-shaven with last year's Beatles cut and cheap, chunky glasses.

He asked if I was Rick Hayworth. I said I was. I believed in always answering that question truthfully, even if nothing good ever came of it. They were shooting a documentary, he said, about influential mathematicians of the past thirty years. Most notably Crystal Singer, of course. Since I'd worked with her so "um, closely," they were hoping I could share some insights about her work, her breakthroughs, and how they came to her. I'd done a few TV interviews with news stations and serious documentarians, and answered questions from a mathematics historian for an academic journal. These materials become important to a historical archive, and since Otis, Priya, Ronnie, and I were the only witnesses anyone could locate, we had to lay our memories down on the balance sheet.

We'd already given out everything we knew, but people still solicited each of us for comments a few times a year. They were a mixed crowd of academics, rabid fans, and kooks, and only Otis gave them any time. These five unkempt kids in their van, though, were on a mission no one else had sent them on, a mission no one else cared about. They probably didn't have enough money for it. They were fueled only by an unearned belief in their project—did they remind me of anybody? Enough so, at least, to make me consider being charitable.

"What's the title of your documentary?"

He shifted uneasily.

"It's a working title," he said.

"What's on the permits?"

I nodded at the guy with the longest beard, who was holding a clipboard.

"We haven't decided on anything yet."

"Show me the clipboard if you want to have any kind of a chance."

The leader nodded to the beard. The beard stepped up to let me take a look.

CRYSTAL SINGER: A HOME ON THE RED PLANET.

"She's not on Mars, you dipshit."

"Where is she then?" asked the leader. "If anyone would know, you would. If she were anywhere on Earth—"

I looked over his shoulder and saw the woman in the crew surreptitiously filming the scene, holding the camera off the side of her hip, where it wouldn't be noticed.

"There are a million easier places to hide on Earth. Get off my property. You don't have consent to be on it or to record me."

I stormed inside. When I looked out the window a few minutes later they were still there, taking a long panning shot across the farmland and narrating who knew what kind of bullshit over it. I thought of the crop circles that had once been embossed into that corn. If they knew the field they were filming had once been the site of a supposed Martian landing, their brains would implode. If I called the sheriff's department, no one would arrive for thirty minutes, so instead I went into the garage and dug through boxes until I found the old .30-30 Winchester my dad had used to get rid of raccoons and possums. It was unloaded, the bolt was rusted shut, and the stock was splitting, but the kids scattered to their van quickly enough when they saw me stride out the front door with it. The young woman, I was happy to see, did not have the presence of mind to train her camera on me before bolting away.

When I got angry, I felt like my dad. I'm not sure whether that made me feel closer to him or summoned the old distance between us. I think it did both. The closeness and the distance were tied together, and I couldn't tug on one without stirring up the other.

Poor stupid kids. They were deluded but didn't know it.

Their leader called my office the next week to tell me they'd pay good money for any correspondence I had from Crystal. I didn't have any, I told him. I'd burned it. After my stunt with the old rifle, I think he believed me. I wouldn't have put it past them to try to sneak into my house if they knew I had an entire file. I don't know what they considered "good money," but if I told him what university archives had offered for the same letters, they would certainly attempt to burgle them. I had lots of letters. Letters were all I had.

*

Dear Rick,

I've never thought math is a miracle. The things we study simply are. They were the rules of the universe before we were here to understand them. They operate the world behind the curtain, whether we look behind it or not, but the rules are already there. Music is a miracle. It adds something to the world that didn't have to be here. Language is a miracle. Every sentence ever spoken and every song ever sung is a new invention. Not only do they add something new to the world, they transmit thoughts and emotions that would otherwise be locked within one person. I hear a song and feel something a composer felt two hundred years ago. I read your letter and hear your voice saying the words. I feel you in the room with me. That's the miracle.

But you forget that I cooked for my father for the first sixteen years of my life. It's not that I don't know how to cook. It's that I'm retired. But a promise is a promise, and you made a good case for the counterproductive nature of starvation. My apartment is bare as a dorm room, but I have soap and shampoo. I have a skillet and a roasting pan. I'm working on keeping my promises.

You'll have to come visit because after experiencing the winter weather here I'm not sure I'm ever coming back to Boston. I can't believe you grew up with this and left it. I can work outside, so long as I keep dodging the dean of sciences, who keeps knocking on my door with trustees in tow. I'm training him out of the habit by not answering.

I hope I'm not torturing you too much being out here, but it's what I dreamed of, what I came for: time to spend in whatever way I see most fit. There are no demands on my time and still there's not enough of it. There's the old Curious Language to formalize. There's the new Curious Language to figure out. There's your pot roast to cook. Enough work, between the three, to fill a lifetime. I don't mind any of it.

A philosophy I got from you—there is work to be done. Those who can do it, must.

Yours always,
Crystal

*

The morning of the 1960 opposition, after we'd taken our pictures and spent a while staring uselessly up at the overcast sky, we packed up camp and drove back to Flagstaff. I swung by the aerial photographer's house to pick up his film roll, and took it and the roll from my Nikon to the one professional darkroom in town for the rush development I'd prearranged. I pleaded with the woman to take the greatest of care with the negatives. In a voice that said, *Sure, guy,* she patiently promised she would treat my film with an even gentler hand than she treated her own. Late in the afternoon, I picked up the negatives and the fat packet of prints. They already looked like something from a history book. I hand-delivered a set to the *Arizona Daily Sun,* while the others addressed packets to New York, Washington, San Francisco, Boston, Philadelphia, Los Angeles, Denver, and Phoenix.

The town that had slept through Christmas ambled to life. We ate sloppy eggs in diners. We drank our coffee without giving it a chance to cool. I'd brought us in on time and under budget, so I sprung for motel rooms. There was no shortage of lodges, even though I'd been right: the clouds had dumped two inches of snow on the town. Since there wasn't enough to ski on, the motels had vacancies. We took scalding showers in their limitless water. The water ran off us brown as chocolate milk.

Crystal and I showered together, close. I'd never seen her more beautiful than she was in those days. Dressing in the bathroom, damp hair falling against her shirt. More than ever, she embodied my mother's ideal of personality as the only makeup a person could need. She was funny, sturdy, hungry, and open. There were no signs of the cracks all of us had noticed on the long drive here. As I'd told Priya, she'd just needed to get through writing the numerals. The sky hadn't cleared and Mars had not seen what we'd done, but she had. None of the major papers had published an article about our work, but the *Daily Sun* published a local interest piece with a picture of us over the headline "Christmas Kids Try Talking to Mars," full of jokes about whether we were trying to signal Martians or reindeer. I kept a pit of doubt in my belly, still worried the Martians wouldn't respond, but Crystal wasn't worried about the project failing, which showed a wisdom I didn't have yet. Priya had worried about what would happen to Crystal if we failed. I had worried about what would happen if we failed. We were worried about the wrong thing. I think she could have handled failure.

Those were the best days of my life. I was finally able to articulate one of the things I had loved about Crystal from the start, which was that she'd always had the confidence I saw in her then, the confidence of absolute understanding. It wasn't pride and had nothing to do with pride, because she didn't see the quality as being about her, but about the world outside of her, which she understood but maintained a greater fascination with than those of us for whom it was an ineffable mystery.

After two days, the clouds cleared. We drove back out to our site at dusk, to make certain that the letters still lit up. They did, and the scope of the project was so grand that you couldn't hold it in your mind when you weren't looking directly at it. It stunned us anew. We didn't want to leave the majesty of it, but we raced back to Flagstaff so we could find a bar with a TV. We sat nursing our beers for an hour before a special report interrupted *Rawhide*. Bar patrons booed the news anchor until they saw the graphic of Mars. Then they listened, while the anchor noted reports from several observatories that blue writing was once again being traced on Mars. The planet had sparked to life again. They had answered us, the reporter said, but who had called out?

While it hadn't yet been authenticated, he said, several newspapers had confirmed receipt of evidence of a massive communicative undertaking in the Arizona desert, just north of the Richter Site, where man had last spoken to Mars. Five young people had claimed responsibility for the installation. They showed the aerial photographer's best shot of Crystal's equation. Then they changed to the photograph of Crystal, Ronnie, Priya, and Otis. I wasn't in the photograph, of course, because someone had to be behind the camera.

The four of them were enough to trigger the recognition of the bartender, who looked over his shoulder at the five of us seated along the bar. The news anchor said they wouldn't release the names of the five people until they were able to confirm the reports. Attempts to contact them had so far gone unanswered. We all stopped to think of our phones in Cambridge, ringing over and over again in our empty rooms. The bartender set another row of drinks on the bar in front of us. He said they were on the house. Tears had formed in his eyes.

*

When I'd heard the documentary van on the gravel, I had looked up hoping it was Angie, the colleague whose horses I was stabling for free on the farm. On another day it might have been. On other days it was. Funny thing about the past: in the present it matters what day a thing happened on. But once the days are gone, it doesn't matter when they happened. You get to call them to mind in the order you want.

*

We were too drunk by then to drive from the bar to Lowell Observatory. Priya, who'd had the least to drink, switched to water and an hour later we all gathered in the van. We pounded on the entrance to the viewing dome, perhaps harder than we would have sober, but knocking at an observatory in the middle of the night is less rude than you might think. That's when all the work happens.

An annoyed man answered the door, wearing a trench coat that looked like a robe or a robe that looked like a trench coat. Public programs were only open during the day, he said. We'd have to come back then. I held up the copy of the *Daily Sun* with our pictures on it. He gaped, then opened the door wide and waved us in.

The viewing platform was a ring around the perimeter of the room. The Pluto Discovery Telescope was a steel column the size of a ballistic missile rising from the center of the ring. The smooth white exterior of the dome belied the craftsman-like interior, which was an elegant latticework of wooden planks and beams. A woman writing something on a clipboard glanced up at us with recognition. She wore a much less idiotic coat. It was freezing in the dome, which was open to a long rectangle of sky in the high desert, twelve days after the winter solstice. We'd left our outerwear in the van, and the beer we'd had an hour before was not enough to warm us. The male

astronomer introduced himself as Dr. Shivers and explained
to his colleague, Dr. Chertow, that we were the ones who'd inscribed the message in the desert.

"Can't believe you were looking at fuckin' Pluto," Ronnie said.
Shivers bristled.

"Neptune," he said.

"You could have given us a heads-up," Chertow said.

"We were on a tight timetable," I said. "Would you have believed us anyway?"

I heard a touch of drunk arrogance in my voice. I glanced
at Crystal to see if I'd embarrassed myself. She hadn't noticed.
She was watching the slow rotation of the dome above us. The
telescope wouldn't be in position to observe Mars until after
4:00 AM, Chertow said. There wouldn't be much time for viewing
before the approaching dawn spoiled conditions until the following night. We were welcome to do the honors, she said. Shivers
gave her a cross look but didn't object. She invited us to catch
some sleep in the bunks of the staff quarters in the meantime.
There was a TV in the break room we could watch. Newsrooms
would have pictures by now from the other observatories.

Crystal said she didn't want to see it on a screen. We ignored
the offer of the bunks and sat around the observatory, though I
made a trip to the van to grab our coats and blankets. Otis fell
asleep against the wall of the dome. Priya leaned against the wall
and closed her eyes for a while. Chertow and Shivers loosened up
and started asking questions. Shivers left the building for a few
minutes and returned. Twenty minutes later, three other astronomers from their team showed up, their long coats misbuttoned
over flannel pajamas. Shivers had dialed them. He wasn't the type

to admit it, but he knew this was a night they'd all talk about for years. They asked how we did it. How we planned it. Where we'd come from. They asked Crystal how she'd figured it out. She said I'd helped her. I looked up, startled.

"In the way a brick wall helps a ball bounce off it," I finally said. "I mostly just stood there."

Crystal tried explaining the Curious Language. They grasped as much of it as the four of us had—some idea of what she was going for without the details clicking into place, but they listened to her patiently until the telescope was aligned. They all stepped aside and looked to Crystal. They'd known us only a few hours but they understood: She was the one. We were the four who ran support. I shook Otis awake. Crystal stepped up to the eyepiece. I leaned back against the wall and watched her looking through the telescope as if it were the only thing in the world. She started writing the new equation on a sheet of lined paper.

*

When I challenged my father with Zeno's paradox it marked, in some important way, the end of his kindness toward me. Not that he never said a nice thing again, but the spirit of our interactions changed. He would still occasionally present me with a difficult puzzle. He would give me space to complete it, as he always had, but the space was different now. It had once been filled with his faith that I would complete the challenge. In some way I could never pinpoint, could never prove in a court of law, that faith was gone.

I set myself up as a rival to him one time, and he hadn't been able to see me as anything else afterward. That was what Crystal said when we talked about it, strolling the humid bank of the Charles River the summer before our journey. Men didn't have the maturity. They couldn't stand to ignore a challenge, even from a twelve-year-old.

Especially from a twelve-year-old, I said.

He had also never sworn around me. Once our relationship changed, he sometimes did.

On a morning a few years later, I was awakened by such an intense bout of swearing I thought a burglar was in the house. My father's sustained shouting was as foreign as an intruder would be. When I realized it was just him, I threw on jeans and shoes and followed the clomp of his boots out the front door. He was already climbing the ladder of the tractor shed, the spot he often went to take a quick survey of the fields, or to take enjoyment in viewing the land he owned, worked, and made useful.

We looked out over our west acreage, where we had cornstalks growing as high as your ribs. The field was imprinted with a series of six concentric rings. The outer ring was widest, its line about thirty feet wide. The line of the innermost ring was only five feet wide. Filling the center of that ring were three equal circles. Twelve gently curving spokes traced from the central ring to the outermost edge, extending slightly beyond to curl into the Martian numerals for one through twelve, almost like the face of a clock. I don't know what we'd have made of the design if we hadn't heard about a similar one from a neighbor of Mom's family in Iowa. A spacecraft had landed

in his wheat field, the neighbor said. He heard strange hoot-
ing noises in the night, and one of his heifers was impregnated
out of rutting season. So this was immediately the same to us:
not necessarily a spaceship landing, but something intended to
look like one. I had my doubts, but I had my curiosities too. My
father had doubts only.

By the time I was up there, on the tractor shed next to him,
he'd stopped shouting. He was muttering to himself, and at first
I thought he'd quieted his vitriol for my sake. Then I caught a
few numbers in the muttering, and realized he was computing
the acreage lost, but in a voice so low and personal he might
have been speaking his own curious language. The mathematics of estimation. He had a brilliance for it.

He was a salt-of-the-earth type, or considered himself one,
but he was always running calculations. Yields, nets, projections.
I'd seen carpenters do the same, talking themselves through a
dozen angles and conversions before nailing in a stud on a diagonal wall. Dad could mentally subdivide an acre in a dozen
different ways, running permutations of different crops he could
plant to rejuvenate the soil, plants that would love the nutrients
this year's crops had passed on and give back to the soil what this
year's crops had taken. I could follow along with what I guessed
was his method—drawing a square around the largest circle, esti-
mating the total area, subdividing the square into four quadrants
to better estimate the percent missing, then multiplying that per-
centage by the total area—but I couldn't put numbers to it the
way he could. I couldn't connect the math to the land.

"Do you think?" I asked, when his muttering stopped.

"Of course not. I think it's a damn waste."

He climbed off the roof without looking at me. I stayed a few minutes longer, looking over the impressive design. I thought not, too. But I was wary of saying *of course*.

*

The slow drive back to Cambridge should have been celebratory. Instead, it was contemplative, almost to the point of being somber. We stayed in motels on the way back, luxuriating on mattresses that might have been thin but were on box springs rather than riding the metal floor of the van. There was no more night driving. The slower travel schedule would make us late for spring-term classes, but it hardly seemed to matter now. We were headed back to a Cambridge in which we would be more famous than our professors. In which our phones were already ringing ceaselessly because everyone in the world was waiting to hear what we had to say. When we got there, we'd be confronted by the big Whatever Happens Next, but none of us were sure what that would be. Or maybe we were just worn out. We were quiet. The radio saved us.

We made it as far as Springfield, Missouri, before Priya asked Crystal:

"So, have you solved it yet?"

Crystal looked up from the sheet of scratch paper she'd been staring at for three days.

"It's about entropy."

"Nope," Otis said. "I don't want to talk about it."

He was terrified of entropy, of the assured eventual heat death of the universe. I took comfort in the assured plain old death of our bodies long before then, but anyone who'd spent time thinking about astronomy had their thing. For me it was black holes. Just two years earlier, David Finkelstein had clarified the nature of a black hole's event horizon, cementing his place in the history of astrophysics and also in my nightmares. For Ronnie it was the scope of the universe, and the impossibility of traversing even a tiny fraction of it. For Priya it was a fear that there was no grand theory of everything, that the universe behaved strangely simply because it wanted to.

"What if as energy gets less organized—" Crystal began. Otis cut her off.

"It's a one-way street. It's a drain everything goes down. It's the endgame."

"The heat death of the universe," Priya said. "I can think of worse endgames. Sounds like a nice bath."

"It's permanent."

"Maybe it's not permanent," Crystal said.

Otis perked up.

"Is that what it says?"

"I don't know what it says. Just what it's about. I can't tell whether the Martians are saying entropy happens faster or slower than we think. So there's a fifty-fifty chance the news is comforting."

"Goddamnit."

"Maybe it's both," I said. "Isn't that their whole thing? What's near is far, what's fast is slow. Thin people are fat and fat people are thin. No one can know anything."

"That's not their thing at all," Crystal said. "That's a lazy misunderstanding. The idea was never that opposite things are true or that we can't know what's true. The idea is that we—we, us—don't see what's true because we're looking at a three-dimensional object in two dimensions. Our whole species has the bad habit of looking at one aspect of a thing and thinking that's all the thing is. It's not that there's anything we can't know. We just don't know anything, unless we look at it more carefully. We're content not to see things fully."

There was no way I could respond to that, so I didn't.

*

We all unplugged our phones except Otis. Every time his rang, he'd pick it up and talk to the reporters as long as they wanted. Some of his conversations stretched on for hours. I imagined journalists trying helplessly to find a tactful way to end the call while their children begged for bedtime stories. Ronnie wasn't so garrulous but had taken the calls for a while. He was a good storyteller and liked the attention, but after two days he tapped out. Priya chose a few reporters to respond to and answered questions by mail. She didn't want anything out there she hadn't had a chance to think through. All this would go in our tenure files someday, she said. Crystal walked into a room with the phone ringing and unplugged it right away. I was surprised. Didn't she want her story to be heard? I asked.

Her story was heard, she said, by whom she'd sent it to.

I asked her what we were going to do now. She was still hoping for Stanford, she said.

"Have they contacted you?"

"Not yet, but I put in my application in October."

"Wait, the postdoc? That's what you were hoping for before you were the most famous mathematician in the world."

"Yeah. Now I'm almost sure to get it."

"You could get a direct hire at any university in the world."

"Which is exactly what I don't want. A course load. Office hours. Public programs and donor dinners. I'm not going to get anything done in a place where I'm the prize pony. I want someplace quiet to think and work. That's why I wanted Stanford before all this and why I still want it now."

"What am I going to do? Stanford's not going to hire me sight unseen. Everyone knows I just drove the car."

I thought of what Karl had said about being the one to take out the trash. I didn't mind being the one who just drove the car. I would take out the trash and cook the food and drive her wherever she wanted to go. A part of me wanted to propose right there and offer those as my vows. But in California, without a job, there'd be no car to drive, no groceries to cook or trash to take out.

We'd figure it out, she said. Or really, I'd figure it out. She was good, she said, at figuring out the Curious Language, and I was the one who figured out everything else. She wasn't good at practical answers, but she could always count on me to be. Through the following weeks, I shopped for her. I washed and folded her laundry. I cooked dinners for her while she sifted through her mail. None of it was anything she wanted to answer, but I think she got some pleasure from looking at each envelope before tossing it into a growing pile in the corner.

One night I made chicken marsala with mashed potatoes and asparagus, or what they called asparagus in New England, which was somewhere between the real thing and the plastic asparagus from a toy kitchen set. Since we'd returned, she'd eaten crackers and cereal except when I made a meal for her. She gobbled up the hearty food.

Immediately upon finishing, she rushed to the toilet and heaved it all up.

She came out of the bathroom crying, apologizing. All the time I'd spent preparing it. All the money I'd spent at the grocery store. I came to her on the couch and wrapped her in my arms. "It's chicken and potatoes, babe," I reassured her. "Chicken and potatoes." She seemed to like the sound of those words together. "There's more in the pan."

She said, as though I hadn't noticed already, that she'd been eating like shit since we got back. Not the food I made when I came over, but everything in between. She'd been focused on other things and didn't like all the attention. Photographers stalked her around campus trying to get pictures. Now she'd trained her body on the closest human thing to dog food and it rejected anything with nutritional value.

"You think you'll throw up less in California?"

"Everyone throws up less in California."

We sat in silence a while. She broke it.

"I thought that figuring it out would free me. I suppose it did. From one cell into the next."

"It won't always feel like a cell. You were at your happiest when you were chasing the answer. Now you have something new to chase after."

She curled deeper into my arm and turned her face up to mine. I gave her a long kiss.

"Can I tell you something?" I asked.

"Of course."

"You need to brush your teeth."

"And now you need to brush yours."

*

My mother would have called chicken marsala fancy, but she would have approved of the chicken and potatoes. Another dinner, years earlier, a few days after the crop circles in our field: my father was no longer too mad to talk about it; he was now too mad not to. Goddamn city kids would get an idea in their heads and not think through its effects. Food ruined to oblige the imaginations of the idle.

"You don't think there's some chance?" I asked.

I myself thought the chances were slim. I asked only to rile him up.

"I'm surprised I have to spell it out for you, but a vehicle landing on a cornfield from above wouldn't lay all the corn down in the same direction like dominoes. It'd break the stalks in half, splay them every direction. You ever stomped on a patch of grass?"

"It would if the landing structure was rotating when it came down."

"Exactly what you want on a landing craft: the opposite of stability. Tell me how many planes you see with rotating landing gears."

My mother laid her fork on her plate and straightened up, a signal that it wasn't dinner while this conversation was going on. The two could not exist simultaneously. Dad would usually have stopped.

"And think about the symbols around the edges of the diagram. They suggest it's some Martian spaceship, is that it? You think they feel the need to filigree 1-2-3-4-5 on the bottom of their spaceship? Why the hell would they do that? Is NASA going to put the ABCs on the bottom of its rockets? And there's the giveaway. The only symbols incorporated into it are the ones we know. There are no other letters, nothing unfamiliar. It's some dope's idea of what a spaceship base would look like. And that city dope's idea costs me, costs us, a thousand dollars and ruins enough corn to feed a small town."

I didn't argue with him now. He had made good points, and I didn't have any counterarguments. I couldn't egg him on any further without revealing the game I was playing. He picked up a chicken drumstick and walked away from the table with it. That was the closest he had ever come to insulting my mother. Her insistence was not on table manners or etiquette so much as respect for the table, for the family dinner, as something akin to church. Walking off unexcused with a chicken bone was like spitting in a pew.

My mom and I ate in silence for a few minutes. I could see she was shaken.

"What do you think?" I asked quietly.

"City kids don't have a monopoly on imagination."

She cleared my dad's plate and scooped his vegetables into a bowl.

I was in high school then, and considered myself to be thinking in more complex ways. I told my mother what I'd

113

thought in response to my dad's outburst—picking a fight with her as a proxy for him. I said Dad was looking at the problem too simply. He was focused on less than a whole acre of corn among millions of acres of corn worldwide. The loss of this acre in a worldwide system didn't cause a food loss. There wasn't some actual person who would have eaten this corn but would now go hungry. In a national economic system, the loss of this acre wouldn't drive the price of an ear of corn up by a full penny.

"There may be some truth to that," she said, "but the simple fact is there was food there and there isn't anymore. That's a loss."

"He's trying to turn his loss into everyone's loss."

She didn't turn around to look at me.

"Yes. He's hurt and he's spewing it all over the place. Sound like anyone else I know?"

*

1967. Hearing tires on the gravel, I looked up to see a horse trailer coming down the road behind a Toyota pickup that seemed too small to pull it. The truck was the green of a brined olive. Angie was my new colleague in the mathematics department. She was the first woman in the department, and acted as if no one treated her differently, though everyone did—a sort of staring contest. It helped that she was tall. She had wavy, reddish hair and a long, serious face with a strong jawline. Her mouth barely moved even when her eyes showed a smile, and despite her teaching slacks and blouses she still looked a bit like a rancher. I had been surprised to hear she was from Oregon. She had an air of unflappable self-reliance I associated with women of the rural Southwest. On days she didn't teach, she came to campus in jeans and work boots. I had been even more surprised by her answer when I asked what had brought her to UC Davis.

She told me I had.

The university had a good enough math department, but she could easily have been in a better one. Like Crystal and Priya, she was an uncontainable force. Her work on locating objects within rotating coordinate frames was being used by NASA as they developed docking procedures for their moon missions. She'd been called to JPL the previous summer as a consultant. She was in her midforties, ten years older than me, and was looking at me with a sort of chagrined wonder, like a child confronted with a magical object. We tend to think of dreamers as undergraduates emerging from the pupae of adolescence, eager to believe for the first time in something of their own choosing. Our communiqué to Mars certainly did something to fire up that generation; few of the underclassmen in my seminars were there because of an interest in representation theory. But I'd seen in the intervening years that the people Crystal's proof had most enchanted were those older than us. People a decade or two older who had believed Lucas Holladay not as children, but as adults, and people in their seventies who had not believed they would ever hear from Mars again.

Priya was at Cornell, and Ronnie was at University of Michigan, Otis was at University of Wisconsin–Madison, and nobody knew where Crystal was. I was here in Davis, teaching upper division classes the other professors thought were rote. They wanted to focus on their research, to publish, to complete the arcs they had imaged for themselves. I just wanted to show up, teach some kids math, and go home. A building needs its architects and its carpenters, and I knew which one I was. The university was fine with that. I was a feather in its cap for what I'd done, not what I'd do. Angie had been teaching in Chicago for ten years. If she moved anywhere colder, she said, her horses would kill her and make it look like an accident. Of the Gang of Five, I was the only one in a viable climate.

"I hope you're not under the impression I can teach you the secrets," I said. "I'm just famous for driving the car."

"I know," she said. "Most people call it the Gang of One."

"Myself included."

"Don't worry," she said. "I just liked the idea of being close to an artifact. If there were a university at the Singer Site, I'd teach there."

"Not sure how I feel about being called an artifact."

"Ha! Try being a woman over thirty."

We'd been working together five months, in the vague way you work with other professors, when she related the trouble she was having with the stables where she housed her two horses. The horses were losing weight from low-quality feed, the stalls were mucked only once a week, and the stable's permit was under review. She was paying a fee for early release from her lease but had yet to find a new stable with openings. I said she could house them at my place. Would I accept what she'd been paying at the old stable? she asked. I wouldn't accept anything, I said. I was already leasing the fields to the university's ag department for nothing to support a longitudinal study. Add in horses and I could complete the illusion of being a farmer without having to do any of the work. I warned her that I had not taken care of the barn, so she might have to rebuild the stables.

Then I went home and rebuilt them myself.

A week later, she brought her horses to my place and led them out of the trailer.

"These are my babies," she said.

She brought out a roan Arabian first, guiding it gently over by the lead rope so I could pet its snout with the back of my hand. This was Jackie, she said. Jackie was her buddy. Then she drew out a shyer one, a bay Morgan horse. Angie let me hold the rope from a distance while she grabbed a bucket of oats from the cab and took the lid off. I would never get close to this one unless I fed her, she said. Once I was holding the bucket, it trotted right over and let me scratch behind its ears.

"This one is Cider," she said. "Cider is my heart."

*

Scraps of 1961—an argument: "I care more about being by your side than about my credentials."

"You shouldn't be reduced to flying in my jet stream. You're brilliant in your own right. You'll be a top thinker in your field, but not if you don't do the legwork. We all have to finish our projects."

"You sound like my dad."

"Am I wrong?" she asked.

"You're not wrong. You're out of perspective."

117

"You're out of perspective. Two years. We each do important work. You get your PhD so you can be my spousal hire."

"I'll change careers."

"Rick. You sound crazy. I have to get on a plane in a week. You're going to change your whole life by then? Work overtime and you can finish in three semesters."

She was cheating, invoking my work ethic. I was already asking myself if I could do it in a year. She knew I was. She knew she was being the voice of reason and I would come around to it. I wanted to listen not to the voice of reason but to the voice of surrender; I wanted to chase after her like she was the greatest mystery in the universe. I wanted to circle around her gravitational well until my orbit collapsed and I fell into her. I wanted to tether myself to her the way she'd tethered herself to the Curious Language.

"Tell me one thing," I said. Her body relaxed, knowing she'd won. She gave me her attention.

"Will you marry me?"

Since she had never pressured me, never brought up a desire for marriage or even the idea of it, I didn't expect her to leap onto me, so when she did, snaring my neck with her arms and my hips with her legs, I almost toppled over. She buried her head against my shoulder. Her hair was spread across my face, but I didn't brush it off. My arms were busy holding her. She let go of my neck to take my face in her hands and kiss me. Yes! she said. Yes. And she leaned back, pulling us down to the bed with me on top of her.

Sprawled next to me on the bed after we finished, she held her left hand up, examining her bare ring finger.

"If there's anyone I pegged as a down-on-one-knee type," she said.

"The ring's in the glove box. This wasn't how I was planning to ask."

"I don't care about that kind of stuff. It's cute that you do."

"I got your dad's blessing."

"Why?"

"It's the gentlemanly thing to do."

"I hope you didn't forget to give him a fat goat for my bride-price."

"You're worth a million fat goats."

I'd go get the ring when she went to the bathroom, so I wouldn't have to lose a moment by her side.

*

I wrote her more letters. Exceedingly long, frequent letters. If I was home and the work on my dissertation was done for the day, I was at the table writing. I was also there writing if my dissertation work was not done and I wanted to delay starting it. I had to set myself a rule that I would send only one letter a week. Even so, that was faster than a letter could get to California and back, even if Crystal were exceedingly punctual about responding, which she wasn't. So when I received a response she'd posted the previous week, she was responding to the letter she'd received a week before, that I'd sent a week earlier after adding to it over the course of a week. Each letter I received was a callback to one I'd written a month ago, and I'd dropped three or four more in the mailbox in the meantime. It was like talking to Alpha Centauri on a CB radio.

I wrote about the strange disconnect in some of our letters, comparing it to the way a fast-moving observer experiences time more slowly, even ages more slowly, while a slow-moving person will observe time in a normal fashion, or what we think of as normal. I liked making sketchy analogies because she was sure to write back to correct them. When I ran out of poetic things to say about distance, I wrote about the snow, supposing she secretly missed it despite all her complaints. Snow caused me frequent frustration but I never longed for my childhood winters without it. I wrote about my parents, because I'd been thinking about them a lot. When you lose the people you spent your whole life revolving around, there is a moment of explosion that collapses into a gravity well, a dark space that only ever pulls you closer. I don't even mean grief—I mean the pull, the inevitability of thinking about them more and more as time passes. Gravity distorts space-time. Absence distorts attention. The empty space pulls your attention into it, but releases nothing.

I think it's a myth that you can't get any closer to the dead, Crystal wrote back. *They can't move closer to you, but you can move closer to them. When somebody is missing, you are able to look at them from a different perspective. The temptation is to say it's a more objective view, but it's not. Nearness can distort your viewpoint as easily as distance. Your father was missing, for you, years before he was gone. I wouldn't be surprised to hear you're closer to him now, across the void, than you were in that little house.*

She wrote back most thoroughly when I was a problem she could help solve. Her responses were shortest when I complained about the distance between us. *Ha!* she wrote when I called the intervening miles a Cartesian torture device. But she didn't have a solution and wasn't willing to accept mine. I still said I'd drop out of the program at a moment's notice. She said I was as eager as a dog with a ball, and equally circumspect.

You still haven't sent me your phone number, I wrote in April. *I know we said we wouldn't bankrupt each other with too many phone calls, but I haven't heard your voice in three months. Give me your number and I'll call you. My bill, and I can handle it. Or call me anytime, and if money is the reason I'll send it to you.* She wrote back:

I never got a phone. Why get a phone when you don't want anybody to call you?

It wasn't the only thing in the letter, but it was the only thing I could see. I responded:

Dear Crystal,

Anybody?

Sincerely,
Somebody

I imagined it was chaotic for her trying to write back to several letters at once, unsure which of her own letters had already been received. After I dropped mine in the mail, I was sure she'd have no idea what to connect it to. When my phone rang five days later, I ignored it, as had become my norm except when I was in a particularly good mood. I had not received a call in the year

1961 from anyone other than reporters and Mars enthusiasts. My mom used to call me late at night once every month or so. She'd wait until my dad went to bed, which was early in California but after eleven Eastern time. He wouldn't have stopped her, but he would have grumbled about the rates.

It rang again and again, which was considered rude at the time. I was trying to untangle a data set and the phone kept breaking my concentration. Finally, I picked it up ready to tell someone off.

"Enough already. If I wanted to—"

"Rick? Rick, is that you?"

"Crystal?"

"Hey! I sent a letter back to you but figured I should call too. You know I didn't mean it like that. I always want to talk to you. You're not anybody. You're the most precious somebody."

"Okay. Thank you, babe. God, it's good to hear your voice. You got a phone!"

"It's the department secretary's phone. I asked her to make some copies for me. This call isn't, uh, officially approved. So I may have to go pretty quickly."

"I'll get you a phone. I'll pay for the bill."

"I don't want one. I'll do this when I need to. Being hard to find is valuable for me. Before I unplugged mine in Cambridge it would go hours without stopping ringing. Everyone else in the department has a little mail cubby and I've got a sack. Go a day without checking it and I'm hauling a Santa bag full of kook letters back to my apartment. It takes me half an hour just to sift through it for your letters and the few other things I want to read. My apartment was—never mind."

"What?"

"Nothing. It's not worth—"

"You know I'm not letting it go."

"My apartment's not publicly listed but I get some random door knocks. A couple weeks ago someone broke in and went through my stuff. They didn't take anything. I might have even left the door unlocked. There were no broken windows or anything. They just left some drawers open, rearranged some papers. Don't freak out."

"One more reason I should be out there."

"Then finish your dissertation. I'll get a rottweiler."

"You realize everything you're struggling with is something I can help you with? I can sort your mail, cook your food, make your copies. Your safety—"

"You can't help me finish faster. You couldn't help slowing me down. Because it wouldn't be you doing it. It would be me. You told me, after Arizona, that the world was different because of what we did. Subtract us out of history and it changes."

"I didn't say 'we.'"

"I'm always thinking about how the things I do will affect my work. Because no one else is doing it yet. No one else is close. I know that sounds arrogant but I've got it all spelled out in my head and I just need to get it onto paper. I need to extrapolate everything I can from it because the answer I gave the Martians was just a fragment of the world as it really is, and I need to draw out the rest from that fragment. I'm trying to hold the whole universe in my head and I have no idea what to do about the—about the—I don't even know if I should tell—"

"About what? Tell what? You're freaking me out."

"Shit, she's back—talk soon."

A clank, and her voice disappeared. I didn't like to think about it, but she was so frantic she sounded crazy. She had called to comfort me and now I had to worry again about her falling apart, only this time she wasn't thirty feet behind me in the next car. She was three thousand miles away in a city I had never seen. She was under immense pressure and had people breaking into her home. Then I thought about the times I'd seen her cook, trying to work on her projects at the same time, leaving drawers open behind her after she grabbed utensils, losing track of the ingredients she'd scattered across the counter. I thought of the mounds of paper that accumulated around her desk, the bills she piled on the kitchen table until Priya organized them. I'd had to buy her binders to keep her work on the Curious Language organized. She wasn't naturally messy, but when she was working, she could focus on a single point, ignoring all else. Maybe she'd lost track of her life to such an extent that she had interpreted her own disarray as the work of an intruder. That wasn't a comforting thought either.

*

Dad spent the week after the crop circles appeared nosing around the farm for clues. Creating such a large design in the dark of a single night was an undertaking that required intense planning and discipline. Doing so without leaving traces of your methodology would be superhuman. He trawled through the channels of crumpled cornstalks, pausing, crouching, examining this break or that smashed ear. He paid special attention to the edge of the outermost ring. He did this all on breaks from the real work he did to keep the farm running, his self-assigned extra credit. From the top of the tractor shed, I watched him wander around the strange imprint.

This was the first time in years I'd seen him overwhelmed by curiosity. He'd told me, in my younger years when we were close, that a man needed both curiosity and skepticism. They were complementary tools. Then he'd adopted a divide-and-conquer strategy, handling skepticism on his own and leaving the curiosity to Mom. I was touched by his search. I could see his befuddlement in the way he'd stoop to examine something, walk on, then return to it a moment later. I went out to join him. I had some idea that helping him with this would work toward repairing our relationship. I hadn't known, would not have admitted, even to myself, that I wanted the relationship repaired.

I'd been looking at the design as a whole, I said. The rings and chambers were all interconnected, meaning only one access point had been needed. We needed to look for the way they'd come in and out. "Why do you think I'm searching the edges?" he said, but with a guarded approval.

"Don't think about the edges. Think about the roads. They didn't start from the inside of the design. They had to come from the outside and get into the middle of the field."

"You were just up there," he said. "Which road is closest?"

"It's pretty well centered, but it's closest to the driveway, over by where it passes the barn."

We went to examine the gravel road. Gravel wouldn't leave footprints, Dad said, but it told its own story. We would be able to tell if they'd walked the margins of it, if they'd dragged equipment down it. We could assume that they'd taken a straight line from the road to the field, and the dirt they'd have had to cross would show their traces. Even if they'd concealed their footprints, we'd see the marks of their concealment. I said it seemed like we should be looking for more than footprints. I didn't see how anyone could make something so massive with anything less than a tractor.

A tractor didn't do this, he said. He would have heard a tractor start in the night.

"You're a pretty deep sleeper."

"Well, I work hard."

"It's not a judgment."

We both laughed a little.

"Besides the impossibility of getting a tractor in without leaving obvious tracks, this isn't the work of a tractor. It's too neat. I've been walking around in it for days. A tractor would rip the stalks up, or shear them off. These are all broken neatly just at ground level."

"Writing with a smaller pen."

"Exactly. I think they dragged something."

"Like an anvil?"

"Anything flat and heavy."

"That would take days," I said.

"When my dad had a problem he couldn't solve on his own, something heavy to lift, he'd send me off to round up the neighbors. One time we lifted the back end of a tractor and pulled it out of a mud patch. That was my biggest lesson from him. You get four or five men together, you can do just about anything."

Heavy things leave tracks, but we didn't find any on the gravel or sprouting off from it. Pre-dusk honeyed the sky. Photographers call this the magic hour. The heat dropped off. We drove around the perimeter of the farm, looking off the shoulder of the road for signs of disturbance, but didn't find any. I suggested we take another look from the rooftop while we still had some light. Get perspective again.

We climbed up and surveyed the field, the design. The problem with looking at something so big was that it drew all your attention to the whole. It was the flap of the magician's cape that obscured what he was doing behind his back. It took effort to scout your eye around the perimeter.

"Jesus, Dad. We looked right past it."

I pointed out where an abandoned stretch of railroad track cut through the field. The straight line of it was tangent to the outer ring and cut through two of the numerals decorating it. We'd built up crossings in the field margins where we sometimes needed to drive a truck or tractor over it. Crabgrass grew between the ties. I'd run along those rails as a kid, then at some point just forgot they were there. We'd been filling in the blind spot so long it took a concerted effort to see the tracks.

He smiled. We'd take a look at it tomorrow, he said.

"This was fun," I said. "We used to do this more often."

"Investigate elaborate pranks?"

"Solve problems. Figure things out."

"Yeah. It was fun."

"Lucas Holladay says ingenuity is its own form of art."

He scoffed.

"Lucas Holladay. Never trust anyone on the TV."

"Even the president?"

"Especially the president."

Something in his demeanor was changing. He was turning back into post-Zeno Dad. I let it pour out:

"For years it's been like you've been looking away from me, treating me like some kind of outcast. For what? Where did the nice dad go? What did I do so wrong as a kid that you couldn't get past?"

He looked out over the fields, then told me, before turning back toward the house, not to stay out too long, because my mother would have dinner ready soon.

We didn't go out the next day. Or rather, he didn't, and my intent had shifted. I spent a few days toying with breaking down cornstalks. With the heel of my boot. With a flat-bladed shovel. With a heavy piece of angle iron. All you needed, it turned out, was a length of two-by-six and the force of your own leg. I looped a short rope around each end and held it like the reins of a horse. I could flatten a stretch by stomping that one board across a row of young corn. Yes, it would take four or five people to create the design in the night; that was all it would take. I didn't tell my dad about my discovery. I did flatten a four-foot space he couldn't help but see through his bedroom window, so he'd know I knew how they did it.

*

Stabling Angie's horses for free opened a door in her I hadn't intended to open. She had come to Davis to look at me like an artifact in a museum—like a boot that was special only because an astronaut once wore it in space. When she came out the next week to ride, she looked at me with a sort of searing attention. I'd just been trying to help a person out. People too easily mistake kindness for love. Maybe kindness is so rare these days it can't help but engender love. Not that I'm saying she'd fallen in love with me, but there's a way people look at you. Her looking at me like that should not have been a surprise now that I kept her heart on my property and fed it apples.

A horse's joy is something to behold. Cider and Jackie danced when they saw her. It was a little dance, but you could see it if you were paying attention. We curried and brushed them both. Angie took a soft brush to their faces while I lifted up a hoof at a time and picked the mud out of it. She spent so long talking to them I got my tools and started putting up nails to hang her ropes and grooming tools on. She got the point and we saddled up and led them out of the barn to mount up. She took Cider and I rode Jackie. We rode around the farm perimeter, and I couldn't help but eye the ground for footprints. I'd had the habit since that day with my dad.

"What was it like?"

She'd resisted asking this, I'm sure, for months. It was easier to ask now, with the horses shifting under us, big sky above, breathing in a bit of dust. And easier to answer. I told her how we'd waited for days for the sky to clear, and the anticipation was as beautiful as anything else. I told her how we stormed the Lowell Observatory and Crystal hogged the telescope until she finished sketching. Eventually we all got a turn. I let everyone else go first, but when I looked through the viewer it was worth the wait. I'd only ever seen pictures of the Martian writing, mostly in black and white; the ones in color were not much better, faded blue on a dusty orange beach. Looking at the glow of the symbols directly, I felt like they were alive. I know they were static symbols, I said, but when I remember them, I remember the numbers dancing.

More tentatively, Angie asked: "What was she like?"

"Is. What *is* she like. She's not dead."

"Some people think she is." She said this gently, compassionately, not to make an argument but to suggest the uncertainty—there was no information, at that point, to indicate whether she was dead or alive, in Palo Alto or Albuquerque or Tibet. On Earth or Mars. In an asylum or a secret government lab. In the absence of data, one could hypothesize anything but prove nothing.

"She was one of those people who felt close when you talked to her. A real listener. She never listened halfway. I'd want to trail off sometimes, to let a point be inferred, but her eyes keyed in on me, waiting for the other half, so I'd have to come up with it and deliver. Talking with her felt very special. But it wasn't like that just for me. She listened to everybody that way. I think it's how she wanted people to listen to her. Her dad was a talker. She was too when her mind started working on something. Most people are either talkers or listeners. She was both."

"There's not much out there about her," Angie said. "Most people have interviews, at least. Letters. Former students eager to say how fantastic or terrible they were. But I always figured she was wonderful. I suffer from the romantic illusion that genius requires a beautiful spirit."

"What?" I said. "Are you in love with her too?"

"A little. I think everyone is."

"You remember Lucas Holladay?"

"You never forget a man who burns you."

"Imagine he'd delivered," I said. "That feeling, the feeling he built up beforehand? Imagine it going on forever."

She didn't cringe, but we rode the next leg in silence. When you say too much, sometimes the air needs a minute to decompress. Angie was a tough one and I wasn't worried about her. She squinted her eyes playfully.

"Female genius, at least," she clarified. "Male geniuses are all assholes."

*

Late in the summer of 1961, Ronnie, Priya, and Otis knocked on my door to roust me for drinks. We were celebrating, they said, and I had to come out of my cave. When Crystal was leaving Massachusetts, she had tossed off the idea that I could finish my degree in a year and a half. My dissertation chair laughed in my face when I told him, but I was racing ahead as fast as I could. Summer was ending but I was sallow. I'd barely been outside. When I traversed the campus, I sped through the subterranean tunnels, interested in the library, not the sunshine. Otis and Priya had not seen me in two months. Ronnie had checked in in July. I told him why I was burying myself, and he let me be.

I let them drag me to a bar. I couldn't resist the three of them together. I thought if we all held hands, we might channel

Crystal to us as in a séance. Ronnie offered the first round, and Otis ordered a whiskey and a beer.

"That's not how it works," Ronnie said. "You can't buy two and call it one round."

"It's a joint round."

"No such damn thing."

"You're right," Priya said. "But you should be careful what you say around Otis. He's immune to reason."

"I have a keen sense of my rights," Otis said.

I was wavering over the bar menu. Ronnie lost patience and ordered a Glenmorangie Signet for himself and one for me. I stared at him and handed our waitress the menu. "What are we celebrating?" I asked. "Did you get an interview somewhere?"

They all stopped and stared at me: "You don't know?" they asked. "We were counting on you to share the inside details." Priya took pity on my bewilderment. Crystal had won her court case, she said. I was still bewildered. "The guy who broke into her place," she said. He'd been convicted: breaking and entering. Intellectual property theft. He was going to jail. Ronnie trotted outside while Priya went into the details.

An associate professor in Crystal's department had been stalking her, trying to steal her work. In fervently trying to explain the Curious Language to him, she'd revealed she was working on a major project related to it. He'd seen it as his ticket to a full-professorship. He started making secret copies of papers she brought into the department office, but she did almost all her work in her apartment near campus. He broke into her apartment three times, going through her notebooks, trying to understand her work well enough to compile what was important.

He was a decent mathematician but a laughable criminal, Priya said. He kept coming back to the scene after establishing his MO. The police caught him on the third break-in.

Ronnie reentered the bar with a copy of the *Globe* in his hand. He set it in front of me and flipped to page three of the local section. The crime took place across the country, but since it involved Crystal, it was local now. Any place that could claim her wanted to. She was local to Boston, Albuquerque, Palo Alto, Arizona—probably every state but Alaska and Hawaii would find a local connection. The article so closely mirrored Priya's summary that I realized it was her only source for it. I skimmed on. Police had staked out her apartment while she was out of it for "an unnamed medical procedure," which she hadn't told me about either.

Although there was not much information beyond what Priya had already shared, there was a picture of her in the witness stand. I didn't like what I saw there. No one looks beautiful on the witness stand, I'm sure, but Crystal's face had both rounded and hollowed out. Besides the direction of her gaze, down and away, seemingly avoidant, the photograph had the somber quality of a mug shot. I'd always known Crystal to have the glow of an idea in her face; even when she wore a pensive or mischievous expression, it was backlit. Now, she just looked weary. I had not seen her in almost eight months and she looked like a different person from the one who'd left.

Had she really not told me any of it? They didn't believe me when I said she had not mentioned anything except her suspicions of the first break-in. I admitted I had not gotten a letter since late May. They offered a round of sorries heavy as condolences, pity I did not want, and a round of beer with them, which

133

I did. "Our relationship isn't dead," I said, "so don't talk about it like it is." Obviously, she had a lot to deal with. I didn't admit to suspecting she'd imagined the attempted burglary, but I did dwell on it. I'd never put those suspicions in a letter, but even so they felt like enough to shift the blame for her silence to me. Who would want to step away from an important project to write to a partner who accuses you of the crimes of which you are a victim? Why would you want anything to do with him?

*

The Russians had docked two spacecraft together the previous week, Angie told me on a ride around the farm. No pilots. After Komarov died in *Soyuz 1*, they decided to do it unmanned. Remote connection of two objects in orbit. The maneuver wasn't accomplished perfectly, but proved it could be done. Think of your first time riding, she said. It feels wild and unpredictable. You don't have a bead on what the horse is going to do. Then it becomes second nature. Docking in space would be like that soon enough, she said, easy as parking a car, and the implications were huge. We'd be able to launch with smaller, more efficient rockets—we wouldn't need to blast a cargo ship into space each time—and connect modular pieces of larger spacecraft up in orbit. We could build a space station. It could grow into a space city.

I remembered telling Crystal things like that, but I didn't have a deeper, broader understanding to offer Angie, the way Crystal had for me. I told her I appreciated her saying "we," humans, rather than "they," Soviets. The government pinned as many flags to Crystal in her absence as they could, but she'd only ever thought of nation-states as crude beasts, dumber and more spiteful than the cells they were made of.

We waved to Ludovico, one of the Davis agriculture professors running studies in my fields. He was guiding a handful of grad students through the field like a museum docent. He waved back and so did they. When we rode up to meet him at the edge of the rows, his students clasped their hands behind their backs and stood upright in a way that told me they'd been instructed to show me respect. The word *benefactor* had likely been used. Like Angie with my stables, Ludovico and the department made too much of me allowing them to unfallow my land.

"At ease," I barked at the students, mock drill sergeant. They relaxed only slightly. I asked Ludovico about the progress of his study. No fuckups yet, he said. For a study with this long a term, that was all you could know at this point, and it was good news. I told him and his students about the crop circles that had appeared in that very field when I was a kid. They had been some of the first ones in the country. They'd become more common since. A rash of them had popped up in the English countryside, some with remarkable fractal patterns that required a knowledge of advanced mathematics to create. The ag students did not care. I could hear them thinking, behind their deference: *How much corn was lost?*

I told them how a stomper worked. They were simple, I said. I could throw one together and show them if they were interested.

"Please do not stomp my research," Ludovico said.

"Fair enough."

We rode on. I'd told Angie about the crop circles, and about my issues with my dad. I really blamed myself for the change in him, she said, didn't I? Her dad had been the same with her two older brothers. Fathers got too attached to being the guiding star. They had trouble when the time came to walk side by side. She could show me the graph. There were a lot of data points. Mothers did the same with their daughters, she said, but snapped out of it after a few years.

"Did your parents die in the house?" she asked.

"Yeah," I said. "Both of them."

"Mine too. It's a lost art. Doctors want you to die in the dying room now."

"Dad had to pretty much fistfight Mom's doctors to let her out of the hospital."

"It changes a house," she said. "Enriches it somehow. The way dead plants fertilize the ground for the next generation. Jesus, that sounds morbid when I say it aloud."

"Haunted fertilizer?"

"It's hard to explain."

"I think I get it."

"Does the house feel haunted?"

She gazed at the farmhouse, which seemed smaller than ever under the weight of our consideration, a little mushroom cap sticking up from the surrounding fields. That little box contained most of my life. Open the lid and there was every meal for eighteen years, homework at the kitchen table, me on my belly watching TV, there was the Tower of Hanoi and the Fall of Holladay. That wasn't what she meant. She wanted to know if I still felt my mother's breath in the hallway, or heard my father's weight on the floorboards.

"No," I told her. "I wish to God it did."

*

After hearing about Crystal's trial and verdict, I flew out to California to find her. Palo Alto wasn't the California I knew. The city was mostly flat but not the way Lodi and the Central Valley around it were: the former smoothed down by tractor and the latter smoothed down by God. They were both small towns but Palo Alto had the bones to grow into a big one. A wide road. Lots of young trees. El Camino Real ran through it with the same pomp Route 66 ran through all those southwestern cities, the last breath of that era when road travel was designed to be enjoyable in its own right, when the journey was supposed to be an experience and not just the shortest line from A to B. I hadn't planned out the trip. I'd gone to the bank to withdraw money, and then to the airport to buy a ticket.

After asking directions a few times, I found the apartment that was on the return address of the envelope I'd brought, a building in the style of a Pacific motel. The long line of doors on the second floor had access from a concrete stairway and an extended balcony with an iron railing. I skipped up the steps and knocked on the door, forcing myself not to pound it. I heard slippers shuffle up, and a middle-aged woman in a robe answered the door. Flyaway strands of her hair were fastened to the rest with hairpins.

"Oh," I said. "I didn't realize Crystal had a roommate."

"What?"

"I'm here to see your—roommate? Crystal Singer?"

"Ah, the math lady. She moved out."

She moved to close the door quickly and I jammed my boot in the way.

"He warned me I'd get crazies," she said to herself. "Jerry! JERRY!"

"I just want to know if she left a forwarding address."

"Scene of your next crime. Yeah, let me give you directions."

She had a Philly accent. Just my luck, I thought—I was trying to find the love of my life and had to rely on the goodwill of a Philadelphian. A man in a near-transparent white undershirt lumbered out of the super's quarters down by the laundry room. I took my foot out of the doorframe, but the woman didn't close it now that Jerry was coming. The thin balcony trembled as he thumped up the staircase.

"Cops are already on their way," he said. "Can you step away from the door?"

"I just want a forwarding address."

"Leave that poor girl alone. Three break-ins. She didn't even have anything nice."

"I'm her fiancé. Look, here's an envelope. My address, her return address. She wrote me."

"Maybe. Or you intercepted her mail."

"How long ago did she move?"

"Kid, I half believe you, which is why I'm telling you you're going to get arrested if you don't leave now."

I wasn't sure he wasn't bluffing, but wasn't sure he was either, so I turned and hustled off the property. The complex was only a couple of blocks from Stanford, so I headed there and started asking students for directions. Sun dusted the sandy facades of the buildings, and the Spanish tile roofs beamed red-orange, and

I couldn't help picturing Crystal walking these quads and corridors for the last eight months, ignorant of how beautiful she was in them. She looked Pacific. Her light brown hair, with color draining out of it, was the hue of beach sand. I wondered about all the thoughts she had while walking the campus, the different perspectives from which she viewed it, which she would have shared with me had I insisted on coming to California with her.

In my politest manner I told the department secretary I was trying to get in touch with Crystal Singer. Did they have any contact info for her? The cheeriness zoomed out of her expression. She was sure, she said, I'd heard about the threats to Ms. Singer's safety and the integrity of her research. To protect her privacy, the university would not release any information about her.

"Please," I begged. I unfolded the letter, which had her handwriting on it and my name at the top.

"I'm Rick. She never mentioned me?"

Her expression changed again. She looked at me as you might a patient with a pitiable illness, or an animal in pain.

"I'm sorry, Rick. We can't give out that information."

And then, more wearily:

"We couldn't even if we knew."

*

My dad didn't haunt the farmhouse after his death, but he did before it. When Mom and I, along with most of the nation, were in the grip of Holladay fever, he turned poltergeist, seen only from the edge of your vision. Cabinets clanked, doors slammed. Faucets went on and off. His hammer pounded against the siding or the shingles. His boots thunked down the hall, but turn and you'd catch only the space where he'd been. It's an exaggeration to say we never saw him—he sat with us for dinner, chewing his roast with a purposeful joylessness before clearing his plate and heading back out to work, even if it was dark. Mom would have the radio in the other room turned up loud enough to hear from the table, and whenever Holladay made a fundraising plea, he'd scoff audibly.

The pressure of Holladay's approaching attempt changed a key thing: how he was with my mother. I was used to my father's dismissive cut-downs and disinterest toward me—"You were more skeptical at seven than you are at fourteen. Tell me how that happened." *Skeptical* was his great compliment, his measure of a man. Not of a woman. He'd always loved that my mother was mostly practical but could get a little dreamy. He would have called that femininity, not something he wanted in a son. When he couldn't look at her either, I knew the rot between him and me had soaked into their marriage. She no longer snickered at his grumblings.

He was insufferable when Holladay's message failed. He walked around the farm beaming. He couldn't help smirking whenever he saw either of us. My mother started sleeping on the couch that week. Dad found that funny for the first few days too—then he became as bitter as ever, and even more angry with me.

He told me, when he knew she was out on an errand, that I had ruined my mother. I was shocked. I had never heard him say a negative word about her, in public or private. He was as stubborn in his devotion to her as in everything else. I told him he'd broken his own relationship with her, after practicing the

140

art on me, but his comment sat with me like a punch. I got angrier and angrier at having to hold it in. I wanted to wound him back, so I passed it on. I told her what he'd said, running my sword through him even though she stood between us.

*

That was it. That was my trip to California.

But when I returned to my Cambridge apartment, there was a letter from her on the floor beneath the mail slot. I recognized the blue-and-red pattern of the Range Conservation stamps I'd sent her. This must have been one of the last ones. I tore it open and sat on the floor to read it.

Dearest Rick,

There are so many things I can't explain to you. That I may never be able to explain to you. They are such a weight on me that I sometimes think I may shatter. I have been through so much in the past year that the calcium feels leached from my bones. My blood feels half water. I feel frail in a way I never have before—that feeling of losing something you never considered a candidate for loss: The stability of a house. The reliability of a body. The warmth of the sun. You once called me fearless. I'm fearful now. Fearful of everything, for myself and the ones I love.

Buy a subscription to Acta Mathematica. *I have an article coming out in the next issue. The half of me that's gone . . . that's where I put it. The half of me that's left, well, that's another thing I'm not ready to explain. I don't know what comes next but there is always more work to be done. As always, the questions will lead the way.*

I know that I have been unbearably distant, but please know that I hold you impossibly close. I see your face first thing in the morning. I see your face when I'm awake in the middle of the night and think I might go crazy. A little piece of you lives with me. I doubt that's any consolation.

With boundless love,
Crystal

P.S. I had to move rather suddenly. I'm sure you're going crazy getting letters bounced back. Write to me at PO Box 72, Petaluma, CA 94953.

I grabbed the envelope from the floor and flipped it over. That was the first letter with no return address.

*

Crystal's article was not *in* the next issue of *Acta Mathematica*. It *was* the next issue. The three-hundred-page issue was composed of her treatise "On the Nature of Static and Kinetic Distances," plus some commentary from the editors on the paper's import. The central idea was that a distance between two objects must actually be triangulated. A third variable was involved. Observing a distance simply as how far point A was from point B was akin to seeing one face of a pyramid and calling the whole object a triangle. She introduced an equation for calculating what she called the "true distance" between objects—though the editors, and everyone afterward, called it Singer Distance.

Imagine a mountain range. Traditional measurement was like measuring from the base of the southernmost mountain to the base of the northernmost mountain in a straight line through the Earth, ignoring the complex topography of the range: not just the varying altitude of the ridge but the differing thicknesses and compositions of each peak. Though she theorized that mapping the actual, exact topography of any distance was a task on par with mapping the universe, she explained how the averages could be calculated, with a detailed process that had to take into account inertial speed or acceleration, medium, and a mysterious variable the editors referred to as the Tanzer Value, but which Crystal named "Intent."

I sort of agreed with the editors, that *Intent* was a troublesome name for the quantity, one that both failed to help visualize how the variable operated and anthropomorphized an inflexible rule; it made distance seem subject to mood swings. I can say, though, that I'm sure she chose the term with—well, with intent. She had a reverence for the naming of particles and forces we couldn't see. She considered it a grave responsibility. Up quarks, down quarks, strange quarks, charm quarks. I could imagine her trying out name after name for the mysterious variable, the way Lucas Holladay stumbled from egg to kite to sponge, not stopping until she found the option that clicked into place and lit up.

Intent could be measured only from within a journey. This was what Crystal had meant on the road trip when she'd said a distance measured was different from a distance traveled.

143

Measured distance was flat. Traveled distance was a dynamic, almost living thing. Singer Distance could be estimated for un-traveled journeys based on the other variables in the equations, but could produce only a range. Her paper explained how the theory operated at both the astronomical and subatomic levels. It had implications everywhere, because no two objects in the universe were not separated by some distance. Even the parti-cles that interlink to form us are separated by distances greater, in terms of relative scale, than the distances between stars.

Her voice came into my mind. It wasn't in the pages of the journal, but I heard her say: *Light-years of distance separate us even from ourselves.*

*

My inability to understand her math was a burden to her, I told Angie. Fair enough. She'd sunk enough time trying to explain it to me, and I wasn't going to get it. Her paper helped. I'd read it three times, and now grasped some elements of the way she saw the universe. Intent still eluded me. It eluded most people, but a handful of mathematicians were popping up who under-stood the elusive quantity. I was not one of them. I could run the numbers but couldn't see what they meant.

"I'm just going to say it: breaking up with someone over math is a shitty thing to do."

"Technically, we're not broken up."

I could see that hurt her, and felt bad for saying it.

"I just wish she could have let it go."

"Maybe she's not the only one who needs to let something go."

"I started writing letters to her PO box in Petaluma. My old pace of one a week didn't seem good for either of us, so I wrote one a month. I'd sent two by the time I got one back, a short little note about how she was trying and failing to understand the Entropy Equation. She couldn't focus the way she used to. She'd moved someplace quieter, but so far it hadn't helped."

Ludovico and his crew were sticking instruments into a hole they'd dug in the field. We waved at them and they waved back dutifully. When Angie wasn't looking, he made kissy faces at me. I flipped him off.

I kept writing once a month, I told Angie, but her letters came three or four months apart. I couldn't predict when one would come. Two of those periods passing meant half a year. By then I had my dissertation done and defended. I saw the University of California, Davis, on the job market and applied right away. They flew me out, dined me well. I didn't let on that I hadn't applied elsewhere. It was the only opening in California north of San Diego, and was within commuting distance from the house I grew up in, which I still owned, and less than a day's drive from Palo Alto, which was no longer Crystal's home but was the last place I knew she'd been. They offered me the job, and I accepted it and gave the current farmhouse tenants notice.

Packing up my stuff did not take long. I'd always led a spartan life. A few boxes of sheets, towels, and books. A toolbox I hadn't found much use for in grad school but didn't feel whole without. The usual plates and glasses. I stacked all the boxes on the porch and cleaned the apartment. Ronnie came to help me load things up. We'd sold the van to the Smithsonian for a mind-boggling sum, and I'd spent my share on a red Chevy pickup. Its glossy curves still had the allure of newness. Ronnie admired it with me as we stacked boxes in the bed. He said I was a bigger man than he was, splitting the proceeds from the sale of a vehicle I'd paid for.

"Is that your way of returning your share?" I asked.

"Don't put words in my mouth."

The value didn't come from the vehicle, but from what we'd done in it, I said. It was only right to divide it up. I didn't need it all anyway. I had a job lined up and a house to live in. Ronnie, Otis, and Priya still had another year living off university stipends. The money would mean a lot more to them. I was holding Crystal's share, as I wasn't going to send that kind of money to a PO box, especially when her scattered responses made me nervous about its reliability.

"What are you going to buy with yours?"

He ran his hand over the fender like he was petting a cat.

"Right now, I'm thinking about a red Chevy truck," he said. "But probably, down payment."

"That's why we got along so well," I said. "Neither of us dreams of Bentleys or tropical vacations."

"*Get* along," Ronnie said. "You'd better come back and visit."

I promised I would, which didn't feel like a lie. I had the vague sense I'd return someday to sit through a graduation or celebrate a promotion. But those ideas felt far away. I didn't have any specific plans for them. My plans faced westward. Ronnie and I embraced and he clapped me on the back. I climbed into the truck and rolled down the window.

"I hope you find her," he said. "I know that's why you're going. But a part of me hopes you'll let her go."

"She's somewhere. I've just got to get myself in the same spot."

We waved goodbye. I stopped to bid Otis farewell. He didn't extract any promises from me, but warned me that he was liable to visit without calling ahead. When it was sixty degrees in California and five below in Boston, I might hear a knock on the door. I thanked him for his help and his friendship, wished him well, and complimented him on the new Airstream trailer parked in front of his place.

My last stop was the apartment Priya and Crystal had kept, which Priya still stayed in alone. She welcomed me in. She'd been the one who'd furnished the common areas and decorated the kitchen, so the place looked mostly the same. Crystal had been the one to supply the place with fresh flowers, so the vase on the coffee table sat empty, chalked with calcium deposits where the water had evaporated out of it. Priya asked how the move was going, and I said my whole life was in the bed of my truck. She laughed and said she'd never heard me sound more like myself. I was glad her old wariness of me had waned since Crystal had left, if also surprised. She paused a moment, lending importance to what she was about to say:

"Rick—"

"You're going to tell me I should leave her be."

She straightened her posture.

"Not at all. I want you to find her. I want to say bring her home, but I don't mean here. It feels like she's *away*, out drifting off to sea somewhere. I think she needs you. She needs a grounding influence."

I hadn't always been a grounding influence, I said. I'd been the one to fill her with Singer Site dreams.

"But that was exactly what she needed. I shouldn't have doubted you."

"Doubting me is never a bad bet. You shouldn't have doubted Crystal."

"A toast to that."

Priya told me that Crystal had taken only half her things when she'd flown to California. I'd be closer to her out there, she said, so if there was anything I wanted to take with me, I was welcome to it. Crystal's room was dusty as an archive and, like mine, relatively spare. A short bookshelf next to the bare bed was still populated with her textbooks and academic journals. Not easy things for her to take on a flight. A tall floor lamp. Also not suited to air travel. Her dresser drawers were empty. Several hung open a couple of inches, and I closed them all neatly. I looked to her nightstand for the one thing I knew I wanted to take: a framed picture of us from a summer day at the beach, taken in our early months of dating, in which the two of us sat together, shielding our eyes with our hands. You couldn't see our faces well, but you could see us growing together, the instinct to lean into each other, to draw closer. That was what I'd loved about an otherwise bad photo. That was why I'd had it framed and now didn't want to leave it behind. It wasn't on the nightstand, though, or in the stand's drawer. It hadn't fallen behind it or under the bed. I searched for several minutes before it even occurred to me that she'd taken the photo with her.

*

The drive across the country was a lonely pilgrimage. I was a ghost passing through the landscapes we'd traveled a couple of years earlier, but with a strange inversion. I'd slept through most of the daytime travel then, and much of the roadside I'd seen had been under the cover of night. Now it was all daytime travel. Half of what I passed was absent from my memories, and the other half was changed in the light. I came into Chicago at twilight and recognized its towers lighting up against the graying sky behind them. I stopped in St. Louis for gas and the whole city was new to me. I'd been dreaming when we passed through. Through Oklahoma and Texas, I tried to recognize motels that had only existed as their neon signage when I last saw them. I saw the same exit signs for roadside curiosities and historical landmarks. I thought I'd eat at a few of the same diners, but after the first, I decided I didn't have the stomach for it.

After four days, I coasted into Albuquerque and pulled into Karl Singer's driveway. I sat in the truck a few minutes, wondering if I might see Crystal's silhouette cross one of the windows, if this was the secret hideaway to which she'd retreated to finish her work. But if she wanted a place to think without interruption, rooming with her garrulous father didn't fit the bill. The chance of finding her here was nil. Sure enough, when Karl saw me at his door, he immediately looked past me to see if I might have Crystal in tow.

He sat me at his table and asked if I'd heard from her.

"Only once every few months," I said.

"Once a year," he said, pointing at his face. "She remembers my birthday. Forgets all the other days."

149

"She hasn't been here at all? I thought she might be here with you."

"The last time I saw her," he said, "was the last time I saw you. I thought she might still be out there with *you*. A hide-in-plain-sight thing."

I looked around at his kitchen, which was well tended. A plate from breakfast was the only thing on the counter. A few neatly clipped stacks of paper were the only things on the table. The southwestern sun blared bright through the windows. Karl asked where I was headed. New Mexico was a long drive for a visit that could have been a phone call. Not that he minded the visit, he said. I told him about the job at Davis and moving back to my parents' house. He congratulated me. He said I'd make a good son-in-law someday. I asked how he was.

"I'm pretty happy for a sad old man with no one."

"That's dark," I said.

"Just a joke. I've got my students. They count for something. But promise me you'll bring her back if you can. You can tell her I'll behave."

"Will you?"

"Probably."

I said I would, knowing I'd have no power to make it happen should I ever find her.

"You kids came through here like you were on a secret mission," Karl said, changing the subject. "Didn't breathe a word of your plans. I could have helped."

"It was her quest. Not the sort of thing she'd want to do in the shadow of a parent."

"I would have loved just to witness it."

"I know."

"Instead, you let me go on and on about Einstein."

"Could we have stopped you?"

He laughed. Then he didn't say anything and I didn't say anything, and the mood dampened.

"I've got a file of all the magazine coverage," he said. "You want to see it?"

"I know all that stuff pretty well."

"I bet."

He invited me to stay the night if I needed a rest. I said I had to get back on the road. California was still a long way off. Karl said he understood. Walking me out to the porch, he told me I should make sure to stop at the site on my way. It wasn't quite as bright as it used to be, but it still lit up. Cold winter nights were when it shone brightest, he said, but even in the summer it was something to see. You couldn't just wait until the sun went down, though. Eleven o'clock, midnight, or even later. That was when the last remnants of sunlight, the traces you didn't even realize were there, would empty out, leaving only the black sky and blue earth.

*

The sun was low by the time I passed Peach Springs, and I recognized the bend in the road that meant the Singer Site was near. You couldn't see the writing from the road. In full daylight, people might pass it without realizing anything was there at all, if not for the signs. With night coming on, the ground north of the highway glowed. Moonlight drifted up out of it. I knew from experience that standing in the midst of it was like being in the center of a heatless flame, the blue light pouring out around you. I imagined Karl there, sitting down inside one of the numerals and waiting from the sunset to the early morning hours, watching the way the light changed. I imagined him visiting in all seasons, perhaps laying flowers, as if at a grave. As soon as I pictured that, I couldn't bring myself to stop.

As I headed west beyond it and the sun sank away completely, I watched the glow strengthen in my rearview mirror like it was trying to call me back. The hills buried it before I got to Kingman, where I stopped for the night at a one-floor motel that smelled like a stale mop bucket. A long haul the next day got me into California and all the way north to Lodi.

I found the farmhouse in disrepair and felt eager to get it back in good condition, but I had something else I needed to do before I began working on it. I went to Petaluma to stake out the post office where I'd been sending Crystal's letters and memorized the location of her box. I rented a motel room by the night and sat on the patio of the café next door for two days, drinking coffee and eating sandwiches. From there I could see through the post office door. The stakeout started Monday. On Wednesday, someone came to pick up the mail, but it wasn't Crystal. It was a middle-aged, secretarial-looking woman: short, curly hair; thick, round glasses. Professional garb. I watched the woman closely while she emptied the box into a canvas tote, trying to discern whether it was Crystal in an elaborate disguise. The woman passed close by me on her way out, and unless Crystal had found a way to make herself thirty years older and six inches shorter, this wasn't her.

A helper, I guessed. An assistant. I'm not proud to say I tailed the woman, whoever she was. She hadn't come in a car and didn't get into one. She walked a few blocks into a suburban neighborhood, heels clacking on the sidewalk, and walked into the smallest house on the block without needing to unlock the door. The house couldn't have been more than six hundred square feet. A branded wooden sign hung from the mailbox: THE PLOVERS. I even went to the edge of the fence to peer into the backyard to see whether there might be some small apartment back there, but there wasn't even a shed, only a weedy lawn and a garage full of dusty boxes. I waited across the street to keep an eye on the house. When the woman headed out again, I checked over my shoulders and, seeing I was alone, hopped the fence. The back door was unlocked.

"You broke into the house?" Angie asked.

"The door was unlocked."

"No breaking, but entering. Is that a plea option?"

There was nothing for me to take, nothing for me to break. The house was all floral print and ceramic ducks, and barely big enough to search. The kitchen was one short countertop between a sink and the electric coils of a small cooktop. The living room was one modest square. I could see into every room in the house from it. One bedroom. One bathroom. The bedroom showed no signs of double occupancy. There was one queen-size bed, sunken with age and overlaid with a floral quilt. One nightstand cluttered with goose statuettes, a plush duck on the pillow next to them. There were no math books lying around or young woman's clothing on the floor. There wasn't a second toothbrush in the bathroom. I checked drawers, cabinets, and closets. The more I failed to find evidence supporting Crystal's presence there, the more I was standing in the house of a stranger who could return at any time.

Crystal, I told Angie, had given me fake contact info.

Angie halted Cider. I stopped Jackie a moment later and had to look over my shoulder at Angie.

"How long are you going to let her drag your heart behind her car like an old tin can?"

"As long as the thread holds, I guess? I've been called a hopeless romantic."

"That's not being a romantic," she said. "That's being a dumbass."

She spurred Cider ahead, and now I was trying to catch up to her. I told her it was rude to hold dumbassery against someone who was born with the condition. Some illnesses can't be cured, only managed. She smiled at my apology, reached out and took my hand. It's hard to hold hands while riding horses, but we made it work.

*

Angie called me on July 20, 1969, to ask if I was watching the TV. I pretended to go click it on, but it was on already, of course. Everyone was watching the TV. The moon mission was underway. I stretched the curly phone cord straight and sat on the couch to watch with Angie's voice in my ear. The command module was orbiting around the moon with Michael Collins inside it. The lunar module, a little tinfoil blob, had detached to lower Armstrong and Aldrin down.

Exhalation was impossible. Breathing out, it seemed, could cause the lander to explode on impact. It touched down and I heard her breathe into the receiver. That the footage was slow and grainy, two glaring spacesuits stuttering around the screen with a starched flag on a pole, only underscored where it was coming from.

"Oh my God," Angie said. "Oh my God."

Didn't it make me feel like anything was possible? Like this step out away from our planet was only a first step, that we were babies stumbling through our first attempt but that someday we'd journey out into space as easily as you might walk to the fridge? A quiver in her voice. God, anything seems possible. Rick, I'm so glad we watched this together. Do you feel it?

What could I say? When I saw that grainy footage, when I heard Neil Armstrong's words, I felt it. But it left quickly. Everyone was imagining themselves up there in those weighted boots, staring out over the desolate lunar plain. I was imagining myself looking up and out, farther into space. Knowing the silent society was out there on Mars, the moon felt less like a magical journey than stepping out onto your front porch to take a look down the road at your neighbor's house, only to see their light was still off. How could the moon feel any less lonely than here?

I feel it, I said. She knew not to believe me.

*

When Angie came down my gravel road, we tended the horses in the barn and rode them around the margins of the property.

She had never been inside my house, which was normal at first because it wasn't a great venue for horseback riding. As we became closer, the idea of her entering the house took on a significance I hadn't intended. She asked for a glass of water and I told her I'd run in and get her one. She brought dinner and I said we'd cook it on the grill. Of her own accord, she used the outhouse the university had built for the grad students.

For my birthday in November 1969, she bought me a porch swing and we sat on the back patio, where I'd poured a modest concrete slab earlier in the year, to assemble it. I liked the way power tools were made in that era, heavy and industrial, not a scrap of plastic on them except the casings of their power cords. I told Angie they should adopt "Lasts Longer Than Your Marriage" as a slogan. She liked dark humor and I wanted to see her laugh. She looked incredible using a drill with a three-quarter-inch bit to punch through a beam. Sweat on her temples, sawdust sticking to it. A red flannel shirt with the sleeves rolled. She slid a long bolt through the hole she'd just drilled.

"Tool guys couldn't help but one-up each other," she said. "The other company would go straight to 'Lasts Longer Than You Will.'"

"My dad would have liked that."

She put on a radio-commercial voice: "Your kids can use these beauties to build you a casket."

We worked for two hours getting the swing together and up on its chains. I grabbed two beers from the house so we could test it out properly. We sat and drank while the stars came out. Venus was in the sky, and I pointed it out to her as if she didn't know. Yeah, she said happily, she knew. It took me a long time, I told her, to wrap my head around charting stars and planets when I was a kid. It didn't come naturally. I was too thrown by the complexity of viewing one distant object in orbit from a viewpoint that was orbiting, spinning, and tilting all at once. Looking up into the sky and knowing where you'd see a particular star or planet seemed impossible when the world had moved so much from the night before.

"How'd you figure it out?"

"I took some paper and charted the position of Mars for a month. Lucas Holladay explained how to do it in one of his radio appearances. You just look up and it's there. And you look up the next night and it's there in almost the same spot. You keep doing it and you see the drift of it, and then you understand."

"Mars. Do you think we'll see the next equation in our lifetime?"

I was surprised she asked. At first, she'd wanted to hear everything about the Curious Language and our attempt to speak it, but the more time we spent together the less she liked to talk about it. The less she asked about any topic that might lead to Crystal. I said it was hard to tell. Eleven years from the 1922 equation to its solution. Almost thirty between that and our solution. It wasn't much data, but it seemed to suggest that the difficulty was increasing at an exponential rate. The Entropy Equation might take a century or more.

I didn't share that I was picturing Crystal hunched over a bare table in a bare apartment hidden in some town with the bare anonymity of an imagined place. I could see the scramble of papers in front of her and dark bags under her eyes. I couldn't tell from the vision whether she was solving the problem or just going crazy trying. Could she overrule the pattern? I'd noted the way Angie phrased her question: would we see the next equation, not would someone—Crystal—solve this one, so I didn't say anything about the aching part of me that believed she would, she had to. Even if Angie shared the same candle of hope, it would only hurt her to hear me say it. Besides, the belief felt too much like religion.

If not for our squabble the last time I'd talked about Crystal's letters, I might have told her I was well acquainted with the feeling of something drifting slowly out of orbit. Crystal's letters had come ever more gradually through the midsixties. Once every four months, five months, seven months, a year. Each letter displayed less and less care in its composition. I could see where she'd left off writing in the middle of a sentence and come back later with a different pen. Sometimes there were childish doodles in the margins. I charted the decreasing frequency of her letters one year, and saw the line of best fit angled down toward an asymptote of longer and longer waits between letters, eventually getting so far apart there was no surety in ever hearing from her again. The last letter I'd received from her seemed to be an attempt to put me out of the misery of waiting. I opened the envelope and a creased sheet of paper fell onto the floor, scribbled with curls of Curious Language so hastily sketched they were nearly illegible. When I flipped it over, I saw there was a short letter she'd seen fit to write on the back of this sheet of scrap paper.

Dear Rick,

I remember when you used to say you could never be close enough to me, that even when you were right next to me you felt the urge to be closer. A blind love can do that, can make you feel like you want to share everything, to be one entity, one mind. But even if I could let you into my mind, I would want to protect you from that very thing. The years have taught me the reason for the space between people. It's a buffer. I did enough damage to you without an open boundary between us. Maybe it's egotistical to suppose you're still thinking about me after all these years, but if I know you, you're holding on. And I want to let you know that you don't have to anymore. Knowing you, you'll think this has to do with you. Please trust me. This has only to do with me.

I miss you. I love you. But you will be okay without me.
Crystal

I felt the urge to drive to her but didn't know where she was, the urge to call her, but I had no number to call. That was all by design, of course. She had closed off all roads to her, and with the finality of this letter I should have known well enough to stop gazing off in whatever felt like her direction. I can't say I did.

That was in late 1967, a few months before I met Angie.

"I'd rather talk constellations," I told her, back on the porch swing. "There's Cygnus."

Taking as much pleasure from stating the known as you could from speculating about the unknown was a disorienting experience. It didn't require having vision beyond what your partner had. It was love with no chasing. *Looks like it's raining*, my father says to my mother. *Yes, looks like it*, my mother says back. I lay across the swing with my head in Angie's lap so I could better point out to her the constellations she already knew.

"Their names are ancient," I said. "The light from some of those stars is more ancient, peeling through space-time for thousands of years to arrive at this very moment."

She laughed.

"You sound like an undergraduate," she said. She ran her fingers through my hair. "Keep drinking."

She tried to tilt my bottle to my mouth and spilled a font of it down my face onto her jeans. She unrolled the sleeve of her flannel and wiped my face. I sat up so she could make a futile attempt to dry her jeans, but I sat closer to her now, right next to her. When my arm draped around her shoulders, she shut her eyes and filled her lungs with air. She breathed it out, then moved her face to mine. I didn't know that I was going to lower my forehead, to block the kiss, until I did it. We sat with our foreheads tilted against each other, and I didn't need to see her face to know her expression.

"I'm sorry. There's a door in me that's shut. Someone else has the key."

"You're going to be locked in there forever, Rick."

"Yeah. I think so."

She got up and smoothed her shirt. She walked in the direction of her truck, pausing when she reached the end of the patio.

I thought she was going to turn and say something, but she rolled her shirtsleeve back up and kept on walking. Her truck rumbled to life and swept off down the driveway. The mind can dream up the feeblest illusions: this time when her truck went down the gravel road, the sound played in a minor key.

*

By the late sixties, the rumors about Crystal were in full swing. She was a secret emissary to Mars. The *Apollo 1* disaster was a smoke screen. The capsule was empty. While the world mourned them, Grissom, White, and Chaffee were actually piloting Crystal across the interplanetary distance. She was at Los Alamos developing a bomb a thousand times more powerful than a neutron bomb. Theorists called it the Continent Killer, the Singer Weapon, or, more funnily, the Intent Bomb. She was at Lawrence Livermore lab developing an instantaneous transporter that worked by creating an RIF, a Reverse Intent Field. The transporter system was eerily similar to the one that had recently aired on *Star Trek*, but try telling the Singer devotees that. The disappearance of the world's most famous mathematician was too juicy a story for people to leave be. No one wanted to believe that, like the Martians, she simply didn't want to talk to us anymore.

But her victory had made its mark. Mars projects inched forward without her. NASA launched *Believer 1*, the first of a series of orbiters designed to study Mars. It rode into space in the nose of an Atlas-Centaur rocket and began the long journey across the void. For five months, the world watched and waited

for what would be the first close-up pictures of the planet's surface, an unprecedented glimpse of the built environment there
that would mark a new era of Martian studies. The probe lost
transmission 12,856 miles from Mars. None of its indicators
showed anything wrong beforehand. None of its diagnostics
gave a warning. It simply went silent. A committee of physicists
published a paper on the Entropy Equation that didn't solve
the equation but proposed two separate, valid interpretations
of it. They were petitioning a skeptical US Congress to fund
a project asking a clarifying question. Caltech, UC Berkeley,
and Stanford were building a new radio telescope array to focus
exclusively on Mars. I even got a call from the project's administrator inviting me to join them for a photo op when it was
completed. I was a part of the history of the Mars quest, I told
her, not its future.

I didn't want to be disturbed.

Angie knew my teaching schedule. She came to get Cider
and Jackie when I was holding an exam. I had a premonition of
emptiness while I drove down the stretch of gravel, that feeling
of an absence you don't yet know the nature of. When I saw the
stables empty, I ran into the fields. I asked Ludovico if someone had left the gates open. Had some of his students taken the
horses for a ride without asking? Breathless, I promised I had
no interest in disciplinary action, I just needed to find them.

"She got them," he said.

"Who?"

"Dr. Parrish. She came with her trailer. I figured she had a
show or something."

"Those aren't show horses."

He shrugged.

"She just picked them up and went. I didn't know I should stop her."

"No, you're fine. No cause to stop her. They're her horses."

"Feels kind of like they're your horses too by this point."

"They're not."

Angie was a tough and practical woman, and I figured we'd talk as colleagues and keep things friendly. If she banged her thumb with a hammer, she'd swear and keep working. I thought that was an approximation of what we'd done: her the tender thumb, me the dumb and useless hammer.

That was not how she approached our severance. She'd learned my patterns well when she came to the department with an intent to put herself in my way, and that knowledge now empowered her to dodge me almost entirely. At department meetings, when being in the same space was unavoidable, she didn't look at me and didn't speak up. I wanted to stop her to talk about it, but she was always the first out the door. She sometimes left a few minutes early to avoid me.

By the time I caught up with her, the school year was almost over. The valley was heating up and the air was dry. Dust from the campus fields drifted in clouds around the horizon. In an act of desperation, I ambushed her as she left her office hours to teach. We needed to talk, I said. We shouldn't just let things rot. Try to stop a fruit from rotting by talking to it, she said. But if I insisted, fine. I had as long as it took to walk to class. I told her my feelings were complicated. I'd never known how to untangle them. There were all these knots in the rope that I didn't know were there until something pulled it taut.

"It's not that complicated," she said. "You've only ever known how to feel one thing."

"That's not true."

She looked at me but didn't stop walking.

"It's true enough."

We were approaching the building where she lectured. My pulse quickened.

"I don't think we should abandon this."

Now she stopped, vexed.

"You don't have any idea what it's like to feel this way about a person who loves someone else more."

I looked at her.

"Or I guess you do. But unlike you I'm not willing to live in it."

Her students were walking into the building, waving at her. She waved back, trying to unclench her jaw. I asked if we could try again, at some point, whenever she felt ready. She didn't believe in nevers, she said. But she didn't believe in right now either. She would have to wait and see how she felt.

I waited too, puttering around the farm through the summer, wishing I had a horse to ride and somebody to ride it with. I had little to do, so I'd stroll the trails with Ludovico and ask him about his plant studies and his students and growing up in Italy. When he wasn't around, I'd sit with a beer and nurse the hope that Angie was feeling the same way, taking Cider out for a ride and then Jackie, wherever she had them stabled. Two horses, one rider. That couldn't feel natural anymore after all our rides together. By the end of the long summer months, I thought, she'd be ready to invite me back onto that empty saddle. When I returned to campus for the fall semester, though, I couldn't find her name among the mail slots. I went to her office and found the name of a new assistant professor there. I went to ask the department chair where Angie's office was.

Evanston, he said. She'd taken a position at Northwestern.

That wasn't ideal weather for her horses, I thought. The selling point must have been that it was far enough away from me.

*

When things were at their worst with my dad, when we couldn't look at each other, my mother sat me down to talk about it. I was going off to college, she said. She was worried I wouldn't come back and revive my relationship with my father. Revive? I said. It was dead. He had turned his back on it and walked the other way for most of a decade. She poked at some nascent tears in the corners of her eyes.

"I don't want you to not love your father."

"What's left? If I tell him I love him, what is he going to say?"

"What I'm saying is don't be overwhelmed by the present, which isn't the whole picture. Don't let the end be the story. Can you remember the boy you were, the man he was? You were so close. So close. The way you feel now wants to erase the way you felt then, but you don't have to let it."

That was sophistry, I said. He'd become what he'd become. It wasn't my job to perform a magic trick to turn him back into the better man he'd once been. I said this even though I knew she was giving advice to herself as much as to me, that she was offering me a medicine that had not yet worked for her. More tears came out of her than her fingers could stop.

"I don't want you to do it for him. I want you to do it for you. To not feel well loved does damage to a person. I want you to remember that you were, even if you have to go back a little further."

I was not ready to do that, but she was planting a seed in me. A handful of years later, when Crystal and I were falling in love and staying up late pouring out our wounds for each other, I told her all about my dad and the painful rift between us. But I found that there was something I could do to soothe the pain. Walking back to my own apartment, I would close my eyes and remember myself in the passenger side of his truck as a kid, curling through the forest roads of the Pacific Northwest. My knees, poking out of my shorts, took on the pattern of the bench seat's quilted vinyl. I had to sit on my feet to see anything more than the treetops. The lone spire of Mount Shasta up the first leg of the drive, then Mount Rainier, Mount St. Helens. The named mountains were just so we could have a destination that would necessitate the journey. He'd point out the changes in trees that came with changes in altitude. Black bears rambled the hillsides and I tried in vain to spot them before he did. We'd stop at every river to finger worms from the mud for our fishing poles.

My father's life savings funded the breakthrough that repudiated his skepticism about Mars communication. I like to think he would have changed his mind if he could have lived to see what we'd done. I know that's not true. But I can imagine the part of him that would have believed it if he were calibrated a little differently, if there were a way he could be reset to some kind of default. Extending that kind of grace to people, seeing them in the light of a goodness they walked out of, requires an intentional shift in perspective, and perhaps an acknowledgment of one's own limits and failings. You might call it eulogizing.

One of the last things Angie said to me was: "You're going to be locked in there forever, Rick," but I had a lot locked in there with me: Angie's fingers through my hair, her laugh as she spilled beer down my face, the feel of her flannel sleeve—it even felt red—the way the texture of it changed as it absorbed the dampness from my face. I still remember the shift of Jackie's saddle underneath me, the strength of the animal feeling like a redirection of her own strength, like it emanated from her. Horses are powerful but sensitive creatures. You can lose one forever, like I did. But with some effort I can remember the way I had one.

And Crystal? The road across the desert, the cafés of Flagstaff while our discovery remained hidden under clouds, her spinning in the waxing blue glow of dusk that accompanied our installation at the Singer Site. I go back there all the time. I go back further, to a time she sang to me. The song was Bobby Darin's "Beyond the Sea," which she'd fallen in love with through the radio. She'd hush me anytime a station played it. That day, she sang the opening bars to me, lines about distance and waiting and lovers meeting again across a great expanse. I interrupted her by belting out the first line of "La Mer." "What?" she said. She didn't know it was originally a French song until I told her. She continued the American version. Over time, she built up the ability to put some real air behind it, to sing it loud enough and clear enough that someone could hear it from across a field. In the calm of a perfect late-April afternoon on the campus lawn, we were so close that she didn't need to. She sang it so quietly her voice almost flickered out, as if she were singing me to sleep. I could have lived in that memory forever. Or so I thought until October 1973, when, thirteen years after we made the Singer Site, I got the call.

*

"Rick? Rick Hayworth?"

"Yes?"

"This is Dottie."

"I'm sorry?"

"Dottie Plover?"

"I'm sorry, you're going to have to refresh me."

"Karl's sister."

"Carl who?"

"Karl Singer. Crystal's aunt."

"Karl never mentioned a sister."

"Figures. I'm not some famous scientist, so why would he? Listen, I know you said you didn't want to be involved but Rhea is insisting on taking a trip down to the Mojave. Some radio thing. I promised her I'd take her but I can't. I'm sick. Like, the Real Sick. I'm not even supposed to drive. Well, she's apoplectic. She's practically on a hunger strike and made me promise I'd call. I already tried Karl. He can barely walk."

"Who's Rhea?"

"Who's Rhea?!"

"Who's Rhea?"

"Who's Rhea?"

"Yeah."

"Who's Rhea. Christ. You mean she never told you?"

*

Dottie gave me an address in Petaluma and asked me to come out at noon the next Tuesday. Rhea would be in school, and we could chat before she got home. When I drove up, it confirmed what I'd started to suspect, reaching back to where I recognized the name Plover from. Dottie's directions led me to the little house to which I'd stalked the aging lady, presumably Dottie, from the post office a decade ago. That woman stepped out the front door as soon as I pulled up. She had a helmet of short curls as tight as toy poodle hair. You couldn't see it without imagining her lined up at the salon with the rest of her bridge club. With her round hairdo atop a wiry body, she cut the silhouette of a lollipop. She was talking to me from the moment I stepped on the walkway, maybe before; she seemed to be mid-sentence when she began.

"Changed a lot over the years, the block; the Rowlands moved back to Sacramento; Eleanor passed on; Walker's kids moved him to some kind of elderly apartments, it's a shame but he could barely walk to the front door; new families moved in to raise their kids but could use some lessons on it if you ask me."

She had me by the elbow and was escorting me up the path.

"I've got tea steeping in the kitchenette. I hope you like chamomile."

I stopped her at the porch before she could toss me in the door.

169

"How's Rhea doing? Is she a happy kid?"

"That child's as much a sunflower as her mother."

I said I didn't know what that meant. It meant she didn't complain, Dottie said, and other things. A sunflower, she repeated. She looks at the ceiling a lot, Dottie told me. "You know"—she cocked her head to the side, gazing up thoughtfully. I laughed. Yes, I recognized that look, I said. I supposed I would be seeing a lot of it. We were about to spend twenty hours in a car together, driving down to the southeastern edge of the state and back.

"She's twelve?"

"Yes, but an old soul."

"And Crystal? You won't tell me where she is?"

"I can't tell you. She doesn't tell me where she goes, she just tells me she's going. She calls it a pilgrimage, she calls it a retreat, she calls it all sorts of things. Ask anyone on the block, telling me a secret is like giving it to the radio broadcaster. Which is probably why she never tells me. She's a smart one."

As Dottie led me in the door, I asked how it never came out, then, that Crystal Singer was living here with her. Her disappearance was a national mystery. Dottie said she had a safe big enough for exactly one secret. Crystal living with her had filled the safe for more than a decade. She'd shared every other secret she knew in that time, but not Crystal's.

You could see most of the house from the threshold. It had the same floral furniture from years ago, the same unforgettable quantity of duck figurines. Since I wasn't here as a detective this time, I was able to take a slower look at things. Across a wood countertop was a small, solid refrigerator that looked like a lead-bellied antique. I could tell the square dining table and simple chairs were handcrafted, perhaps by the absent, unmentioned Mr. Plover. The dining space was separated from the living space only by a step down and a transition to carpet. There was a schoolhouse desk in a corner of the living room now, topped with a scattering of lined paper. Dottie insisted I sit while she brought over the tea, carrying the cup with both hands. Her pace of life was so frenetic that I hadn't noticed her tremor until she held out the teacup, rattling on its saucer and spilling tea over its lip.

"I'm sorry. Like I said on the phone, the Real Sick."

I grabbed the cup from her, eager to relieve her of it. The tea looked like water a child had bathed in. I didn't want to drink it, so I asked Dottie to tell me more about Rhea. She said Rhea kept a lot to herself. Like a lot of young girls. Like a lot of women, too. Like her mother. "Not like me," she said with a laugh. The gears were always turning, but you couldn't tell what they were connected to. Did she have trouble in school? I asked. All As, Dottie said, except for physical education, and failing that was a sign of character. But she wasn't one of those kids the teachers gushed about. She sat quietly in class, did her homework quietly at home, and turned it in quietly the next day.

"To be honest," Dottie said, "I think the time is coming when you may need to take over with her permanently. I'd keep that child till kingdom come. My doctor thinks my kingdom is not too far down the road, so I'm planning ahead for her. She doesn't need to be here for the ugly parts. I don't know if that's a thing you want, but she's your blood, and she needs somebody."

"Of course," I told Dottie. Even if I hadn't anticipated this question, and then spent the entire trip to Petaluma considering it, I think I still would've told her yes. I felt it was my duty, as a father, to care for Rhea if that was something she wanted, though I was still trying to wrap my head around the fact of her existence. "As long as she's okay with it. But I'm sure you've got some concerns about handing her off to a stranger."

"I can't say I don't. But you've got good references."

"What did Crystal tell you about me?"

"She said you didn't want to be involved. I guess that was some grade-A horse cake. But the rest was good. She said you wore faux-humility like a ten-gallon hat, but that otherwise you were the best man she had ever known. I always wondered how 'best man' squared with 'absent father.' It makes a lot more sense now."

"I would have been here if I had known."

"I can tell. I've got a sense for people. Rhea does too. She doesn't announce her insights, but she has them. She'll see who you are. This little trip with her will be a good trial run."

Some radio thing, Dottie had called it. When she gave me directions it was clear she was talking about the Cibola Radio Astronomy Complex, the ambitious new array of radio tele-scopes built to focus exclusively on Mars. It had failed to secure congressional funding but the universities had managed to as-semble a trove of private grants. It was opening in a few days, set to send its first broadcast at the heart of the opposition period. That was the thing driving Rhea's pilgrimage there. It saddened me to think of her fixated on something so far away at such a young age. What other connections on Earth was she missing while she directed her gaze at the sky? A little tan suitcase with a handle was propped against the door of the single bedroom, alongside an army surplus duffel bag. Behind it, I could see two cots next to the main bed, one with sheets in disarray and the other with no bedding at all. The cots hadn't been there the last time I'd come, so many years ago—perhaps Crystal had been away then, I thought, and she'd taken Rhea with her. At this point, I had no idea how much or how little Rhea would be leaving behind in this house. She'd lived her whole life here but it still had the atmosphere of a temporary living situation. The farm where I'd grown up, her potential future home, had felt full of everything when I was a kid, and then devoid of anything when I was a teen. I resolved to be the difference between the two for this child.

"I can tell you're nervous," Dottie said. "You don't need to be. That kid knows how to get along."

A word was missing from Dottie's sentence. Rhea knew how to get along *without*. Dottie was telling me she knew how to get by without her mother, that she had little need of a father. She needed someone to buy groceries and sign the forms that came home from school. She needed a roommate who wasn't actively dying, and that was it. I understood what she meant. It was impressive that a child without a single reliable parent wasn't ditching school and starting fights. But I knew well enough from my own teenage years, when I too could have gotten along on my own, that there was a difference between managing your life and living it. Anger at Crystal swelled in me as I thought of the damage she had caused, much of which I might have prevented if she had involved me. I would look, to Rhea, indistinguishable from a father who didn't care enough to show up.

Dottie had been speaking while I processed all that, and she must have noticed my distraction because she raised her volume until my attention returned to her. If I wanted to take any of Crystal's correspondence, she repeated, I'd be doing her a favor. Those boxes were too heavy for her to move, and who knew what the neighbors would do with them after she passed. She spoke of her funeral like a party she might attend. Which, I supposed—she went on to say she knew there were people who would want those letters preserved, even if she didn't understand why. Oh, she understood the writing and the reading of letters, just not the keeping of letters.

I stiffened the moment Dottie mentioned Crystal's correspondence. I owned half of the conversation I'd had with Crystal over the course of the sixties: the letters I'd received. The other half, the letters I'd sent, were out in Dottie's garage— along, perhaps, with other conversations she'd carried on with other people. I knew she'd been in contact with some mathematicians and astrophysicists around the publication of her article in *Acta Mathematica*. I told Dottie I'd be happy to take it off her hands, and she led me out to her unofficial archive.

I'd pictured a few bundles of letters, mostly my own, tied together with string. What I found, lit by one uncovered bulb on a pull chain, was a reef of cardboard boxes from the perimeter of the garage inward. The progression of the structure was signaled by a decay in organization. The earliest boxes, those in the outermost ring, were filled with vertical file folders and had their years written in marker on the flaps. The boxes from the middle of the decade also contained file folders, but they were stacked flat on top of one another. Those from the most recent years, presumably—they had no organizational markings on them—were filled to the brim with yellowed envelopes in a heaping disarray as if they'd been put there with a shovel. Crystal hadn't disappeared from her own life. She had converted it into letters.

"Are there any you want me to leave?" I asked Dottie.

"For what?" she said. "To put in my coffin?"

My stomach buzzed as I started loading boxes into the bed of the truck. I began with the oldest, most orderly boxes, whose lids still fit. Handling them coated my arms and shirt with ten years' worth of dust. Those were the years she wrote back to me, but these boxes contained much more. The shadow life she'd been living, absent from my view, would have its traces in them. This was a trove of evidence beyond anything a cold case detective could imagine. I layered them in the truck one by one.

The messier boxes sprouted with bundles of paper like unkempt houseplants. Those were my top layer, since the others wouldn't stack on them. I was carrying one of those out when Rhea arrived on the sidewalk. She stopped when she saw me. I stopped when I saw her. She had Crystal's long straight hair, the color of unfinished wood, and her piercing eyes. Her expression did not light up the way I remembered Crystal's so easily did. She looked nothing like me except, poor thing, in the eyebrows. She looked me over with an air of neutral appraisal, in which neither judgment nor approval lurked. Her gaze lacked warmth but didn't register as coldness either. It was fair enough for her to take my measure. She'd just been dropped in the lap of a new parent with all the abruptness of an arranged marriage. But I didn't need any time to appraise. Here she was, my daughter, with her thumbs tucked into her backpack straps and a T-shirt that said *Believer 2*.

PART III
THE RIVER BACKWARDS

////

We curled south on Highway 1, across the Golden Gate and through the city, then down that narrow strip of road that follows the same curves as the coast. We rose up and down the emerald hills, green with fresh grass from the first autumn rains. Out past the windshield, white surf bubbled against the beaches. This wasn't the fastest route. A straight shot down I-5 or 99 was much more direct, but this was a drive I had always wanted to take.

When Crystal left Boston before me, I had fantasized about driving this route after I came out to join her: me behind the wheel, gliding us through the turns while she watched the hypnotic churn of the sea and pondered entropy. I imagined driving through purple dawns, the sun lighting the ocean before it lit our side of the mountains, and her bouncing her ideas off me, trying to explain her breakthroughs, the way she had on our pilgrimage to Arizona. But that hadn't come to pass, and I'd had little urge in the years since to take the scenic route. Rhea had assented to it, so long as we reached the Cibola complex before Thursday, the official date of opposition, when it would turn its dishes on.

Rhea spent most of the next few hours in silence, watching the landscape change outside her window. "So, are you a believer?" I finally asked her.

"Dottie drags me to church every Sunday," she said, "but I can't say it does much for me."

"No, your shirt." She looked down at it, at the assembly schematic for the probe and the big text that said *Believer 2*. The press was full of griping and worrymongering about this probe, after the unexplained loss of *Believer 1*, and scientists were legitimately concerned about its prospects. We were lucky to get a second chance after doing a disappearing act with one hundred and twenty million dollars. We all knew there would not be a third. Rhea said she didn't like the name *Believer*. It forced the beholder to answer a yes-no question. Are you a dupe? Or are you a cynic? It required putting a wager on one of two outcomes, but that was shortsighted because the situation would evolve and challenges would be met. She said it would be better for the probes to be named for the qualities we would need when we met them. Grit. Perseverance.

I said that was very Vulcan of her.

"Thank you," she said.

"Though I don't know how inspired anyone is going to be by *Grit 1*."

"Fair."

"Funny to think of it out there, clipping through empty space. It'll intercept around the same time they start broadcasting at Cibola. Two attempts going out at the same time. Which do you think will work?"

"I feel like you weren't listening to what I said about putting down a wager."

I laughed.

"Well, I'm not asking you to put money on it."

She looked out at the surf while she thought about it.

"I think they're both long shots."

"This is a long drive to make for a long shot."

She rolled her eyes at me.

"I'm not going because I think they'll get an answer. I'm going because they're sending Mom's message. Something she came up with. I think she's going to be there to deliver it."

The floor dropped out of my stomach. I suddenly regretted choosing the scenic route. We were on the long, isolated stretch of California's central coast, and there would be no way through the coastal range for a hundred miles. But I was being irrational. Our route added hours, not days.

"What makes you think that?"

She told me about a letter that had come for Crystal last month from Dr. Rivera, the lead administrator of the Cibola Radio Astronomy Complex. The letter implored her, almost begged her, to deliver her message to them in advance. Dr. Rivera wrote that she understood Crystal's reasons for not wanting to do so, but that her own team would need time to assess the message and prepare it for transmission.

"How do you know she didn't send it early, then?" I asked.

"Well, one, she didn't get the letter," Rhea said. "Two, Mom's paranoid. That's what Dr. Rivera means by her 'reasons.' She'd never trust someone else with her work."

She did once, I thought.

I asked how long it had been since she'd seen her mother. Three years next March, she said. *Three years!* I said. I was incredulous, angry. Rhea said it wasn't usually like this. Crystal would typically leave for three or four months. Sometimes she'd go and come back two weeks later. She had gone missing for more than a year only once before, when Rhea was five or six, and after that, living in the little house alone with Dottie always felt normal enough. Dottie was the constant, her mother the variable. Lots of kids had dads who went on deployment or long work trips. You just have to adapt to the circumstances of your life, she said.

"You shouldn't have to adapt to that," I said.

"What's my other choice?"

I honked at an oncoming convertible that was drifting into our lane. I held the horn longer than I needed to. When my heart rate settled, I looked at her for as long as I felt comfortable taking my eyes off the road and said: "You know I didn't know you existed until Dottie called last week. I would have been there from the beginning had I known."

"Dottie told me."

"I *wanted* to have a family with Crystal. Didn't just want— that was the only future I could have imagined."

"It's not your fault. Mom ruined a lot of things."

She turned to look out the window again, putting a kind of terminal punctuation on this line of conversation. Gray waves beat against the rocky cliffs of Big Sur. Sea spray foamed off the top of massive boulders settled farther out in the water. It was a nice enough drive to withstand the silence.

*

Rhea and I sank into the Mojave basin and drove down to Palo Verde, then fifteen miles west of it on the dustiest dirt road in the world. The truck's vents coughed the dust into the cab and it was through our self-created haze that we first saw them: the dishes so big it was hard to fit all of them into your vision at once. You could comprehend an arc, a sector, but not the whole thing—at least not until the dust died down. Something about the scale of them made them seem organic, if alien, like enormous mushrooms with their caps flipped up. In the deadening dust that drifted slower than snow, they seemed the monolithic artifacts of a dead civilization, outsized and ineffable. I started explaining how a Cassegrain antenna works, how the hyperboloid secondary reflector interacts with the parabolic big dish. The first of these was built little more than a decade ago in this same desert. Most people couldn't tell them from other types of antennae but the advantages were manifold. It was an adaptation of a much older technology invented for optical telescopes by—Laurent Cassegrain, Rhea said. She knew. He was a French priest, 1672. She'd read all about it.

"Rick!" a voice called.

A silhouette wandered toward us through the haze. It got closer and turned into Ronnie. He gave his khakis a few useless claps before wrapping me up in a hug. He stepped back to look at me.

"I thought you were a farm boy," he said. "Don't you know how to drive on a dirt road?"

I mocked offense.

"I prefer gravel."

"Ah. Those gravel farms. What are you doing here? Dr. Rivera said you refused to come."

"I'm chaperoning," I said, nodding to Rhea.

"Who's this?"

"Our daughter."

"Our?"

"Me and Crystal."

He cocked his head, startled by the news.

"Didn't know you two had a kid. Seems like the kind of thing you'd mention?"

"Seems like the kind of thing she would have mentioned to me."

As Ronnie looked at Rhea, I could see him doing the math back to 1960 in his head.

"I have a name," she said. "It's Rhea."

He shook her hand and introduced himself. I asked if we could get inside. The wind was strengthening and blanketing us with the fine dust. He waved and led us to the control building, where we clapped off as much as we could under the shelter of the awning. We followed him down the main hall and into a small, mostly empty cafeteria, quiet at this mid-afternoon hour. At a few tables, small groups of center employees played cards or paper football while they sipped at their coffees. A Ping-Pong table went unused in the corner. The far wall was a line of tall plexiglass windows that looked out at the receiving array, and the farthest row of tables was up against it. Otis and Priya were at one of those, drinking from Styrofoam coffee cups and arguing about something. Ronnie walked to their table with the two of us in tow. I wanted to hear the source of their debate but they fell silent when they saw me walk up.

Priya rose to give me a quick hug. Otis stayed seated and said hello, but his smile was laced with a grimace. I wanted to ask Otis if he was okay. His skin was jaundiced, his hair all white. I could diagnose him as an alcoholic from a glance. In grad school, he ate like his brain missed a shutoff signal. Not ravenously, just ceaselessly. My guess was that he drank that way now. Priya, on the other hand, looked the same as when I'd last seen her, except for crow's-feet and some streaks of gray hair that made her look so dignified and authoritative I thought she might have put them there on purpose. Ronnie, like me, had a midthirties paunch but looked otherwise the same. I pulled up a chair for Rhea and another for myself.

"This is my daughter, Rhea," I said. "Mine and Crystal's. I just found out about her last month."

Otis fell into a coughing fit. Priya was less obvious, but her expression still revealed her surprise.

"So is Crystal coming?" Ronnie asked. "Dr. Rivera made some weird hints on the phone."

"She's not here?" I asked.

"No one's seen her in more than ten years," Priya said.

"I have," Rhea said. "For me it's been less than three."

I explained that she had come looking for her mother. She thought we'd find her here. We probably still would, Rhea said. She'd sweep in as late as she could and deliver her message. She might come under the cover of night. *What?!* she said, glancing from face to face. I realized I was looking at her the same way

Ronnie, Otis, and Priya were, the way you look at a child who's expressed a naïve hope.

"What do you think her message will be?" I asked, eager to lend her some support.

"She only ever worked on one thing. The Entropy Equation."

"You think she solved it?" Ronnie said. "I can't imagine she'd try to transmit it if she didn't figure it out."

"How exciting! No one has made any progress in years," Priya said in the empty, enthusiastic tone of a skeptical parent. She didn't believe a word of it, not that Crystal would come or that she'd solved the Entropy Equation. She believed in being kind to children but not in their ability to see through bullshit. Sensing we were on tenuous ground, I shifted the topic to my old friends, asking them to catch me up on their lives and cities, their universities and research. They talked about their work and offered simplified explanations of their fields to Rhea. We found a deck of cards and played hearts and drank more coffee as the afternoon passed. Pages occasionally sounded from the overhead PA system, summoning this or that person to this or that place, so dry and businesslike that Ronnie had to clue me in when one of them used my name, or rather, a version of it I rarely used. *Dr. Hayworth to Dr. Rivera's office, please*, repeated twice.

"Time to go to the principal's office," Otis said.

Dr. Rivera's office was adjacent to the facility's control room, which I peered into as I walked past, a sort of amphitheater filled with computer banks, the long desks populated with the backs of a dozen heads. Her office was small but neat, with a view of the transmitter dishes through the windows behind her.

Framed magazine covers of Crystal, Ronnie, Otis, and Priya adorned the walls, pictures I'd taken, as did two maps of Mars, a modern, scientific one, and an old hand-drawn one from Percival Lowell's notebooks. Dr. Rivera herself was a diminutive middle-aged woman with a short, styleless haircut and dowdy clothes. She looked like a Wisconsin mom, but her voice was commanding and assured. As soon as she saw me she turned and held out her hand. "Dr. Hayworth," she said warmly. She'd spent time studying our photos, I supposed.

She motioned for me to sit across from her and began thanking me for coming to the complex. She was surprised to see me, she said, given how cold a reception I'd given her when she called a couple of years ago, but she was delighted by my change of heart. She wasn't shy about lineage, she told me. The whole Cibola Radio Astronomy Complex was the manifest destiny of the work we'd done in 1960. It was much like the Goldstone complex in technology but quite different in intent. Radio telescopes had of course tossed messages in the direction of the red planet. Big dishes had scanned Mars in their off-hours, but their time was primarily dedicated to intergalactic matters. They thought the solar system was small potatoes. This would be the first dish network wholly dedicated to communication with Mars. We'd sent radio signals before and they'd made no attempt to send something back to us. That didn't mean they weren't using radio communications among themselves. If they lived underground, as the current theories suggested, radio signaling would be fairly contained and muffled. The stray waves would be very faint. But the big dish was sensitive enough to pick them up. We'd be poised to listen not just for a direct response, but for any ground chatter they'd make among themselves when they heard our message.

"It's an impressive facility," I said. "I hope you get a response."

"You seem underwhelmed."

"Don't take it personally. This isn't my first time in a situation like this. I found I liked what came before a lot more than what came after."

"Do you know how old I was when she solved the distance equation? Thirty-four. The most boring of all ages. I wasn't some starry-eyed kid, but I felt like one for the first time in years. I had to haul my old telescope down from the attic. That's how long it had been since I'd used the dusty thing. I had access to the university observatory, and I went a few times to see the Martian response in full scale. But I plopped my own telescope on my deck and went out pretty much every night until Mars was out of viewing range. Just a little red marble, with a smear of blue too small to read. I had to look at it. You can spend your whole life knowing the history, but it's as dead as any other planet until something like that happens. For me, what you all did in the desert brought Mars to life for the first time."

"I know what it did for other people. It did something different to me."

"I understand. Though I'm not sure I understand your visit in that case."

"I'm here for Crystal. I'm here with her daughter, who feels certain Crystal is here somewhere, or will be before the dishes go on tonight."

The wind whipped up a cloud of dust, erasing the dishes from view in the window. As the dust settled, their outlines reemerged. Dr. Rivera wriggled in her seat a little. I could tell she was wrestling with a discretion she didn't really want to exercise, so I added: "Rhea hasn't seen her mother in three years. I hope you're not prepared to break her heart."

Dr. Rivera exhaled.

"She was already here. She came and went. Got here Sunday. Left Tuesday morning before Ronnie arrived. She spent the whole time trying to convince me to turn them on early. I kept telling her there are outside controls. There are regulations."

"She never had much patience for bureaucrats. No offense."

"Bureaucrats and dreamers aren't mutually exclusive. You can layer one over the other. Protocols have their own poetry."

"If you told her that, I'm not surprised she left early."

"She never planned to stay. She didn't tell me that, but as soon as she heard your friends were coming, it was like she'd heard the countdown for a bomb. I really wanted all five of you here. Like I said, this is the continuation of your work."

She hoped it would be, but we'd have to wait and see. I looked again at the framed pictures of the Singer Site on the wall and saw them in a different light now. Dr. Rivera, her crew here, and her backers in the academy believed they were the next generation of great communicators. They wanted a photo connecting our generation to their own. They would have to settle for the four of us.

"She didn't let you take a single photo, did she?"

"It was always about what I could do for her. And I accepted that."

"How did you even get her down here?"

"She called me to ask if she could choose the first message. That's why she wanted me to fire up the observatory so bad."

"So she solved it. The Entropy Equation."

Dr. Rivera delicately retrieved a file from the drawer of her desk, holding it as gingerly as if it were fissile material. Inside the folder was a cellophane envelope, and inside that, sandwiched between two sheets of thin foam and backed by cardboard, was a weathered sheet of binder paper that had clearly not always been treated with this level of care. It had been crumpled and uncrumpled. On it was a looping, irregular script that I could identify as Crystal's. Dr. Rivera let me take the page, though the abundance of caution with which she handed it over inspired me to take the same pains. I took some time to look it over. It was a page full of human numerals drawn almost as if by someone barely familiar with them, irregularly sized and in some places hardly legible. They crowded on top of each other and next to each other in places, and in others they were widely spaced. The messiness did not seem entirely accidental, though. Numerals intersected with each other, joining like ligatures, in too many places to be unintentional. Still, I couldn't discern any meaning from the page.

"This is just a random sequence of numbers," I said.

"That's what it looked like to me too," she said. "And that's what my math people thought."

I tried to focus on the page, on the transition from each number to the next. Then I held it farther away from me and tried to take it in as a whole, as if relaxing my eyesight would convince it to offer up its secrets. I wondered if it were an arithmetic or logarithmic sequence. I checked to see if it was some kind of riff on the Fibonacci sequence. I wondered if it was something like Morse code. It did seem to have some kind of pattern, some repeated subsequences that hinted at an order. Some of the numerals were drawn too large and others too small, as if the sequence was a dashed-off doodle, but that was attributable to Crystal's penmanship. The more I stared at it, the more I was staring at myself trying to infuse it with a meaning it did not contain. It was a jumble of numbers. It didn't even contain an equal sign. I handed it back to Dr. Rivera, and as I watched her repackage it as if it were a rare artwork, I felt a new tenderness for her. For all indomitable bureaucrats.

"How did she look?"

"Older. Older than in the pictures, obviously. That old look like she had a belief in something—permission to speak freely?"

"Granted."

"She looked like that belief was broken. She looked weary. But she didn't talk like it was broken. She loved the idea of the dishes. 'Building an ear just for them,' she called it. To be honest, she kind of reinspired me about all the stuff here that's become so routine."

I glanced at the page on her desk again, repackaged in its many layers.

"Did she seem—did she seem like she was losing it?"

"She seemed very convinced that this sheet was important. She had specific instructions for how to broadcast it as a radio signal, and kept quizzing me on them. I don't know if that's crazy."

I followed her gaze as she turned to look out the window at the monolithic dishes towering above the little control building.

"I guess we'll know when you turn them on."

*

From the door of the cafeteria, I could see Rhea and Ronnie absorbed in a game of Ping-Pong. Priya and Otis had resumed their debate from earlier, or started a new one. None of them noticed me, so I slipped out of the building and walked to my truck. The wind was calm for now, but I pulled a couple of boxes of the letters into the cab to riffle through in anticipation of it picking up again. Until the late 1960s, the letters were filed by sender. Most of the folders were thin enough for me to know they contained only one or two sheets of paper. Those were the one-offs, seemingly every letter a fan, critic, or crank had ever sent her. I didn't know why she'd kept them all. Thank-you notes. Love letters from strangers. Yellowed envelopes from the older years, their skins leathered but fragile, holding query after query from magazine writers, newspaper reporters, and television producers.

I started pulling the thickest folders from their boxes. I wanted to see the way her conversations had spooled out over time. Dr. Lorna Meyer. I knew that name. She was a luminary in astrophysics. Marianne Mosley, another name I knew. There were many groupings I didn't understand the nature of. Musicians and musicologists. Poets. A few young mathematicians whose particular research sparked her interest. Cartographers. Linguistics professors. A random schoolteacher from Ohio named Ed Callahan.

I startled when the truck door opened behind me. Rhea took a look at what I was doing.

"Trying to untangle the web?" she asked.

"I can't say I've even fashioned it into the shape of a web yet."

"No. You're right. A web is made with precision and intent."

She had that same dagger of wit Crystal had, though Crystal had only used it playfully, a fencer tapping you not to draw blood but to let you know she could. With Rhea, it came out primarily in reference to her mother, and I wasn't sure how playful it was. They were assembling the fogeys, she said, and I was being called for. Ronnie, Otis, and Priya stood by the door of the control building, alongside the director and a photographer with heavy equipment. The sun hung low over the horizon. It was the golden hour, and Dr. Rivera wasn't going to waste it.

After they'd shuffled us out in front of the dishes for an array of photos exhaustive enough to rival any wedding shoot—the old gang, the new gang, the old gang with the new gang, and so on—my old classmates and I hung back in the darkening evening. Dr. Rivera led the new gang back into the control building so they could prepare the dishes to go online at the stroke of midnight, as soon as the official date of opposition arrived. The dishes worked day or night. They could have been turned on months ago with almost the same efficacy, but Dr. Rivera was waiting until opposition day to turn them on. I couldn't blame her for her concern with symbolic gestures, not after choosing to paint the Singer Site across the street from the Richter Site.

Rhea hung back as well, but stayed a few feet behind our circle, either feeling out of place with us or slightly repelled by us. We walked the path that curved from dish to dish. Priya slowed her pace so that she was the last of us, inviting Rhea to catch up and match her. Rhea maintained her distance, declining the invitation. Otis's pace kept the rest of us from getting too far ahead. Anything more than a stroll made him start to pant.

They wanted our photo from the desert, I said. The one that made all the magazine covers. But they were making a copy of a copy and the results would be as stale as a senior portrait. Dr. Rivera seemed a talented administrator who hadn't lost her spark, but that was different from being a visionary.

"I know you can't imagine anyone measuring up to Crystal," Priya said. "That may have more to do with your imagination than with the rest of the world."

"I'll be as excited as anyone if they get a response."

Ronnie chuckled.

"I will. I'm not expecting it, though."

"You're just here to find Crystal," Ronnie said.

"I'm here for the kid, who's here for her mother."

"I'm sure it took a lot of prodding," Priya said. "Oh, Rick. You work so hard not to know yourself."

"Still chasing the dragon after all these years," Otis croaked.

"Don't call my mother a dragon," Rhea said from behind us.

"Oh, sorry."

"Just kidding. I like dragons. He came because I asked him to."

We were between two of the dishes now, close enough that each occluded a sector of the sky. Around those dark outlines, stars were beginning to shine in the velvet. Desert nights have a special depth. The lights on the dishes came on all at once. Several floodlights illuminated the bases and armatures of the structures, and the inside of each dish was lit by three lamps set at equidistant points around their outer circumferences, embossing them with spokes of light.

"Wow," Rhea said. "Does that mean they're transmitting?"

"The lights switch on automatically when it gets dark," Ronnie said. "Happened last night at the same time."

"Shall we head in, then?" Priya asked. Her arms were crossed; she was indifferent to the magic of the giant dishes that seemed to hover in the still, dark air. I don't think she noticed the way desert air changes not just in temperature but in texture as the night comes on. My youth was an open sky with a saddle between my legs and the tassels of cornstalks brushing my elbows. You learned to notice the way a leaf dries out, the way the soil in this row shifts differently from the soil in that one. Priya grew up sheltering in her terraced house to keep out of the London rain, so all these outside details were as invisible to her as the action of these giant transmitters and receivers, which would soon be bullhorning a message into space and listening for a whisper from thirty-five million miles away. But then, we all had these private languages. For Priya, it might have been the difference between a rain you could walk in and a rain you couldn't, the ability to sense whether it was waxing or waning. Or it might have been some other thing entirely, something I couldn't conceive of, because that's the nature of these languages.

Out there I heard the language I thought Crystal and I had shared, an ability to be overtaken by the natural world and the world of ideas and the rare physical places where they overlap. I could tell just the spot she would have chosen to stand and it exerted a gravity on me, pulling the direction of my stroll. But

I imagined she would say we had been speaking different languages and wrongly assuming we understood each other.

I scanned their faces to see if anyone else could feel the energy, could read the air. Ronnie seemed happy to be here. He seemed to half get it. Then I saw Otis shivering and rubbing his arms, his posture hunched. Whatever was going wrong in his body was short-circuiting his thermostat.

"Sure, let's head in," I said. "Let's go see what Mars has to say."

I let the three of them walk ahead so that I could fall back to walk alongside Rhea. When I told her that her mother had already come and gone, leaving only the message she wanted to transmit, Rhea turned her face away from me long enough for whatever expression had overtaken it to pass. It was not a short amount of time. She put her palm to her mouth. She wiped her cheeks with the back of her hand. When she turned back toward me, her eyes were red but she was in control of her face again, the same distant stare that I was coming to learn was her default.

"That's Mom for you," she said. "Always one step ahead."

*

Radio communication with Mars would be more like a letter than a phone call. We think of the radio as instantaneous, as obliterating distance, but the distance is still there. Earth distances are just made infinitesimal by the speed of light. Interplanetary scale stretches things out. The electromagnetic waves had to originate from us at the communications complex, then embark across the vacuum and keep going until they hit something. About four minutes, in the case of Mars. Then Mars would have to transmit its own message, a new voyager that would mosey its way across thirty-five million miles to land in the bowls of these dishes.

Hello, Mars?

Eight minutes later: Who's calling?

As the dishes switched on at midnight, Dr. Rivera reminded everyone of these delays. A whiteboard on the side of the room listed what she called the Minimum Possible Response time at seven minutes and twenty-eight seconds. That was if Mars started broadcasting a response the moment our signal reached them. Below MPRt was a Minimum Effective Response time of twelve minutes and twenty-eight seconds, allowing them five minutes to gather their thoughts before they began transmitting. Most important to remember, she said, was the Likely Response time, which was listed as: *Days???* . . . *Months???* Below it was a list of bullet points:

· decoding
· technical adjustments
· equipment construction
· scientific debate
· political/bureaucratic hang-ups

If Mars sent an official response to our signal, we had no idea what that timeline would look like, how long protocols would delay a response. I didn't pipe up to say that Mars had gotten back to the Gang of Five within six hours. But, Dr. Rivera emphasized, MPRt and MERt were crucial to watch closely, because that would be our best chance of overhearing incidental communication between the Martians themselves.

Despite her disclaimers, there was more fragile hope on Dr. Rivera's face than anyone else's as MPRt and MERt arrived and passed. She was working to maintain her emotional equilibrium. I was watching Rhea most closely, and I saw she was in a similar state, alternately watching the monitors in the control room and the big dishes out the window. She was much more engaged with the radio contact attempt now than she'd been before. I thought I understood what she was feeling because I felt it too—the vague, ridiculous intimation that if Mars responded, Crystal would suddenly appear. Minutes went by. No waveforms wriggled across the computer screens. There was no crackle of static. No one shouted, "I've got something!" There was nothing in the room but breath and the ticking of a wall clock.

I gave Rhea a pat on the shoulder.

"We should head to bed."

Ronnie showed us to the bunkroom where the three of them were staying and set us up in the one next door. I hauled in our suitcases so we could change and brush our teeth. Afterward, we lay in our beds, listening to heavy wind sweep the side of the building. Maybe I was starting to learn the rudiments of Rhea's language, because even in the dark, I could sense she was in a different emotional state. She'd gone from a line with slack in it to a line with tension.

"You don't think they'll answer?"

I wanted to offer her good news, but knew how quickly she'd sniff out a lie.

"You're supposed to tell kids hopeful things, so I wish I could say yes. But no, I don't think so. Every indication is that they're creatures who want little to do with us. They know where we are. If they wanted to reach out to us, it would be the easiest thing in the world for them. There's something about us that just doesn't appeal to them. I don't think they view us as equals, and they're probably right not to." That was a bit more hopeless than I'd intended, so I added: "But your guess is as good as mine. The young are naïve. The old are jaded. Neither is the same as wisdom."

"Mom's message. Do you think she got it right?"

"I don't know. I'm not equipped to tell a right answer from a wrong answer. But it didn't look right to me, didn't even seem like it was addressing the right question. I've been over and over her work on the distance equation, and I never fully got it, but I could see the symmetry between the question and the solution. The sheet Rivera showed me just looked like a bunch of numbers. Like she was rolling dice and writing down the results."

"Oh."

"Did she ever say she had it?" I asked. "Did she think she was on the right track?"

"She never shouted eureka, if that's what you mean. There were times she felt she was on the right track, and times where the idea just fell apart and she fell apart with it."

"Fell apart?"

"She'd have these bouts of excitement. She lit up when she thought she was getting it. She didn't talk about it with me, but she'd write all these letters—you've seen the letters—and she'd get all poetic about everything. About streetlights and leaves and pressure cookers. She was a fun mom then. But then she'd get off track and it would be like she was emptied out. Sitting on the couch, staring at the TV but you could turn it off and she wouldn't notice. Aunt Dot had to put a plate of food in her lap sometimes."

"I'm sorry. That's a hard way to grow up."

"At first I loved when she was so excited. Then I dreaded it because it meant the sad days were coming. Then even the calm periods worried me because I knew she'd get excited and then sad again. When she'd go away, I wanted her to come back so bad but I'd be scared of that too, because coming in the door meant she was on the path to going back out."

"That was usually when she left? When the equation was troubling her?" I asked.

"I think that's the reason."

"I'm sorry."

I told her how my dad never ran out on me but turned away from me emotionally. It wasn't the same, I knew, but the change was so abrupt and total that it felt like he was gone. If I'd known some way to track that part of him down, I would have taken pains to make it happen too. She asked if we hadn't made up with each other when we were older. No, I told her. When he died, we hadn't spoken to each other in more than two years. She went quiet. "But I don't think that's what's going to happen with you and your mom," I said too late. She sat with my response a minute.

"Good night, Rick," she said quietly.

"Good night, Rhea," I said. I stayed awake listening, until the rhythm of her breathing told me she was asleep.

*

In the morning, we found Ronnie and Priya in the next room over. They looked terrible, and it was immediately clear why. Otis's raucous snores would cut off abruptly and he'd go silent for a minute at a time. Then he'd gasp for breath and do it all over again. Ronnie had spent the whole night thinking Otis had just died. Priya was sitting up in bed with her face swollen, her eyes red. It was hard to hear each other over the volume of the snore, then the silence was sudden enough to be startling, and the gasping was as desperate as if he'd been pulled out of a lake. Priya and Ronnie said they wouldn't have stayed up so late in the control room if they knew what the night had in store.

We stopped in the cafeteria to load foam cups with coffee, then walked down the hall to the control room. Had they heard anything from Mars, someone would have woken us. No one had woken us. Therefore, they had heard nothing. I knew this from the moment I woke, but we headed in anyway to hear the lack of news. Dr. Rivera repeated her spiel about the difference between the minimum response time and the likely response time. We'll keep listening, she concluded. *Ah,* I thought, *now we have two senses trained on the planet that ignores us.*

"There wasn't even a blip?" Rhea asked. "The kind of incidental chatter you talked about?"

"Not yet," Dr. Rivera said to her kindly. "But it's a long game. Resist the temptation to give up on it prematurely."

She busied herself wandering the room, looking at the monitors on which nothing was happening. Occasionally, she'd slip the headphones off someone and slide them over her own ears. We recognized the signs of someone distracting herself and left her to continue the ritual. We went back to the cafeteria and feasted on cold cereal and muffins, reminiscing about our grad school professors, the ones who bumped into tables while they lectured, the Fields Medal winner who plucked hairs out of his head when he was concentrating. Rhea was silent through it all, even when I steered the conversation toward topics more her speed.

"Hey, kiddo," I said quietly to her. "Game of Ping-Pong?"

She shook her head slightly and looked back at her empty cereal bowl.

We'd talked away an hour and a half of the morning when two dozen of the scientists at the facility rushed into the room and ran to the television mounted in the corner. They turned it on and gathered in a crowd to watch the special news report that had interrupted the usual morning programming. We hopped up and gathered behind them. Rhea snaked her way through to the front so she could see the screen. Once the sound of everyone's shoes had settled, we could hear what Walter Cronkite was announcing:

". . . million miles away, trying to learn more about our quiet neighbor. Not since 1960, and since 1933 before that, have they shown any signs of life. That's twice in half a century. Today is a sad day as we have to put another dream to rest. We've just received news that NASA's ground control has lost all communication with the *Believer 2* probe. The disappearance was sudden and unexpected, and as with the *Believer 1* probe of 1969, it happened when the probe was exactly 12,856 miles from Mars."

We lost what he said next to a chorus of groans. What a sad end it was to the probe program, all we'd hoped to learn about Mars reduced to a single fact: the limit of Martian airspace.

Ordinarily, I'd attribute the complaints of these scientists to academic concerns—it was going to be harder than ever to get grants for anything related to Mars—but Dr. Rivera had vouched for them as true believers, and they seemed genuinely despondent. Disappointment was clear on my friends' faces as well. And Rhea? I shouldered through the crowd toward where I'd last seen her, but she was no longer in the front row. I scanned the cafeteria just in time to see her slinking out of the room. By the time I got back through the crowd and out the door after her, the hallway was deserted.

Finding our bunkroom empty, I searched the rest of the building. The other bunkrooms, the control room, Dr. Rivera's empty office. The hallways and stairwells. I had Priya check the women's restroom. I finally found her out in the cab of my truck. The passenger seat was still crowded with letter boxes, so she was in the driver's seat, her forehead against the steering wheel, tears on her cheeks. There was no room to sit next to her, so I put my hand on her back and she didn't shrug it off.

"She'll come back to you," I told her.

"Yeah?" she said. "How long have you been waiting?"

Shit. Twelve years. The entire span of Rhea's life.

"I'm not her kid. I'm just an old boyfriend who can't let go."

"She doesn't care that I'm her kid," Rhea spat. "If she did, she wouldn't have gone in the first place."

"You deserve better."

"I never should have come here. I'm sorry I dragged you along."

"This," I said, "is the most important thing I've done in a long time."

It was. Despite my doubts and cynicism, despite some strained moments between Rhea and me, this was the first time in years I'd been shaken out of the farmhouse, out of the routines in which I'd entombed my own life. I never felt closer with my dad than when we did long drives like this, had big conversations with the countryside passing by our windows, and then spent hours in silence drifting down a lonely highway, sharing the peace with each other. My eyes wandered to the boxes of letters next to Rhea.

"The trip doesn't have to end here," I said.

I grabbed my road atlas from the pocket behind her seat and asked her to grab me the thumbtacks from the glove box. I pulled the box of Crystal's most frequent correspondents across Rhea's lap and put it on the ground by my feet. Pulling one of the bundles from the box, I handed her a tack.

"Lester Cuttleman. Lincoln, Nebraska. A cartographer she wrote to a lot in the midsixties."

"Funny, she never seemed very interested in carts."

"Cartography is the study of maps."

"That's the joke."

She poked a tack into Lincoln. I pulled a letter from one of the bigger bundles.

"Lorna Meyer. University of Denver. They wrote back and forth for years about entropy."

She added a tack.

"Madison, Wisconsin. Marianne Mosley. Astrophysics."

"Why are we looking at a map, Rick? You want to drive all the way to Wisconsin when we could just call them?"

"Crystal's been in hiding for twelve years and people are

still trying to track her down. People still call me asking questions. Soon as I hear a stranger say her name, I hang up the phone. I'm on her side, not theirs. These people are on her side too. They know she doesn't want to be found."

"So why would they help us at all?"

"We're not strangers."

I held out another tack. She looked at it and considered. Finally, she took it from me.

"Hans Böde. Chicago. Professor of musicology."

"What does that have to do with entropy?"

"I have no idea."

"Have you considered that some of these are just private friendships and not part of some grand puzzle?"

"Yes. Ed Callahan. Youngstown, Ohio."

Rhea didn't ask about him, which was good because I knew only that he was a random schoolteacher. His letters were the biggest bundle, and for the life of me I couldn't understand why this guy who taught trig to ninth graders had the ear of the world's most brilliant living mathematician. She wrote to the leading minds in mathematics and astrophysics to mull the nature of the universe, and they wrote back. And she had always had an interest in maps and codes and music. I wasn't surprised that she had reached out to experts in those fields. My only theory about Ed Callahan was that whatever connection Crystal had to him was personal.

Rhea put a tack in him.

"If we're doing a road trip," I said, grabbing one last tack, "there's one more place we need to stop. Luckily, it's on the way."

*

We said our goodbyes to Priya, Ronnie, and Otis, and went to the control room to thank Dr. Rivera for hosting us. I had Rhea call Dottie to get her permission to extend our trip a week or two, and to ask her to notify Rhea's school, then sent Rhea to poach snacks from the cafeteria while I popped back into Dr. Rivera's office to grab the sheet she'd shown me the day before. After that, we were on our way. Little desert highways took us north from the radio complex. The monolithic dishes faded out of the rearview and, it seemed, out of reality. Flatness and random sandstone quarries. Towns anchored by gas depots. A rising sun that could make you think it was all some feathery dream. That changed when we got to I-40, which was Route 66 with the wild parts paved over and its crooked teeth straightened. This was a wide, modern freeway. Even where there were only two lanes, they were rifled neatly and turned in soft arcs so long they drifted into the horizon. The sun hit I-40 differently, maybe because the distant perspective of the road kept you more focused on where you were going than where you were at the moment.

The landscape was less desolate than I remembered, stubbled all over with creosote scrub the color of olive leaves. There were dips and rises too: nothing dramatic, but low, noticeable swells of them. There was enough subtle variation to make me want to turn off the radio, but Rhea was enjoying scanning the options. I asked her if she was interested in the same things her mother and I were. Math. Physics. Science. Sort of, she said. She wasn't a genius. There were parts she didn't get.

"Like what?"

"I don't get space-time."

Think about the sea, I told her. There's a sea of time and a sea of space, but really they're the same sea. Imagine standing at the edge of the ocean, watching the surface toss itself around. We used to think of space as being like all that water with no motion. All the oceans, still as a fish tank. But you have to think of space-time as something that can move and swell like the tides.

"So space is a medium in constant motion?" she asked.

"Well, it may or may not be a medium."

"What does that mean?"

"There's nothing there. But the nothing has characteristics."

"Characteristics?"

"It can bend. It can twist."

"Like a wave."

"Yeah! Not an exact match, but a useful framework. Now imagine a stick floating in the water, moving as the water moves, and a fish swimming forward through the water. The stick experiences the wave but the water doesn't experience the wave. The water just is the wave. As the fish moves away from the stick in the moving water, their distance increases."

"But how is that different from a fish swimming away from a stick in still water?"

"Well, uh—imagine that the fish and the stick are both wearing watches."

"I think you've lost control of your metaphor."

"Yeah, that's fair."

"I'll think of another."

Space-time, relativity—these were counterintuitive concepts. Even the people who studied them found they slipped out of socket like a dislocated joint and needed to be popped back in. I took great comfort in the nature of Rhea's curiosity, which was expansive without being as desperate as Crystal's had been. She wanted to understand things but could bear the state of not understanding things yet. Crystal would have said this quality limited her, that one needed a desperate speed to break through the perimeter of human understanding. I would have agreed, before Rhea, but relativity took me a while too. I could recite its principles long before I could comprehend them. I don't think I got there any sooner for all my hunger for it.

I rolled some analogies around in my head. My father's mock-folksy voice popped in: *Things look different if you watch from different places.*

"I've never been," Rhea said.

"What?"

"To the sea. I've never been."

"Are you kidding me? You grew up thirty miles from it."

"Mom was too busy. Dottie said it was too cold."

"Too cold for swimming."

"Why else would you go?"

"Just to see."

"To seeee the seaaa?" she said.

She smiled like a kid. It was the first time I'd seen her do so. Most of the time she squinted off into the distance like she was trying to win an Oscar, which had been enrapturing in her mother but was a bit sad in a twelve-year-old. It was not a normal expression for someone her age, but Crystal was her only model. If you feed a kid nothing but carrots, they'll turn orange.

To seeee the seeeaaa? To see you smile again, kid.

"I'll get you there," I said.

Her smile dropped. I'd approached too directly.

"Tell me about entropy. What's all the fuss about?"

"It keeps some people up." I made a corny ghost sound.

"Oh," she said. "The spooky math."

Things fall apart, I told her. Entropy is the breakdown of all matter and energy into gradually less organized forms. Every time you chop a carrot, you're increasing entropy. If you make a cabin out of Lincoln Logs, that's ordered matter. Over time, it'll grow disordered. Something will knock it down. Maybe a person or an animal. Maybe an earthquake. Maybe it eventually just leans and falls over like an old barn. If you wait long enough it will come down. But you can wait forever and the cabin won't put itself back together. Gravity's not going to reassemble the cabin.

"That's what scares people about entropy," I said.

"People are scared of entropy?"

"Nerds are."

"It's just a cabin."

"The example is just a cabin. The index of things subject to entropy is: everything. Everything degrades as time moves forward."

"But I can rebuild the cabin."

"By adding your own energy from outside the system. But in a closed system, it's decay, decay, decay. Entropy is a one-way street. That's what scares people. It's the direction of the universe, and it flows only in the direction of nothingness. Things will only ever fall further apart. The river doesn't run backwards."

"The Entropy Equation—it's supposed to be about the rate of decay?"

"Far as anyone can tell."

She stared out the window, not interested in the desert, but interested in looking away from me.

"Your mother wrote—not to me, but to one of her scientist pals—that it's impossible to fully appreciate entropy on an endlessly generative planet. How can you watch a dead tree erupt into new plant and insect life in the jungle and believe the direction of the universe is unremitting decay? Even something like mold—leave a piece of bread on the counter and it will seem to create new life. These gains are small on the cosmic scale, but they are vivid. Most of what's lost to entropy is in spectrums we can't even see. Matter to light to heat to nothing. An infinitesimal fraction of the sun's energy is responsible for all the abundance of our planet. A good thing we can't see the torrent of waste, the enormity of what's lost. Imagine pouring a jug of milk down the drain. The droplets of leftover milk in the sink? That's what we live off."

I had not meant to drop all this on her. She asked the right questions, and I answered honestly. In truth, I'd been thinking a lot about entropy in recent years. I'd felt myself slowing down, my energy stagnating. Otis's body was falling apart. Ronnie and Priya—they weren't disintegrating the same way, but their hope, their energy, were sapped. When Angie left, I lost all sense of progress, or even stasis. My sense of self, of organization, of capability, was a pile of Lincoln Logs scattered across the floor. All this wanted to pour out when Rhea asked me about entropy. I held back what I could. You don't want to withhold the truth from a kid. You also can't tell them: *Entropy will be the story of your life.*

*

In Kingman, we stopped at a sporting goods store to buy camping gear. I wanted us to sleep outside at our first stop. Two sleeping bags, a tent, matches, fire supplies. We had a late lunch, then Rhea slept through the afternoon. Impossible to say how much my monologuing was to blame. We were almost to our first stop when she woke up, though she didn't know that. She rubbed her eyes and took stock of our surroundings. This was the old road. It was narrower, more rugged, than the one she'd fallen asleep on, enough so that it seemed a different universe. Rhea looked out at the southward expanse and took note.

"There was a fire."

"A very specific fire."

She sat up straighter, as if a couple of inches would give her a proper vantage. She looked back over her shoulder, and then far and away up ahead, trying to grasp the scope, but the burn extended farther than the eye could see in both directions.

"This is what you wanted me to see."

"No," I said. "But you're warm."

The Richter Site, given Einstein and Richter's resources, given their maximalist intentions, was much larger than the Singer Site. It was also oriented horizontally along the highway, whereas we had to fit our message north–south, with the narrow edge against the road. So we drove along the scooped-out and charred message a while, noting the occasional cars that dotted its numerals. I'd read that the dirt blowing into them year after year had started to erase the message. Satellite photography showed that only the outline of the script remained clear. The row closest to the road was occasionally dug out to maintain the site, but after long enough, maintaining the site would require the same amount of work it had taken to excavate it in the first place.

If the Richter Site was carved. into something less than stone, the Singer Site was printed in something less than ink. I was expecting to find a blank stretch of desert where we once shouted to the Martians. I was ready for it to break my heart.

As we approached that topography I could never forget, we saw two vans parked on the north side of the road, just off the little parking lot at the entrance. One van was a sparkling blue, and the other was the color, to put it generously, of dirt. The back doors of the brown van hung open, and the inside was cluttered with what looked like five-gallon buckets of paint.

We got out of the truck. I lost myself for a moment staring at the two vans. They were so tall and wide, the interiors so cavernous, that I was dumbstruck by envy. These vans were built for the type of trip we'd made in 1960. If only we could have had one then. We heard laughter from the other side of the vehicles, and we walked around the vans to find three young couples walking toward us from the desert. All had the same long hair, which could have come from Old Testament paintings, and the men's beards were at prime apostle length. But that was all that was religious about them. The women were in flowy skirts and crocheted bikini tops. The men were in shorts only. It was sixty-five degrees out, so it took a lot of commitment to dress like this. They were all so deeply tanned their skin seemed less like a part of their bodies than like old fruit peels ready to come off at the touch. Each of them was coated with random patches of light blue paint—this one's knees and palms, that one's whole back.

"Fellow travelers!" shouted the tallest of them. He had a thin, boxy chest, a torso in the shape of a cereal box. His shoulders bobbed side to side when he walked.

I held up a hand to signal I'd heard him. *Never wave to a hippie,* I heard my dad say. He passed before hippies were a thing, but enough of him lingered to say this to me, only half joking. Rhea held a hand over her eyes to block the sun. As usual, it was impossible to tell whether she was judging or reserving judgment.

"You've reached the sacred site!"

We were close enough to return conversation now.

"Sacred?" I said.

"What else would you call it?" asked the young woman next to him. She had dangly earrings in the shape of humpback whales.

"You're here," said the tall one, "so you must see something in it."

"Maybe we were just passing through and wanted to see what was out here."

"That's a weird thing to be hypothetical about," said one of the other women. This one had the kind of bright blue eyes that seemed designed to burn the dishonesty out of whomever she looked at. She and the apostle next to her were both streaked with paint down the whole of their left sides. I realized with horror that the patterns of paint on each pair indicated the positions in which they had recently coupled. I prayed to God Rhea wasn't drawing the same inferences.

"Is something wrong, dude?"

Instinctually, I'd looked away, as if I'd come across them naked.

"We saw your dust cloud," laughed the tall one. "Don't you know how to drive on dirt? Come on, have a beer."

"I know how to drive on dirt."

Rhea laughed. The guy was already grabbing me something from the cooler. He looked at her.

"We don't have, like, juice," he said.

"Beer?" Rhea asked speculatively, her pitch rising at the end.

"Water," I said. "Nice try."

We settled down with these strangers in the shade of their vans, using spent paint buckets as stools. I cast another covetous look at the vans and asked how they drove. Get you where you want to go, said Francine, the hippie with the honesty-eyes. It was an ill-fitting name, but that's how it goes. Children are named long before their generation invents its way in the world. Tall-boy Lloyd was clearly the leader, but it was the third woman, Pearl, who was small and thin-boned and had seemed shyest until now, who started talking to us about the place we were in. This was Hualapai land, she said. To the extent that any land can be ascribed to a people. They were its custodians. Then they were shot down and forced out over a road. Not this road, but one enough like it. And the roads kept coming, kept evolving.

Her voice was so reverent it became clear she was the one who'd picked this location for their pilgrimage. The others might have been as happy in the Grand Canyon or at any beach. She continued:

A road erases the land it runs through. The land becomes a vessel to bear the road, and we no longer see the land. We see the strand of black thread for which the land is just a background. Our eyes follow it to the horizon and our cars follow it farther. If you blow a tire you're stuck in the middle of nowhere. As if the land itself does not exist. This place is sacred because it draws the eye back to the land. First the Richter Site and then the Singer Site drew the eyes of the world back to this land we've tried so hard to reduce to the time it takes to traverse, which we quantify as lost time. These sites made the land exist again. Even across an interstellar distance, they made this land seen.

Interplanetary, I thought—*not interstellar.*

"What I love," said her boyfriend, "is the chorus it created. We sang a song to Mars and they sang back."

Less a song, I wanted to say, than a very technical and complicated math problem. But I wasn't planning to tell them my relation to the site. Crystal's disappearance let everyone fill the empty space with whatever they wanted to believe, and belief can be a volatile material.

"Is there something about this place?" Rhea asked Pearl. "If it happens again, will it happen here?"

"There must be. For it to happen twice here? There's something special."

"Is it, like, chakras or magnetic resonance or something?"

Rhea was deadpan enough that Pearl didn't realize she was being teased.

"I don't know. But can't you feel it?"

"I can," Rhea said.

I looked out toward the site. Our hippie gang had splashed blue paint over several hundred square feet of it, coloring in a small fraction of the last symbol in the equation. I estimated it to be one-hundredth of a percent of the message. In other places, there were patches of more faded blue paint on the ground, so apparently these six weren't the first to perform the ritual. Still, the vast majority of the message was bare earth now, the curves of the numerals marked by metal posts every twenty feet. The posts had loops to hold chains, but the chains had long ago been stolen to sell as scrap.

The sun was getting closer to the horizon.

"The temperature's going to drop real hard out here soon. You all have jackets?"

"Aw," said Francine. "You really are a dad."

"We've got a good blanket. What the Sherpa use in Nepal," Lloyd said.

"One blanket for the six of you?" Rhea asked.

"Some fleece and some body heat. It's all you'll ever need."

I turned to Rhea.

"We should set up camp before it gets dark."

"Can't we stay a little longer?"

I was in no position to deny her a thing, so we hung out with the hippies longer. They shared more beer and we shared our trail mix. I built a fire and we sat in a circle around it on our paint buckets while the sun set and we talked of other things. Smaller things. Places we'd seen in the country. Best songs for the highway. Saddest things we'd seen in a small town. Most surprising shows of kindness. Rhea hadn't been around to collect many of these, so they kindly asked about her favorite subjects and worst teachers. She answered openly, in a way I knew she wouldn't have for me alone.

I passed my bottle to her and told her: "One sip."

She raised her eyebrows, but couldn't hide a little smile. She took a swig of the lukewarm brew, then spit it violently in the sand. We all laughed while she wiped her tongue with her forearm.

"Let that be a lesson to you," I said. "Everything that makes you long for adulthood is actually self-punishment."

Francine cackled and turned back to Rhea.

"My dad was just like him. This gruff, country-dad stuff. Couldn't show weakness."

"Am I that gruff?"

The group nodded in unison.

"Am I?"

Rhea shrugged affirmatively.

Well, here came the drunk-sads. For a moment I was ready to tell them about my dad, about the open door closing and the way that stayed with me. The moment passed, but left me urging myself to remember in the morning: don't do to Rhea what my dad did to me. Cars moseyed by on the highway now and then—not many, and not very fast. This was 66, not I-40. Their headlights pulled them on right past us. I agreed with Pearl: it was sad, the rest of the land erased. I scooted my paint bucket next to the blue van so I could lean back against it. That was another sad thing, that I didn't have a van like this. *Maybe I should trade in the truck?* I thought.

Sometime later, Lloyd rustled me out of sleep. I heard laughter. The three young women were sitting on either side of Rhea, and they were all laughing together. I couldn't hear what they were saying, but Rhea was showing another smile

I'd never seen—a smile that seemed attached to a part of her I'd never met. Lloyd told me it was a miracle I hadn't fallen off the paint bucket. He and Luke had a wager on it, with an over/under of thirty minutes. I was outside the campfire's radius and it was freezing. Luke and Ted were setting up their camp for the night, which didn't take long; it was just spreading a giant fleece blanket out closer to the fire than I'd call wise.

The women stood and stretched. Each gave Rhea a hug. This was the transition to bedtime. Lloyd said there was plenty of blanket if we wanted to share camp with them. I looked at Lloyd with his blue knees and shins, and his girlfriend with her blue knees and palms, and declined as politely as I could. I stumbled out to the truck and set up our bags in front of the headlights so Rhea would be able to see her way over, hoping this was far enough to be out of earshot of any nocturnal activities. I headed back to get her, figuring I'd have to talk her out of sharing the blanket, but caught her already heading my way.

We brushed our teeth out of a canteen. She tied her hair back. She settled into her bag and I turned off the headlights and got into mine.

A car drove down the highway with its high beams on and I turned away from the road. Only then did I see it. Without the light of the campfire in the way, the ground of the Singer Site glowed. It was nothing like the day we'd put it down, when blue luminescence seemed to pour out and infuse the sky. This was as faint as a river under moonlight. There were miles and miles of these faded runes carpeting the space between us and the hills, like the gentle presence of a light left on for you in the next room over.

218

*

Past Ash Fork, we were on I-40 again. Route 66 was subsumed by the interstate, so were we traveling on it, or was it gone? Whichever road we were on, it lifted us into the Coconino National Forest, where jutting red buttes were strung with lines of pine trees as if decorated for Christmas. Passing through Flagstaff was an experience that turned emotional pain physical. I saw the motel we had stayed in and the diner we had eaten in, and it felt as if someone had lodged a grappling hook in my ribs and was pulling it downward arm over arm. Rhea noticed I'd gone quiet. The domes of Lowell Observatory floated by, and she must have been pleasantly surprised not to be conscripted into a seminar about it. She didn't know that to me it was less a historical site than a scar.

But our mood—my mood, and therefore fifty percent of the overall mood—rose when the urban development started to thin and the road lapsed back into its gas stations and motor lodges and roadside relics. We were still in the high country, if coming down out of it. After our drive through the low desert, the greenery here seemed a ridiculous abundance. And we were lifted by the previous night's encounter. Rhea joked that the hippies were more in tune with the moon than they were with Mars, but we both smiled when we talked about them. Friendly strangers. Allies in a hostile terrain. Devotees, in their own way, of Crystal's work. When we'd begun talking with them, I'd thought of it as a meaningless devotion; in their combined lifetimes the six of them would never understand a fraction of the equation they were there to celebrate.

Today, that seemed to matter less.

Winslow. Holbrook. Petrified National Forest. The meaning-lessness of a desert border flew by and we were in New Mexico. We stopped for lunch in Gallup and turned north on the Devil's Highway toward Denver.

"The river doesn't run backwards," Rhea mused, some-where past the Colorado border.

"What?"

"You said it about entropy." She affected the deep voice of a simpleton: "'The river doesn't run backwards.'"

"I don't sound like that."

"We learned about the Chicago River in history last year. They made that one flow backwards. What's so funny?"

"No, you're right. They did reverse the flow. It's just funny that you bring it up. That was one of my dad's favorite things. He loved to talk about it. The miracle. The miracle of engineer-ing. When there's shit in the water, he said, people can engineer a miracle to make someone else the one downstream."

"I mean, better than drinking it?"

"Indeed. So, does this connect to a theory? Are you making some kind of analogy?"

"Not really. It just seems meaningful somehow."

"Maybe it is," I said. "It never hurts to chase that feeling."

*

Lorna Meyer's house was an elegant brick cottage hiding un-der a magnificent sycamore. It suggested a desire to live in the shadow of a great tree, and a willingness to die if it fell.

Not until we were parked at the curb did it strike me that we'd look like maniacs, showing up unannounced to ask about the details of a decade-old private correspondence. Not having thought of this earlier suggested that I *was* a maniac. I cycled through different things I could say if she opened the door, and each seemed crazier than the next—*We drove here from California to see you*—*We've driven a great distance to untangle the nature of entropy*—*I've been reading your letters*. Bored with my vacillation, Rhea hopped out of the truck, and she was knocking on the front door by the time I caught up with her. The woman who opened it was a little shorter than Rhea, so she peered upward at us. Her hair, though steel gray and striated with white, still flowed straight and healthy down to her neckline. The face it framed was only lightly wrinkled but ruddy, and overall she presented a curious mix of elegance and earthiness.

"What can I do for you?" she asked. She sounded eager to show us away.

"Did you know Crystal Singer?" Rhea said.

Dr. Meyer seemed a bit stunned by the question. Her glance shifted to me and became more suspicious. She looked at Rhea again, scrutinizing her now, her eyes darting to the girl's cheeks, chin, nose, the straight strawberry rope of her hair. Her mouth dropped open a little.

"I did," she said, with some playful caginess.

"She's my mother."

"Rhea," Dr. Meyer said, her voice now friendly and beguiling. "I'm sure you don't remember, but this is not the first time we've met."

She turned and walked back into the house, leaving the door open for us. I followed behind Rhea, who was clearly the guest of interest. We caught up to our host in a plant-laden kitchen with leafy vines snaking from the windowsills down to the countertop. Dr. Meyer was at the tap, filling a kettle shaped like a rooster. She lit a burner and set the kettle there.

"Do you like tea? My granddaughter Nedda is a little younger than you and she'll drink it all day. Her mother hates it, says that's why she never naps over here. If I could freeze time, I'd keep her this age forever. But when she's older, I'll tell you the thing she's going to remember about her Nannie."

"I don't know," Rhea said. "I haven't really tried it. I used to smell Aunt Dottie's chamomile and gag."

"Chamomile tastes like an old floral sofa. It's time to expand your horizons."

Dr. Meyer scooped some loose-leaf tea from an unlabeled glass jar on her counter and set up an infuser in a teapot that was already on the table. She motioned for us to sit. The kettle whistled and she filled the pot, then went to the fridge. She told Rhea the best thing, if you were new to the art of tea drinking, was a healthy splash of milk. She dithered around the kitchen gathering spoons and saucers, and when she set them on the table for us, she sniffed the air once and poured the tea into the three cups on the table. She added a few glugs of the milk to Rhea's and a tiny splash to her own, and left mine alone without offering.

As soon as all this was completed, she disappeared from the room. Rhea inhaled some of the steam rising off her cup and shrugged. A much better nose, she said, than Dot's tea. It's Earl Grey, I told her. Okay, she said skeptically, as if I'd tried to

222

bestow a knighthood on her tea. Drawers clattered and banged from another room.

Dr. Meyer returned and put a four-by-six photo print on the table between us. It had been taken here in this shady room—you could see the same weeping willow outside the patio door—and had so little color it looked almost black and white. There she was, Crystal, looking so much like the last time I'd seen her it was as if Dr. Meyer had pulled the photograph from my hippocampus. The camera had caught her in three-quarter profile. Her chin was down, her hair hanging over a third of her face. Her smile was just this side of laughter; it was pregnant with a laugh that was about to come. Rhea, maybe two at the time, was riding straight as a board on Crystal's far shoulder, her legs sticking out in front of Crystal, her shoulders and face behind. Crystal's hand was tickling her ribs, and Rhea's back was arched slightly, her eyes rolling up, grinning with that searing purity of emotion only toddlers have.

Dr. Meyer sipped her tea while we took in the photograph. I soaked it in. Rhea looked at it a moment, then turned her face away.

"That's why you wouldn't remember," she said. "You were just short of two. Such a joy, but too young for memories."

"I remember that tree. Sort of. I remember the feeling of it, if that makes any sense."

Dr. Meyer smiled.

"Makes perfect sense to me," she said.

"This was the last time we visited?"

"It was the last time you visited. She came a couple more times after. But not like she had before. I saw a lot of you when

223

you were a baby. I did everything but nurse you. My daughter was in high school by then, and didn't think much of me. I was eager to smuggle a little baby time back into my life."

"We came here a lot?"

"Your poor mother—she was so grateful to your aunt for taking you both in. They barely knew each other before then. It was an act of great faith and generosity, she said. But your aunt drove her crazy half the time. She talked too much. At least, that's what Crystal told me. She'd be doing her Crystal thing, trying to fit the whole Entropy Equation in her head at once, the way those chess masters do. Then the screen door would slam and Dorothy would come into the little house saying: *You'll never guess who I bumped into at the nursery, did I ever tell you about Clem Potter, and boy is downtown getting crowded.*"

"Sounds like Dottie," Rhea said.

"I never knew if she was exaggerating. Sometimes she thought *I* talked too much. From the stories she told, I don't know if anyone could be as chatty as all that."

"She wasn't exaggerating."

"Crystal felt guilty, of course, for being annoyed when she was also indebted. But she had little enough quiet time already, with a baby, that losing the little she had drove her crazy. I think this was her refuge, not just from the interruptions but from the guilt. Even here, she couldn't go out to work. Couldn't go to a café or a library. But we have a cozy guest room with a heavy door. I keep a nice garden. She liked to work out back while I played with you."

"What happened?" I asked. "Why'd she stop coming?"

Dr. Meyer looked over at me to receive the question and back at Rhea to answer it.

"That same trip from the picture, I convinced her to take a walk. It had just rained. The weather was brilliant. This is a quiet neighborhood now and was even quieter then. She put on a ball cap and sunglasses. I told her she looked like a narc and she took off the glasses but kept the hat. Just two women walking around the neighborhood, I thought. Who would even give us a second glance? But the rumors started to swirl, I guess. A couple of days later, news vans began prowling the neighborhood. They even knocked on my door. Someone must have told them I was a physics professor. They never got enough to report, but for a while after that, I'd see these well-dressed, binocular-toting creeps I *knew* didn't live around here. When things calmed down, she left. She didn't come back for a long time. I understood, but it made me sad. I saw her again two more times, but that was really the end of the friendship."

"But you were writing her letters as late as 1969," I said.

She looked at me, alarmed, and set down her tea. Rhea immediately picked up her own and leaned forward to recapture Dr. Meyer's attention. It was a savvy move. "He's obsessive," she said, "but not dangerous." Dr. Meyer assessed Rhea's confidence, and seemed to decide that as long as Rhea was my keeper, rather than the other way around, we could continue. "She was different the next time you saw her, wasn't she?" Rhea asked. "In the late sixties?" Dr. Meyer asked how so—not as if she didn't know, but as if she didn't want to go first.

"Like she'd lost something."

Dr. Meyer nodded solemnly.

"She came in 1964 and 1966. She seemed"—she stirred the air with her hand, searching for the word—"ragged. When we'd talk about a possible solution, when we'd riff on it and feel like we were on its tail, I thought she was like a house on fire. When she visited those last times, she was more like a burnt-out house. I don't know if you could feel me worrying about you from afar. I hoped what I saw wasn't what you saw. That you were insulated from it. It doesn't sound like that was the case."

Rhea shook her head slightly.

"Did you make progress in all your discussions over the years?" I asked. "Were the two of you close to solving it?"

"Progress is a nebulous thing. It's not like a road that brings you steadily closer to your destination. We always felt like we were on the verge. Her especially. She said she was on the edge of understanding. She said it felt like looking at a picture that was abstract but still representational, that sometimes she could see what it represented for a moment but it would slip away before her mind could articulate it. There was the moment of recognition that made her turn toward it, but as soon as she turned toward it, it would retreat. She was saying that as early as 1963. It was terribly exciting to her then. In 1967, it was the same phenomenon but filled her with desperation. Was she closer? Who can say?"

"Do you think she's still working on it?" I asked.

"I can't imagine otherwise."

"Do you think she might have solved it?"

"I wouldn't know any better than you."

I pulled out the folder I'd been hiding by my side and laid it on the table. It was the distorted message Crystal had given to Dr. Rivera. They had Xeroxes of it taped up in the control room, so I hadn't worried about taking their only copy. But this original, this page written in her own hand, was something I wanted in my possession. When I flipped the folder open, Rhea gasped. Then she smiled at me with a new respect. Dr. Meyer was intrigued enough to forget her skepticism of me and scoot her chair around to our side of the table. I unwrapped the document using the same doting care as Dr. Rivera. Dr. Meyer scooted even closer, hovering over my shoulder. Her eyes darted over the page on her first read. Her brow furrowed as she read it again. After the third time, her shoulders sank.

"Does it mean anything? Does it fit into any of your theories together?" I asked, though her posture had already answered the question.

"This has nothing to do with anything we ever talked about. And frankly, I don't think it means anything. It means she's in a bad place, if she thinks this is something to share with the world."

"With two worlds," I said.

"Dr. Meyer, do you know where my mother is?"

Dr. Meyer took Rhea's hand and squeezed it. Near tears, she answered fiercely, "If I did, I would tell you. If I did, I would call her myself and tell her *go back to your* fucking *daughter.*"

I stared back into the message on the page. Again, I wondered about the strange, childlike writing, trying to parse some meaning from the variations in size, the horizontal stretching of some of the numerals, the way they bumped into each other. Though it didn't make any sense, staring into it gave me a strange nostalgic pull, the sort of effect that comes from an eerie work of art, not a numerical sequence. I almost asked Dr. Meyer if it gave her the same effect, but I didn't because I knew the real answer: it called me back to the past because that was where I wanted to be called.

*

Denver to Lincoln was a day's drive, long and flat, though far more verdant than the Southwest. Green grass sprouted from the fall rains, but the trees were almost bare. I chided Rhea for calling them the not-so-Great Plains. Over fields of wheat we could spy patterns of farmhouses and silos as regular as a metronome. Then we'd take a turn and be walled in by tall fields of late corn. I loved all this, but felt a certain uneasiness being off the Mother Road. Route 66 felt like the route that would take me to Crystal. I'm not given to mysticism, but what is it they say? When you've lost something, retrace your steps. Think about the last place you saw it.

And perhaps those misgivings had some merit, because Lincoln, Nebraska, was a wash. We stepped onto the porch of Lester Cuttleman's Craftsman bungalow and gave a knock. We heard slippers shuffle to the door. He opened it only partway. Rhea tried to repeat her trick from Denver, but as soon as he heard the name Crystal Singer, he closed the door in our faces and latched the deadbolt. *She's my mother!* Rhea shouted. The slippers shuffled away.

Burgers for dinner. A Lincoln motel. Hot showers.

"Why Cuttleman anyway?" Rhea asked. "Wasn't he the cartmaker?"

"Cartographer. Yeah, they wrote a lot in the midsixties. He created a famous map projection. Didn't become the standard or anything. Not like shipping companies are using it. But it's influential in cartographic circles, apparently."

"Map projection?"

"The map you've seen in every classroom in your life is wrong. Every map other than a globe is wrong, because when you try to take a sphere and map it onto two-dimensional space, things invariably get distorted. If you keep the shape of things accurate, their size will be distorted. To preserve latitudes, you distort longitudes. You can't keep the shape of things and the distance between them accurate at the same time. You have to decide what you're willing to sacrifice, and that has implications. Boy, could he get pissed off about the Mercator projection."

"You think this has something to do with entropy? Sounds more like her distance stuff. 2D and 3D values."

"I don't know that it has anything to do with anything. Crystal had all kinds of side interests. I just know she visited him in early 1967. I hoped he could shed some light on what was going on with her then. I guess that's not happening. Oh well. Our next stop is Madison, so at least we're closer."

*

The first snowfalls had come early to Iowa and Wisconsin, and Rhea watched carefully through the passenger window, studying the way snow extended into the distance, the things that stuck up out of it, the people in the roadside towns who went about their lives in it. She wouldn't have seen any of this in

Petaluma, and if there were no trips to the beach thirty miles away, I couldn't imagine there were any three-hour drives to the mountains. The truck's heater couldn't quite beat the cold, so we were in our jackets. I let Rhea crack the window for a few minutes so she could feel the air so crisp it almost snapped like glass. We pulled through downtown Des Moines for lunch and found it surprisingly magical, draped in lights and carpeted in white.

"So, entropy," she said, inhaling a tuna melt, imitating me again—"The river flows one way"—then back to her normal voice: "but a river can be reversed."

"By changing the direction of its flow. But downstream is downstream, even if downstream is somewhere else."

"But that's just thinking about the river, isn't it?"

"What do you mean?"

"I mean the whole problem was the river, and all the sewage in it, flowing into Lake Michigan. They switched it to dump into the Mississippi. So the river may be the same, but the *place it flows into* is changed."

"But you're talking about open systems. The Mississippi River is changed because of an input from outside the Mississippi River. Just like our planet receives surplus energy from the sun. The problem is that eventually the sun burns out, the river dries up. If you zoom out enough, it's all one closed system."

"Couldn't the Entropy Equation be exactly that—some untapped source outside what we think of as a closed system? Isn't that the point, that they understand things beyond us?"

I sipped my shake and thought about it.

"Wow," I said. Rhea looked up at me, startled.

"What? Did I just figure it out?"

"I have no idea. But it's an interesting theory and one I haven't heard before. If we find your mother, you can ask her."

Her expression darkened.

"I'm not so sure she's still the authority on it."

She was thinking of Dr. Meyer's interpretation of Crystal's sketch, the way it showed nothing about entropy but a lot about Crystal's state of mind.

"We can call Dr. Meyer and see what she thinks."

Rhea considered this, but decided she needed to think it through more before she put the theory to the test. We drove on to Madison and Marianne Mosley, who was an astrophysics professor and another of Crystal's correspondents about the Entropy Equation. *Entropy isn't really that complicated,* she had written to Crystal. *It's not difficult to understand. It's just difficult to bear.* But they had spent the early sixties writing back and forth about the nuances of the subject, and there had been a few visits during those years as well. Dr. Mosley invited us in and served coffee for herself and me, and gave Rhea a soda can.

She seemed much less suspicious of me than Dr. Meyer, but was less rosy on Crystal and her foibles. What she could tell us was along the same lines of what Dr. Meyer already had: Crystal chasing a better understanding of what the Entropy Equation could mean. Flights of excitement. Depths of depression. It was very bad around 1967, she said. She was very worried for Crystal, and offered to refer Crystal to her own therapist. Crystal demurred. She told Dr. Mosley she just needed to get away for a while, her quarters were too cramped, as was her mind. She said something about a cabin in Montana. Dr. Mosley didn't know if it was a place Crystal owned or rented, but said she had worried some sheriff's deputy would find her there swinging from a rafter.

Dr. Mosley didn't notice the way Rhea's posture stiffened, but I did.

She had met Rhea only once, she said, when she was a baby too young to walk. When Crystal visited in later years, she said the weather was too harsh for such a young child, and if she needed time in the cabin it certainly wasn't a hospitable place. I asked Dr. Mosley where in Montana the cabin was and whether she thought that was where Crystal might be now. She laughed and asked if I'd like the whereabouts of Lucas Holladay and Amelia Earhart while I was at it. Rhea asked her some of the same questions we'd asked Dr. Meyer. Did she know other places Crystal went? Did she think Crystal was getting close to an answer? Certainly didn't seem like it, Dr. Mosley said. 1967 was the last time Dr. Mosley had seen her in person, and she'd smelled like desperation. I showed her Crystal's message from the radio complex. Lacking either Dr. Meyer's tact or her affection for Crystal, Dr. Mosley took one look and said:

"A crazy person wrote this."

"You don't see any connection?"

"It's not just no connection. Look at the handwriting. The letters are all distorted. Look how uneven the lines are. It's a mess."

Rhea looked downcast. Dr. Mosley softened a little.

"I do hope you two find her, hon," she said. "It looks like she could really use the help."

*

A short drive, finally: Madison to Chicago. We got there before night fell, but didn't try to seek out Hans Böde. After our dispiriting chat with Dr. Mosley, we weren't up for the risk of another dead-end contact. Rhea and I tried piecing our mystery together as we waited for Chinese takeout and checked into the hotel—a real hotel this time, nothing five-star, but a big step up from roadside lodges with linens that felt like the shed skin of other people. We spread out the most important chains of letters on the table and ordered them by date.

For the first half of the 1960s, Crystal gleefully chased entropy. She kept private but traveled. She visited Lorna Meyer with Rhea. She visited Marianne Mosley. She drove some of the great expansive country, as we were doing now. Her earliest letters and visits to Böde were in 1962, but they continued on into the late 1960s. He was one of her more regular correspondents, if a less frequent one. They talked music. They recommended albums to each other.

In 1964, she was nearly spotted in Denver. Her anonymity was more fragile than she thought. She bunkered down in Petaluma. Her only company was Aunt Dottie. "And a meddlesome toddler," Rhea added.

"I didn't want to say it."

Now there was only one mind to bounce her ideas off of: her own. It was not fun anymore. She frayed. She still wrote to Meyer and Mosley and other scientists, but the Holladayan optimism was drained out of her writing. This, maybe, was when she got her cabin in Montana. A refuge. A place she could go to think or just hide out. "That's the lead," I said. "The thing no one knows about but us."

"Montana," Rhea said, "is big."

"Well, I don't think she'll be in the phone book. But there are public records. Registries of landownership. There are ways to look."

She forked some broccoli beef and asked me to go on. Midsixties. Crystal fraying. Et cetera.

A lot of her conversations dropped off in 1966. There was a gap in the letters, and when things picked up, the patterns were different. She wrote Meyer only on occasion. No more Mosley. Not much of anything with physicists. But she wrote Böde more. She started writing Ed Callahan much more frequently—"the teacher guy?"; "exactly"—and he was her primary correspondent thereafter. 1967 was when she started writing Lester Cuttleman, the map guy. 1967 was the last year a letter came to me, though the last one before that had come in 1964.

She was gone more then, Rhea said. After she turned seven, her mom's trips were longer and more frequent. But what happened? Rhea asked. Where was she? Montana? I told her I didn't know. I asked Rhea if she had any clue where her mother might have gone after that. Had she said anything about where she was going? Rhea said sometimes she didn't even know Crystal *was* going except by her cooking. The more worn-down Crystal got, the more she cared about breakfast. She'd make French toast, pumpkin pancakes. She'd hand-whip cream and melt sugar into caramel on the stovetop. The smell of walnuts toasting in the oven would permeate the whole house. Crystal would be spent the rest of the day. She might skip lunch and eat crackers for dinner. She could do this for weeks, Dottie struggling to keep up with the dishes. Then Rhea would wake to a lonely house and fix herself a bowl of cereal.

"She made visits to Böde and Callahan long after she stopped visiting the others," I told her. "If anyone can tell us where she is, it's them."

*

Böde's condo was small but had a big window that looked out, from a distance, over the spread of Lake Michigan. The wall surrounding the window was concrete, but little of it was visible. It was covered by built-in shelving, custom fit for row after row of 7-, 10-, and 12-inch records. Most of the shelving was for those standard sizes, but others were fit for older record formats, and some bins in the bottom right corner were filled with early cassettes, wax cylinders, and punched player piano scrolls.

Böde was a tall, tube-shaped fellow in a T-shirt, perpetually pushing his wire-rimmed glasses up the bridge of his nose with his pinkie. In his other hand he held the smallest cup of coffee I'd ever seen, a thing more like a thimble than a mug. He had to pinch the tiny handle between his finger and thumb. Rhea seemed entranced by this. We sat with him around a square little wood table that shared a minimalist aesthetic with the rest of the place. He offered to brew us cups of what he was drinking, but we both declined, unsure how long it took to fix, and not entirely certain he wasn't drinking out of doll furniture. Some kind of chaotic jazz played quietly in the background. It sounded as if someone was trying to play a saxophone and repair it at the same time.

I asked him if Crystal's theories on entropy had something to do with music.

"To be honest, we never really talked about entropy. I tried to ask her about it early on. And the distance thing. Who wouldn't? It was fascinating. The whole world wanted to hear her thoughts. She demurred or dodged. I got the idea these visits were restorative for her. A vacation from all that. She'd show up, usually unannounced, and tell me to play her something unlike anything she knew."

He waved his free hand at the wall of records, then pushed his glasses up again.

"At first it was easy. Early Americana. I knew her dad was an émigré, so she would have missed that stuff. She soaked it up and wanted anything I could throw at her. Yodeling. Tuvan throat singing. Ancient dirges. Every brand of modern pop. She loved almost anything. She'd go to the wall and pull an album without even looking at the sleeve. Anything but corny folk. We'd just lie around listening to records and talking music theory like a couple of stoned undergraduates."

"Like what?"

"I'd tell her music is math. She hated that. She said that math undergirds music but that music is not just math. Math can map the interlocking rings of ripples rain creates on a pond, but the math isn't the rain. I remember her riffing on how the human mind has grooves built in for music. The grooves in the records, she said, were negative images of those. There were infinite possibilities for the arrangement of sound, but only certain combinations registered as music. Every piece of sheet music, every record and cylinder, arose out of those patterns built into our brains. The shape of instruments arose out of those patterns. Every dance is a response to those patterns."

"Just stuff like that? Nothing about Mars?"

"Just stuff like that. But these open-ended conversations could go on for hours. What would music sound like in a hundred years? Could I *hear* music by reading sheet music? Yes, but then we'd debate over what constitutes hearing. If I could reinvent music notation from scratch, what would it look like? What a stoner question, but also very flattering to be asked, as a musicologist."

"What was your answer?" Rhea asked.

Oh boy, I thought, *don't give him the runway.*

"Erase staves. Erase bars and flagged notes. Get rid of all that medieval shit. I felt sad saying it, surprisingly, as if I had killed it all off by saying so. But it was liberating to consider the more complete possibilities made available by sweeping out those old cobwebs. You could have a purely graphical system, or a purely numerical system. You see, music on staff notation is like a two-dimensional map, but music is like a topographical map. What staff notation doesn't show is the relationship between the notes. Pleasing arrangements of sound come from harmonic relationships, but look at a piece of sheet music and you won't see, unless you've studied to see, the different notes that align into a chord and notes that chafe against each other. You can't see the spatial relationship between a third and a fifth. The difference between notes is a difference in the frequency of their waveforms. That difference, as Crystal would say, is not numerical—I guess I would ask her, what is, if you look at it that way?—but like so many things it can be represented as such."

I decided to change my tack.

237

"When she visited in the late 1960s, did she seem . . . different? Less put together?"

"Broken," Rhea added. "He doesn't want to say it."

Böde shrugged.

"She seemed more tired; I suppose. She was in her thirties. She was a single mom. Who wouldn't be?"

"She didn't seem like she was falling apart?"

"Not at all. But like I said, her visits were a vacation, I think, from everything else in her brain. She loved music as much as anything. When she was here, all she had to do was listen to it. This was part of a whole restorative circuit for her."

"What do you mean?"

"She'd go to her cabin—"

"You know the cabin? Do you know where it is?"

"Minnesota? Montana?"

"You don't know the address, then?"

"She was pretty guarded about it. She'd mention it, but without any details. She'd spend a while there. Then she'd come see me on the way to seeing Ed."

"Ed Callahan?" I blurted.

"I don't know. Same thing. She'd talk about her friend Ed, but no details. I think he lives in Ohio?"

"Youngstown."

"Ed was the one who'd tell her when she needed some time in the cabin. When she needed some rest. She trusted him on that kind of thing. Her emotions. Her psyche."

"Were they in love?" I asked. Rhea slapped my shoulder.

Böde pushed his glasses up again. He'd been sipping at his coffee, but somehow a little pool remained in his tiny mug.

"I know what music she loves. I don't know what people she loves."

I asked him a dozen more questions about the cabin and Ed Callahan, seeing if I could suss out any more information about either. I wanted to head west from Chicago with her cabin pinned on the road atlas. That was her hiding spot. That was where she'd most likely be. And truth be told I felt a certain aversion to visiting Ed Callahan. I didn't want to know what he looked like. I didn't want to know how tall he was and what his voice sounded like. I'd read enough letters like this one:

My Dear Crystal,

Let's drop the veneer and let me ask you how are you doing? *Not in the way you might greet a stranger in a grocery line, but in the way an old friend might ask, late in the night. How is your soul? I want to tell you that the pain I feel when you write to me that your life has fallen apart, that you have made yourself a disaster to everyone around you, is equal to the pain you feel. That, of course, is foolish and insulting, but there is something to that foolishness. The human tendency to want to bear someone else's pain if it eases their burden, or even if it doesn't, is the best of us. Our species is so venal, so happy to stumble into war and walk all over each other, but it's all cantilevered from a core desire to give and receive empathy. I don't mean to call my own reaction to your difficulties the best of human nature (ha!). I just mean to say a constellation is formed by points of light that are not*

*connected to each other by anything other than the ob-
server. You are a point in a great constellation. When you
say you feel distant from everyone and everything, that's
only because you cannot see the axis that unites you with
your distant stars. And of course you cannot see the axis.
You're on it. Perhaps you are it.*

With love,
Edward

Smooth-talking son of a bitch.

If anyone would know where she was, it'd be Callahan.

Who knew? She might even be there with him.

*

"This is the last one, huh?" Rhea asked.

We watched northern Ohio slide by. A row of tollbooths for
the turnpike sat ahead of us, and I told her we'd be seeing them
the whole way, but the way was not much longer.

"No, the last pin in the map. The last stop."

I told her I didn't want to go home. That my little house
felt adrift from time, an empty space where my life had gone
stale. I felt better here, on the road with her, on the trail even
if the trail was cold. I once wrote to Crystal: *However far apart
we are, a line connects us, a line that never gets any longer despite the distance.* Even all these years later, I would rather be
dragged along behind her by that line than believe it didn't
exist.

240

"But you're ready, aren't you?" I asked. "You're ready to go home."

No, she said. She felt the same. She felt closer for being on the trail.

"Youngstown," I said.

We turned off the freeway and it was a short drive to the return address I'd seen on so many envelopes. It was the plainest house we'd visited yet: a bare concrete path bisecting a ratty lawn; a small, square house with worn white siding. There was not a flower or a decoration or the slightest iota of a personality, just a big TV antenna poking up from the backyard. I looked at the place and thought: *No one could fall in love with someone who lived here.* As always, I let Rhea lead the way. She knocked and asked the man who answered if he knew Crystal Singer. But I was not listening to his answer.

The man had a short graying beard, and hair trimmed close and parted to the side. He was in old khaki slacks and a pilled tan sweater. He had slippers on his feet and a small glass of bourbon in his hand. He looked every bit the burnt-out teacher on the weekend. But I would have recognized the thick arch of his eyebrows anywhere. The recognition was immediate, and I couldn't believe he didn't face it every time he shopped for groceries. I thought I must be crazy, so I listened to his voice and that, too, was unmistakable: A voice like cognac with the sun shining through it. The same voice I heard from the radio all those years while my mother washed the dishes. My jaw fell open. The file I was holding dropped to the concrete.

"Well, you know who I am," he said. "Why don't you come on in and tell me who you are?"

He shuffled back into the depths of the house. I mouthed to Rhea: *Lucas Holladay.* She shrugged, unfamiliar with the name. I gingerly retrieved the file and we caught up with him at the kitchen counter, where he was pouring me a couple of fingers of Wild Turkey. He eyed Rhea, paused, and turned to the fridge to pull out a carton of orange juice. He handed us our cups and waved us into the living room, where there were two recliners that had once been a matched set. One was barely used; the other was nearly worn out of existence. The cushions were deflated and the fabric looked like an old dog bed. He gestured for me to take the nicer one as he dropped into the other. Rhea sat cross-legged on the rug, between us and a TV playing golf at a hushed murmur.

"Your name would be a good start," he said.

"I'm Rick Hayworth. I was one of the four—"

"Ah, Rick. The one that got away."

That was so absurd I wanted to laugh, but no laugh came. Hearing it just hurt.

"I'm surprised she talked about me."

"She talked about a lot of things, but none more than you. And you, Rhea."

"What are you doing here, fifty miles from where it all happened? You're more conspicuous here than anywhere."

"I spent ten years in Oregon. My dad got sick and I had to come home to tend to him. I spent a year in a trench coat and sunglasses like some poorly disguised federale. Had this terrible mustache. I looked like Frank Zappa. From the neck up, at least. But no one gave me a second glance. I ditched the coat. I ditched the shades. Shaved the mustache. No one noticed.

Twice in ten years someone's asked, 'Do you know who you look like?' I just say, 'I get that all the time.'"

I sipped at my bourbon.

"Not as many people are looking up at the stars as we like to think," he said. "To us it means everything. Most people don't know how to see it."

"You were on TV."

He laughed gently. Rhea turned from the golf tournament to eye him with more interest.

"It burns me up too, believe me. Infamy, it turns out, is rather hard to enjoy."

"Crystal found you."

"She did! And that turned out to be enough."

"How did she track you down?"

"Through my letters. I wrote begging her to explain the Curious Language to me. The Distance Theorem. I wanted to understand it so badly. It had been my whole life. I threw my life on the pyre for it. And then the understanding was out there. Someone understood it. I needed her to help me understand. I wrote under my assumed name, this name. Some signature of my writing, some fingerprint of phrase, must have given me away. She felt me out with the exchange of a few more letters. Then she showed up on my porch saying, 'Evening, Mr. Holladay,' and let herself inside."

"Did she?" Rhea asked. "Did she teach you?"

He nodded beatifically. "It took a while, but she did."

"Did you ever meet me?"

He winked at her.

"You were eight months, and walking already."

243

"Just the once?"

"She got a lot more cautious after she was spotted in Denver. And a bit paranoid, if I'm being honest. That's when I started to worry about her."

"She was deteriorating by the midsixties, wasn't she?" I asked. He nodded.

"Did you buy her the cabin? As a getaway?"

Now he stopped. The angle of his head changed. The arch of his eyebrows softened. A sadness entered the frame.

"I don't know if I should be telling you this. But I always thought she should tell you. Always told her she should let you back in. You sounded like you would have given her the care she needed. It took a lot to break her reluctance to get help. She felt the care got in the way of the mission. That the health of her mind was a small price to pay for the answer she was seeking. Which was stupid, I told her. Like saying the health of your boat is a small price to pay to cross the ocean. You need the boat to get there."

"Can you tell us where the cabin is? We'll go find her. Bring her back down to Earth."

"There is no cabin."

"We know there's a cabin. We know you told her when to go there."

"The cabin was our code for the Rock Harbor Psychiatric Haven outside Santa Fe. She made an attempt on her life in 1967, pills, and I drove out to Flagstaff to get her out of the awful county psych ward. To get her transferred to Rock Harbor. I—I spent a little time there myself, a long time ago. I had my doctor there call to arrange the transfer."

"How—" Rhea asked. Her voice cracked. "How close did she get?"

Holladay gave her a long, significant look.

"Too close," he said. "You're lucky not to have lost her. I know you lost her, in a sense, but it could have been much worse."

Tears started to form in Rhea's eyes. She asked, "So every time she 'went to the cabin,' that was a suicide attempt?"

"Oh! No. Just that first time. The others were times she was worn out. Times she was spiraling. Times I was worried about her. She trusted my words of warning. She knew I'd been in some of the same dark places. I understood the pressure, the sense of failure."

"But she was the real deal," I said. "You were a fraud."

He took a sip of his bourbon.

"It feels the same," he said.

"Was she making progress. Late in the sixties? Was she figuring it out?"

"It?"

"The Entropy Equation."

"She came out of Rock Harbor saying she didn't care about entropy. She hardly wanted to think about math. Said she'd given too much of her life to it. She didn't want it to be king anymore."

"But she went back to it," I said. "It kept driving her back to the edge."

"Not that I know of," he said.

"Then why'd she keep going back to the facility?"

"She could obsess over anything. Music. History. Geology, for God's sake."

"She kept working on entropy," I told him. "She thought she'd solved it. You didn't hear about the Cibola radio message? She didn't talk to you about it?"

"It's been a while since we talked. But no, she never mentioned it."

I pulled Crystal's message from the file and passed it over to him. I told him she thought this was showtime. She had them broadcast it to Mars. Did it look like anything she'd talked about? He took his time looking it over. Reading it again and again. I almost laughed when he turned it upside down, shook his head, and turned it right side up again. As he scrutinized the paper, the years shook off him and he stood up much more quickly than he'd sat down. He paced the room, rubbing his mouth with his hand.

"Do you understand it?" I asked.

"No!" he said excitedly. "Did the radio people figure it out?"

"I wouldn't be asking you if they did."

"I can't see what it has to do with the Entropy Equation."

"Some other energy source?" Rhea asked.

"Hang on," Holladay said. He snatched a piece of paper from a little desk against the wall and put it and the message we'd brought onto the kitchen counter next to each other. He combed noisily through the desk's drawer until he found what he was looking for. He held it up to display it for us: a permanent marker with a bright blue cap. At the counter, he started writing on his blank sheet of paper, except that the motions of his wrist were more like drawing, tracing slow, deliberate arcs. Rhea and I gathered around him, watching him slowly translate Crystal's page into the Curious Language. It was always useful, he said, to look at a thing from as many angles as possible. He translated not just the meaning of each number but also its distortions. For a two that was stretched horizontally, he stretched his Martian numeral the same way. For a six that was amplified, he amplified the translation. I tried to make sense of it as he drew, but all I could see was the same sequence in a different script, a series of numbers with no mathematical relation.

I didn't want to interrupt him, though. It had been decades, I imagined, since he'd been so energized. On the TV, a golfer swiped at a ball and it shrank away to nothing in the sky. Another camera caught a close-up of it bouncing along the turf down the range. Holladay was still hunched over the paper. Rhea was still watching him eagerly. Her pupils darted as he translated each new symbol, even though the original was right there in front of her. He finished his writing and held the page out in front of him, tilting it back and forth again as if to roll around the numerals he'd sketched on it. He and Rhea cocked their heads in unison. I froze.

"I can't say this unlocks anything," he finally said. "It's a curious sequence. It doesn't mean anything to me. But I'm sure it means something to her. She's a very deliberate woman."

I didn't know what it meant either, but I knew I recognized it. I stared at Holladay's page, wondering if my memory was playing tricks on me.

"She was at the Cibola center two weeks ago," Rhea said. "Where would she have gone after? Back to Rock Harbor?"

"I don't know. I don't know where she's been living. The last time she visited me was in 1970. She was troubled then, and I did tell her I thought a stay at Rock Harbor would do her some good. But three years is much longer than she ever stayed before. I think it's doubtful."

"Can we get the address?"

While Holladay scribbled it on a piece of stationery, Rhea cast a look at me that wondered why I was so fixated on the translation that she'd had to take over questioning. As soon as he put the address in Rhea's hand, I swept up the two papers on the counter and started shepherding us to the door. I thanked him for his help and said it had been a pleasure meeting him. We could stay for dinner, he offered. I said that we had a long drive and needed to get on the road. I turned the door handle and stepped out onto the porch. Rhea raised her eyebrows at me, astonished by my rudeness.

By the passenger door of the truck, she held up the address and shouted to him, standing there in his doorway, that we would let him know if we found her. And if we found out what the sequence meant, we'd let him know that too.

"If she's not there," he said, "your guess is as good as mine. Maybe she really is on Mars." He invited us to come by again sometime. He didn't get many visits, he said, from people who knew the right name.

I gassed up the truck in town, preparing for a long haul, and we headed west with my foot on the accelerator. When we blew through Chicago and kept on I-80, Rhea grabbed the road atlas and furrowed her brow at it. After a few minutes, she asked why we weren't taking Route 66. If we were headed to Rock Harbor, that was the most direct route. I told her we weren't heading to Rock Harbor. Not yet, at least. She said, "What are you talking about, Rick? We solve the mystery and you're too scared to follow through?"

"There are a lot of directions Crystal might have driven when she left Cibola," I said. "Rock Harbor is the best lead we've ever had, but I know something better than where she is. I know what she wants."

"Which is?"

"It sounds too crazy," I said. "Can I ask you to trust me?"

I looked at her while I waited for her answer. I held her gaze longer than I should have given that I was behind the wheel, but the road was long and straight and empty. The road was the distance between here and home, the distance between the same two terminal points, but a distance could be properly measured only from within a journey, and this distance had never been shorter. If I could move through glass I would have reached through the windshield and touched my farmhouse.

Rhea finally returned my gaze. Yes, she said, she could.

We stopped into a motel before 8:00 PM so I could call California to make orders and schedule deliveries. Rhea took some money from my wallet and came back twenty minutes later with sub sandwiches. I was still on the phone when she came in—*not four* hundred *gallons, four* thousand *gallons. Yes, I have a card. It's got a high limit.* Rhea was curious but decided to live in the curiosity rather than try to solve it.

We ate. We slept. Continental breakfast and the gas station. We tore west again and watched the country change from snow to wet grass to bare earth. I felt the distance reel into me like a fishing line. Two days like this and we were almost home, staying in a lodge in Truckee, two hours away.

249

The next morning, we pulled down the long gravel drive, the exact sound of home. I leapt out of the truck, grabbing Holladay's translation of Crystal's message, and ran to the filing cabinet in my bedroom where I kept the letters I had before all the other letters: the letters from Crystal to me. I'd filed them chronologically, so it was not hard to find the very last one she'd sent me, the only one in the 1967 file. When I'd first opened the envelope and pulled out a sheet of paper with nothing but Curious Language on the back, I'd assumed it was just scratch paper, that she'd grabbed whatever paper was at hand to dash off her last letter to me.

Now, I flattened it on the floor. Next to it, I placed Holladay's translation of Crystal's message from Cibola.

It was the same message.

Though the numerals were all the same, the sheets were not quite identical. The later message had more of what I saw as distortion, but lined up next to the earlier message it was clear the numerals were all distorted along the same curve, all stretched in the same direction. In this way, counterposed against the original or first draft or whatever what she'd sent me was, the second message looked not like a distortion of the first but a different draft of it.

I was about to go with the later message when I noticed a faint pencil line cutting diagonally through Crystal's message. It was too perfectly straight not to be intentional. The folds in the paper, too, were made with exacting precision, forming it into a grid of perfect squares just like a map—I took it to the window and looked out at where the train tracks cut diagonally through our field. I rotated the paper. There it was. Crystal must have thought I'd see that diagonal line and know it was the railroad track I could see from my bedroom window. I saw it every day, she must have figured, so I was bound to recognize it. But I was seeing that track from Earth and she, drawing the farm from some map of it she'd found, was picturing it from orbit.

I ran to the yard with the paper and climbed the ladder to the tractor shed, where I could survey the west acreage and see the way Crystal's message was designed to fit into it. Since the message was mapped onto a grid and positioned by the railroad track, all that needed to be worked out was the scale, and she'd made that easy for me as well. One square equaled one acre.

Within fifteen minutes I was pulling the university's combine out of the barn. Dad would have killed to have one of these, or any of the array of industrial-grade tractors in there. None of them would even fit in the old tractor shed where Dad's little John Deere sat rusting. I took it out to the field and started cutting lines into the canola Ludovico had planted there, turning back and forth to widen them. The stroke width took three turns. The size of this message would be much smaller than the Singer Site. Either Crystal had worked out further inferences about Martian telescope capability or she was taking it on faith. Whichever she was doing, so was I.

I saw Rhea perched on the top of the tractor shed, shielding her eyes to watch me.

I carved the rails first. The combine did most of the work but driving it was still enough to make you sweat in November. The morning wore on. I carved a numeral and returned to the rail. I carved the next. Carving a message I didn't understand into the familiar earth of home should have felt tedious, like reading phonemes from a text in a different language, but work had never felt more meaningful. Each foot drew me further into the future, and at the same time folded the work of making the Singer Site over the present on top of me.

Then I looked up at the tractor shed and Rhea wasn't there. That was a sixteen-foot drop. I stopped the combine and sprinted to the base of the shed. Her body was not in a crumpled heap on the perimeter. But I heard her swearing from the inside of the shed between the weak chugs of an engine trying to turn over. She was on the seat of the John Deere, twisting the key so hard she could snap her wrist.

"That tractor hasn't had its battery charged in a decade," I said.

She looked back at me with a kind of desperation.

"Follow me," I told her. We headed into the barn and she took in the stable of backhoes and loaders. I led her to one of the muscular modern tractors. She sat in the seat and I stood on the side rail while we guided it over to the harrow attachment. She backed it up gently and I latched her up.

In the field I went through her first numeral with her, showing her how to scale out a curve from the rail and how to orient herself using the tracks and the acre lines. She took to it naturally. The focus she showed—this was new, a look I'd never seen in her eyes. Rhea as I'd known her had a fencer's poise and a defensive patience. This was the first I'd seen her with *intent*. She drove the tractor as if it were ferrying her to her mother.

We carved into the afternoon, our tractors curling through the canola in tandem. We stopped for water but not for food.

Five huge delivery rigs arrived just before three, their backs tiled with rows of black oil drums lashed together with shipping straps. The trucks crawled up the gravel and their drivers set up ramps to slide the drums down in front of the house.

We were starved by the time the trucks left, and all the food in the fridge was bad, so I called out for pizza and while we waited for it to come, we climbed the shed and surveyed what we'd done in the last of the light. The hour was beautiful on its own, the blue sky going lavender to the east, while the strips of cirrus clouds to the west were just starting to glow, a manifold designed to catch and diffuse the light. The relief in which our letters were carved was shallower than the crop circles Dad and I had found, which had been smashed into tall corn, and at this hour the lines were growing faint, but I knew they'd pop when they needed to. But we weren't there yet. We had half a day of carving left, and more to do after that.

"What's in the barrels?" Rhea asked.

"Blue," I said.

*

I woke to bright sunlight and the ceaseless burr of my alarm. My father liked to say that a man who couldn't make the alarm clock his boss would find someone else in that position. When I slapped the alarm off, I heard the sound underneath the sound, the thing that had really woken me. Shouts from the west acreage. Through the window I saw Rhea on the seat of the tractor, halfway through a new numeral, but the tractor was stopped and there was a man pounding on the side of it with his fist. Having slept in my clothes made it easier to sprint out the door.

The man's back was to me, so I didn't recognize him until I was halfway there: Ludovico. As soon as I saw him my worry switched. As erratically as he was banging on the tractor, I knew he'd never harm Rhea. I was less certain she wouldn't put the tractor in gear and crush him with the monster tire he was foolish enough to stand in front of.

I shouted his name as I approached and he wheeled toward me with his arm up. He left it up for a second before deciding he wouldn't hit me. Instead, he screamed so hard spit threads fell to his chin. A ten-year study, he wailed. What did she do? What did she do?

"I did this," I told him.

"Ten years."

There is no anguish like academic anguish. His tenure review was coming up in two years.

"You're breaking my life, Rick."

"I'm sorry. I'm so sorry."

He sat in the dirt where his canola should have been and put his head in his hands. He spent some minutes like that. He finally looked up and asked us what we were even doing.

"Do you remember 1960? Arizona? The Singer Site?"

He nodded solemnly.

"We're doing that."

Ludovico nodded again, and stood to walk back in the direction of the barn. Rhea waved to me, then put the tractor back in gear and started cutting down the canola in front of her again. I walked to the barn, where Ludovico sat disconsolate on a short stack of hay bales. I left him to feel whatever he had to feel and pulled the combine out of the building. The work continued.

The previous day we'd done most of the numerals on the first rail, and that was where Rhea was this morning. I set to work carving the second rail and then branching the numerals off it. The tractors filled your eardrums with a uniform thrum, making for a quiet kind of work despite the noise. Like anything that mutes a sense, it inflamed the others. The air was rich with the wet, grassy smell of cut canola and the tang of disturbed soil. The levers of the combine rattled in my hands. Through the seat I felt every bump and dip in the land, as if I were driving over the field's fingerprint. Rhea's tractor made long scythe-like sweeps into the canola, as did mine, and we swept toward and away from each other, working sometimes in parallel, then cutting away to follow the logic of our next curve on the map.

An hour later, Ludovico walked toward us through the channels we'd carved. Something about his walk made me stiffen. His arms didn't sway. His pace was too slow. I looked at his hands to see if he had a gun. Empty. Still, I pulled around so he'd reach me before he reached Rhea, and I stopped the combine in front of him. I climbed down from the cab to face him man to man. Are we really doing all this, he asked, to talk to them? He pointed to the sky. Yes, I told him. We're trying, at least. His study was ruined, he said. It was the work of his life. None of it was salvageable. He asked if this was the work of my life. I nodded.

"It is."

"Then can I help you?"

"Of course you can," I said. I pulled him into an embrace. "I'm so sorry. I'll make it up to you."

He didn't know if that was in the cards, he said. Just tell him what he could do. I told him to hook up a tractor with a water tank and an irrigation rig, and explained how to mix the solution in the drums into the water tank. All he needed was the concentration. He knew all this equipment better than I did. Rhea had finished the first rail and was working with me on the second now. It wasn't long before I saw Ludovico pulling into the first rail and starting to spray it down.

We stopped for lunch soon after. The work was ahead of schedule now, with a third crew member, and some of yesterday's fever was gone. We could see what we'd done and to the end of what we needed to do, though seeing anything beyond that was impossible. After lunch, Rhea and I finished the rest of the cutting, and the three of us took turns driving the irrigator.

To busy myself, I dug my old Nikon out of the closet and put a new roll of film in it. I took pictures of the work we'd done, and of Rhea and Ludovico as they did it. The full drums and the spent drums of blue dye. The ruts of the tractor wheels. The places where the canola sprung undisturbed next to the bare spaces we'd cut. I didn't know whether these pictures would end up in history books or be used against me in a court hearing, but they would testify to something.

The site was starting to glow, still faint under the daylight but there. It looked so much like magic I had to remind myself we wouldn't know until later whether it had actually cast a spell. I took my turn driving the irrigator, winding it down the broad avenues we'd carved, driving it along the long curls of Curious Language, inking in the lines. We were finished before dusk. Ludovico shared a sandwich he'd brought for himself and a big thermos of minestrone.

The farmhouse sat on a hill slightly above the level of the fields. We watched the sunset from there, standing on spent oil drums. There was no loss of light as the sun dropped below the hills. For every ray of light draining out of the sky, leaving a purple-gray backdrop, the blue glow amped itself higher. It was brighter than it was fifteen years ago, I thought. Much brighter. That was false, I knew. The chemical composition hadn't changed. Some things were just impossible to remember in their full depth. Some feelings exceeded our recording capacity.

Ludovico wiped his eyes with the backs of his wrists.

"How will we know if it worked?" he asked.

"Keep an eye on the morning papers," I said. "They'll let you know."

He went inside to phone his wife and explain why he was so late, though what explanation he offered I couldn't guess. After that, he took his leave.

"Come on," I said to Rhea.

I led her over to the tractor shed, where we hadn't taken a vantage yet. The building blocked our view of the site, so as we climbed the rungs of the ladder, the night looked like any night. We summited the roof and stood to take a look. The sight could punch the wind right out of you. The luminescent script didn't stretch as far as the eye could see the way the message at the Singer Site did, but it stretched further in another dimension. Déjà vu is the feeling of the past reaching forward to touch you, but the déjà vu I'd felt on the road when I saw Crystal's message from Cibola was not the past reaching forward to me at that moment, but the past reaching beyond me to this moment. The message she'd sent to me and the message she'd given to Dr. Rivera were, like all maps, encodings. Now the map was made the territory.

Rhea leaned against me and put her arm around my back. I wrapped my arm around her small shoulders and she put her head against my ribs. This point, this very point in space, was where I had learned the first lesson of distance twenty-five years ago. Standing up here with my father, I looked out at the same design as him but saw something entirely different. Now, I knew, my daughter and I saw the same thing.

"So this is entropy," she said. "What do you think it means?"

I thought it meant a river could flow backwards.

"I have no idea," I said. "But it looks beautiful."

We looked out at it again.

Then, together, we looked up.

*

DERANGED PROFESSOR RUINS AGRICULTURAL STUDY. That was the gist of the morning headlines. The papers put it more gently, but not by much. Rhea chewed cereal while I read the articles. Mars: the planet that managed to rotate constantly and still keep its back to us. I thought of Dr. Rivera's Minimum Possible Response time, Minimum Effective Response time, and all the anticipated delays beyond them. How desperate those considerations had seemed.

Out the front window I saw a few news vans taking footage of the site. A few photographers wandered the property. A cameraman was on top of the tractor shed, panning from east to west. I didn't bother shooing them away. They were doing their jobs. A deranged professor was newsworthy. The dean of sciences called to put me on a temporary leave that, he assured me, would be permanent soon.

"Let's go to Rock Harbor," I said. "Maybe we should have gone there from the start."

"No point," she said.

"You said you wanted to go."

"I called from the motel while you were asleep. They can't confirm she's there. Can't pass along a message. Can't ask her to call. 'Our reputation rests on our discretion.'" She said the last part in the same dopey voice she used to imitate me. "I asked if, say, a patient's *daughter* showed up in person, could they not at least inform the patient? They said no and hung up."

The reporters were doing their jobs, but watching them walk around the property made me feel like I had ants crawling on me. I'd have to get Rhea back to Dottie soon—or make more formal arrangements to move her here if Dottie could no longer care for her—and back to school and her normal, or abnormal, life, but I wasn't ready yet for our voyaging to end.

"Let's go somewhere else, then. Get out of town for a couple of days," I said.

"Where are you thinking?"

"To see the sea."

*

In jeans and sweatshirts, we stood on the beach. The wind came in cold and stiff, like a lash of wet hair, blowing our clothes

259

against our bodies. Everybody wanted calm, sunny beaches, I said, but this was the beach just the same. This was truer to the sea. That icy wind was what roiled the waves into impressive whitecaps, while the dull overcast sky cast its shadow on them. Cypress trees leaned into the wind the same way we did. They grew that way. They were used to it.

I couldn't be out here, I told Rhea, without thinking about some ancient human standing on the shore of the Atlantic, thinking it uncrossable. Even then, sailors were navigating the Mediterranean and the continental coasts. Vikings crossed to Canada and home again without much fanfare. Polynesians crossed most of the Pacific in outriggers and double-hulled canoes. We have so little idea of what's possible, I said. Some impossible things turn out to be easy. Other things that seem within reach turn out to be bound by natural law. Did she want me to try explaining space-time again?

"No," she said. "I'll get there."

She set off toward a tangle of driftwood, and I followed behind but gave her space as she picked up a piece and took stock of it. She knew branches, of course, knew wood, but not this bleached, fossilized twist, light as a bird's bone, so dry in its skin you'd think it could soak up water like a sponge. It was new to her. The briny knots of kelp were new to her. If I had been able to bring her here when she was five, I would have called them mermaid hair or sea-monster thread. I'd have arranged the driftwood pile into the form of some mythical sea skeleton and asked her to tell me about the creature it had been. For a moment I felt such a fury rise up against Crystal for what she'd kept from me that I imagined the line between us igniting.

Then I thought of her on the floor after chugging a bottle of pills and the fury evaporated. The line cooled.

"Dad?" Rhea asked.

"Yeah?"

"Do you still feel connected to her?"

"If point A and point B both lie on a Cartesian plane, are they by nature connected? Is *being on* the plane enough to connect them?"

"I don't know. You're the math professor."

"It's not a math question. It's a philosophy question."

Rhea angled her piece of driftwood to the ground. Now it was a walking stick. She walked along the swash line with her shoes in her hand, wincing as the frigid water washed her feet. I paced her on the damp edge of it. She was an inexperienced beachgoer, but had a natural sense for how to enjoy the place.

"If they are, then we're connected to everybody. No more or less connected to her than to some stranger in Kamchatka."

"You'll make a good mathematician."

"Or philosopher."

"Or philosopher."

"But that seems like horseshit," she said. "How can we not be more connected to her than a stranger is?"

"Maybe if the two points are both oriented toward each other it creates a connection. That's not very good math or philosophy, but I believe it."

"But we don't know if she's oriented toward us."

"We know we're oriented toward her. So if you feel a connection, that means she's oriented toward us."

"I didn't take you for a mystic."

"That's just algebra."

Seagulls picked at bagels left on the dry sand. The strand of beach highway behind us was dead today. The empty seaside diners huddled on their piers, a few waitresses smoking silently in front of them.

"Dottie told me she might need you to come stay with me. If you're interested, I'd love to have you."

"I'd like that."

We fished at an inlet a little way up the beach, but didn't catch anything. We ate the salami and cheese I'd brought instead. Rhea wanted to camp on the beach, so we unrolled our bags above the tide line. We hiked to the wooded hill nearby to gather branches and some fallen logs, and I built a fire as night fell. Rhea noted how long it took for the sun to set with nothing between us and the rim of the sea.

Once it was gone, the wind howled even harder. The fire couldn't keep up with it and neither could our sleeping bags. We suffered a couple of hours before deciding to call it. It was only a few hours home. She slept in the truck while we wound through the Coastal Range and caught the eastbound interstate, descending into the flatland of the Sacramento Valley. The glow of our field was visible from miles off, like a full moon pouring light off the earth.

The number of cars traversing these agricultural backroads was unusual, more than I'd seen the rest of the day put together. I saw them navigating the mile-marked avenues, their headlights towing their dark silhouettes through the night, driving parallel to me but faster. A big van pulled into the left lane to pass and as it slipped by us, its flank flashed in our headlights:

KVLA – News & Weather – Los Angeles. It pulled in front of us and, a few miles later, turned left in the same place I'd be turning left.

My stomach tightened. These headlights, and all the other headlights, were converging on something, and there was little doubt what it was. Sure enough, the house was surrounded. Rhea woke when we hit the gravel road. I could barely squeeze down it between news vans and other cars. I could see tracks in the fresh fields where vans had driven through them. The tops of the tractor shed and the barn were both dotted with the lights of TV cameras. Reporters crowded the house windows, trying to peer in through the curtains. I pulled in as close to the house as I could and readied the door key. Rhea and I made a run for it, squeezing past microphones thrust in our faces and through the front door.

A great commotion erupted as we closed the door behind us and locked it. The phone was already ringing and the first thing I did was unplug it. I told Rhea to turn on the TV while I checked that all the curtains were fully closed. Its screen showed a view of the message in our yard. An announcer spoke over it: "—appeared yesterday in the field of a small farm in Lodi. It was presumed to be a hoax or, like so many private attempts, not to say anything of importance. Indeed, scientists we've contacted have been unable to find any mathematical meaning in the message. But the message was not addressed to them, and the recipients appear to understand it."

The screen changed to a picture of Mars, the same Acidalia Planitia that spoke to us in 1961, only this message was much bigger. The letters weren't bigger. The canvas they'd selected was bigger. There was more written than any of the equations we'd seen before. The text was more crowded. Like Crystal's, this writing had unexplainable shifts in the distance between numerals, the size of them, and the way some seemed pulled in one direction or another. But there was more beyond the changes we'd seen in Crystal's. There were gaps between some numbers. Numerals bloomed above and below the rail lines, and sometimes sprouted from one another. There were places where numbers were superimposed over one another, or tied together as if in cursive, and many of the numbers seemed to be trying to say something with their individual shapes. The numerals seemed imbued with *feeling*, which was the least mathematical thing I'd ever thought.

I looked at Rhea to see how she was reacting to what we were seeing. She was not just watching, God bless her. She was taking notes. They cut back to the reporter. Rhea complained that she'd only gotten half of it down. Don't worry, I told her. They'd have it on a loop. Next up they rolled footage of us scrambling inside the front door, not answering the questions. I laughed when they said this appeared to be the breakthrough of a "gentleman farmer" with no interest in the spotlight, but within the next hour they'd learned my name and pieced together my connection to the Singer Site. That threw another round of gasoline on the fire, and for half an hour they knocked on the door. Some assholes even started knocking on the windows, but after a while they gave up.

Once the noise died down, the adrenaline wore off and I passed out on the couch. Rhea was snoring on the other end of it when I woke the next morning, but her sketch of what reporters were calling the New Language was complete. She'd even gone over it in blue marker. She'd muted the TV but the screen was on, so I didn't need to open the windows to check the situation outside. I could see it as a camera panned from the field to the farmhouse, which was still crawling like a bug den. There were the reporters and some sheriff's deputies to maintain order, and now even flocks of tourists who had come to see the inspiration. The newscaster called them pilgrims.

*

Half the reporters left after the second day. Another handful left the day after that. The last third was persistent. *What does it mean? What does it mean?* they called at us when we went out for groceries and when we returned. I told Rhea to never respond; anything we said would only feed the frenzy. One time she couldn't help herself from shouting, *It means go fuck yourself!* at a rude reporter. Their deadlines would pull them away, I told her. The TV crews couldn't keep showing footage of our closed curtains and empty truck. The newspaper reporters would have to chase new headlines. It was the magazine reporters who'd stick around longest. They'd be allowed a lot of lead time.

They interviewed my neighbors and colleagues and got what information they could out of Ludovico. My dean called to let me know I was no longer on administrative leave, and to invite me to give the keynote lecture at the annual science symposium. I said I would think about it. We camped out inside. I checked out long books from the library for both of us. Rhea spent chunks of time staring at strange patterns of the

New Language, which she'd made into a poster and tacked onto the wall with her mother's smaller message beside it.

There were so many differences from every previous message, she said, that the differences were their own category of information. They opened up a whole different angle from which to view the Martian civilization. Yes, I said, but we didn't know how to read that information. We didn't know what the differences meant. *Yet*, she said. We'd been staring at it for weeks and the differences hadn't resolved into their meanings. We couldn't figure it out, but then, neither could any of the world's second-best minds in mathematics.

We got so used to the noise of reporters and passersby skulking around the property that it was as hard to sleep when the last of them left as it had been to sleep in the beginning. After the call from the dean, I'd left the phone unplugged the whole time. Once or twice a week we got a knock on the door and ignored it. Those tapered off. We only left for the grocery store and library; it took so little to trigger a new media blitz. But I felt time stretch out again as the days went on: not something to be borne, not something to be ridden, just a great expanse with infinite horizons. Dottie had mailed Rhea's schoolwork to my address, and the school had agreed that given the frenzy surrounding us it would be best for Rhea to wait until after the holiday break to return to in-person classes. A week passed since we'd made the site. Another week and a half. They felt the same.

*

Cars all sounded the same on the gravel road, but when I heard tires on it on a cool morning in mid-December, I knew right away. I unlocked the front door and called Rhea out to the couch from her room. What? she asked. Just sit, I said. She heard the car door close in the driveway and her posture tensed. She looked at the door like a deer might look at the sound of boots.

Crystal opened the door without knocking and stood in the doorframe, a faded red rucksack slung over her shoulder. She had the same ranchwoman leanness as my mother. Her hair was straight and longer than I'd ever seen it, and had lost its color without going gray. It looked like straw in a sepia photograph. She looked ten years older than she was. I saw so much of her old self in her face—her wonder, her playfulness—veiled but not occluded by the screen of worry hanging in front of it. She had been scared to come, I saw. Rhea and I both had the power to break her.

"How do you say hello to two people who can never forgive you?"

"The same way you'd say it to anybody," I said.

"Hi, Rick," she said, stepping across the threshold. She shifted a sheepish gaze to Rhea. "Hi, baby girl."

Rhea didn't answer, but didn't look away. Crystal's gaze drifted to Rhea's poster of the New Language and she smiled at it. Rhea softened a little, realizing her mother was an egg containing the answers to all the questions Rhea wanted answered. I prayed Rhea would hold that egg up to the light rather than crack it open. Crystal owed the two of us so many apologies, but I'd spent enough years imagining extracting those from my father to know that wringing someone else out didn't make you any fuller.

Crystal walked toward us hesitantly, as if we might have laid traps on the floor. I nodded to the love seat, which was closer to Rhea's end of the couch. Crystal sat in it and tucked her knees in sideways. She and her daughter both looked past one another with such intent they were actually looking at one another, focusing their peripheral vision. Crystal finally looked back to a safe place: Rhea's poster.

"You did it," she said to me. "You called and they answered."

"I wasn't calling them."

"No," she said. "I figured you weren't."

"You couldn't have sent some instructions with the map?"

"I was falling apart at the time. Ed talked to you, I know, about the pills. I sent that to you the night I took them. It was my Hail Mary."

I knew what Rhea was feeling, because a little coal of it was still going in me. I had not believed this moment would come. I had disbelieved it in the fervent manner of a new atheist, disbelieving but letting it lease a lot of space in my brain. I'd certainly imagined the flood of emotions that would overtake me upon her return, though I hadn't known if that would be love or anger or lostness or foundness. Crystal looked down at the floor.

"I know I've been distant a long time," she said. "Most of the last ten years I've felt distant even from myself. Off floating in space, as Dad would say. But I want you to know that I always held you near to me."

"Distance—" I said, but I had no idea what to say about it and I trailed off. Everything felt so distant and so close all at once. For the first time, the house felt haunted. I heard my father's boots on the floorboards. I heard my mother turn on the sink. I heard the fuzz of the radio and Lucas Holladay speaking into the house from miles away and years past. I felt Crystal slap my arm and tell me to wake up when I wasn't asleep. I saw her eyes glowing from nothing but the dashboard lights.

"Distance hurts," Rhea said.

There was the simple truth of it.

"I'm so sorry, baby," Crystal said. "I hope I can make it up to you."

"Ask her your questions," I told Rhea. "It won't solve everything, but it's a step on the path."

Rhea looked back at her sketch of the New Language, and at the smaller paper with Crystal's message, which was tacked up next to it. What did it mean? Rhea asked her. The Entropy Equation?

"I don't know," Crystal said. "I never solved it."

"What do you mean?" Rhea snapped. "We carved it. They answered. They wouldn't have answered if it was wrong."

"It's not the Entropy Equation."

"Then what is it?" I asked.

"I got so tired of solving their problems. Of failing to solve their problems. I wanted to change the conversation. So I decided to send them something else."

She went to the paper she'd sent me in 1967 and unpinned it from the wall. She motioned for the two of us to follow her and led us to the other side of the dining room table, where my mother's old upright piano was wedged against the wall. Crystal sat on one side of the piano bench and patted the other side

269

of it. Rhea took the spot next to her and I stood behind them. Crystal uncovered the keys. She folded down the music rack and set the paper on top of it.

Crystal took hold of Rhea's hand and gently guided it to a middle C. She pointed to the first numeral in the message and pressed Rhea's ring finger into the key. Crystal pointed to the next symbol with her finger while she pressed Rhea's finger to another key a few notes up. She pressed the pedal and held the note a long time. My mind leapt at that pair of notes, knowing them before I could name them. Crystal waited until she saw recognition light up my eyes, but when it did she walked Rhea's fingers up a few more keys and she began to sing along to that song I'd heard her sing so many times, so long ago: "Beyond the Sea." A song about distance. A song about waiting. A song about the beginning of the ocean and the end of it.

Crystal pointed to the next numeral in the sequence but let go of Rhea's hand. Rhea squinted at the numeral, then the keys. She shifted her fingers over one at a time and pressed her index finger into the next A.

"Yes!" Crystal said.

Rhea ran through the next measure without trouble, but hesitated when the following notes dropped lower.

"Can you just do it?" Rhea asked. "You know it all."

"You can do it," Crystal whispered.

Rhea shifted her hand lower, looked back at the sheet, then shifted it back up a note. She played the next three notes. The following line came easier. Then easier than that. There was a natural relationship, I realized, between the numeral placements and their relationships to one another. I was looking at the theoretical musical notation Hans Böde had suggested to Crystal, something completely unlike standard notation but with its own intuitive logic. Maybe the Martians hadn't received Crystal's radio broadcast. We'd never observed anything that looked like our radio dishes on their surface. Or maybe they had received it but needed to see the whole thing laid out to understand. Crystal had always been beyond everyone else when it came to seeing the music behind the numbers. Maybe she was beyond them too.

It was not a long song, but by the end of it, Rhea had picked up the pattern, and though she was playing slowly the stutter was gone. There was a look in her eyes of chasing something, and she started right back in from the beginning. Crystal joined in, playing the notes for the left hand, and I saw there on her finger the gold engagement ring I had slid onto it twelve years earlier. She sang the words, her voice clear and full of peace. I sang the bass key, even if my voice was cracking. My father had never cared much about music. There wasn't much opportunity to listen to it when you spent all day in the fields. He never bought a record of his own, never put one of my mother's on or turned the radio knob himself, but he'd get excited when Wagner came on the classical station, and any time my mother sat at the piano, summoning Debussy from her girlhood lessons, he'd stop as if caught in a snare. How I wished they were here to see me and Crystal and their granddaughter singing together at her instrument.

Rhea stopped after the second playthrough and looked over her shoulder at her map of the New Language from the Martian landscape, crowded with superimposed numbers and shifting lines.

"So that's . . . ?" she asked.

Crystal smiled slowly. I was amazed she'd been able to hold her secret this long.

"Can you play it?" Rhea asked.

Crystal shook her head.

"It doesn't work on piano. But—"

She leaned over her rucksack and carefully retrieved a vinyl record in a blank white sleeve.

"Are you ready to hear music from another world?"

Not yet, I told her. First, I want to hear your song again.

ACKNOWLEDGMENTS

A book starts as an individual dream. Then miraculous people come along and dream it with you. My agent, Kerry D'Agostino, has been a consummate guide and support through new and confusing waters. My editor, Elizabeth DeMeo, brought *Singer Distance* into its best possible form, solving its problems in ways I could never have done alone. Her tireless work and passionate advocacy for this book have buoyed my spirits constantly through the long process of bringing a book to print. No writer could hope for a better editor.

Tin House has been a joy to work with. Thank you to everyone there, including Craig Popelars, Nanci McCloskey, Becky Kraemer, Alyssa Ogi, Masie Cochran, Diane Chonette, Jakob Vala, Alex Gonzales, Sangi Lama, Alice Yang, and Phoebe Bright. Thank you to Lauren Peters-Collaer for the beautiful cover, and to Meg Storey and Allison Dubinksy for copy editing and proofreading. Thank you as well to Kerry's teammates at Curtis Brown, Ltd: Sarah Perillo, Mahalaleel M. Clinton, Holly Frederick, Maddie Tavis, and Madison Greene.

I could not have drafted this book without the help of Brian Gleim, who patiently answered many questions about astronomy. My ignorance on the subject is too broad for any one person to contain, so any inaccuracies are mine alone, while anything I did get right is due to his help. Thank you as well to Jessica Sweet, for help with questions about farming and agriculture.

This book owes a debt of inspiration to Ken Kalfus's 2013 novel *Equilateral*, whose alternate history provided the seed of this alternate history. In an age of billionaires using money that could save the planet on vanity spaceflights, his powerful critique of imperialistic hubris and myopia has only grown more relevant.

I'll feel eternal gratitude to the early readers whose generosity made this book feel like it had found a home long before it hit shelves. Erika Swyler, Matt Bell, Adrienne Celt, Karen Thompson Walker, Kevin Brockmeier, Kate Hope Day, and Drew Broussard: you are saints. To past and present members of my writing group: Carole Firstman, Sally Vogl, Talia Lakshmi Kolluri, Jim Schmidt, Phyllis Brotherton, Connie Patton, and Erin Cook, thank you for your help with this book, but even more so for your friendship. Writing once felt very lonely, but not with all of you along for the journey. Thank you to Liza Wieland and Steve Yarbrough, whose personal and professional guidance have been an enduring gift. Thank you to Evelyn Rodriguez of Grace Rose Photo for the wonderful author photos. Thank you to Jefferson Beavers, Lee Conell, and Elizabeth Schulte Martin for your support, advice, and friendship.

Thank you to my parents, Tom and Sylvia Chatagnier, for a lifetime of love and support.

Thank you to my children, Ishmael and Colette, for bringing joy into my life.

Thank you to Laura, love of my life. I hold you impossibly close.